A BODY OF FATES

KENNETH EVREN

 FriesenPress

One Printers Way
Altona, MB R0G 0B0
Canada

www.friesenpress.com

ISBN
978-1-73893-801-8 (Hardcover)
978-1-73893-800-1 (Paperback)
978-1-73893-802-5 (eBook)

1. FICTION, LITERARY FICTION
2. FICTION, MAGICAL REALISM
3. FICTION, SAGAS

Distributed to the trade by The Ingram Book Company

Special thanks to my talented editor Arlene Prunkl and my first reader friends Johnny Seguin, Kathy and Aubry Farenholtz and Janelle Dwyer. And very special thanks to my exceptional and creative wife, Barb for her many brilliant ideas, support and extravagant love.

PREFACE

The Ideas Behind the Story—Science, Mythology, and Ineffable Life Questions

I am addicted to unanswerable questions. The ineffable is my crack. Love is ineffable. So too is the act of telling a story, singing in harmony or becoming a parent; all are shared experiences, therein lies the intersubjective mystery of being a *self*. Is the *self* real? What is real? Only the physical as against what some might call *information*, others *the mind*. Is the disembodied magic of mathematics, imagination, and meaning real? What of scientific mysteries such as emergence and complexity, the origin of life from chemistry or the multiverse? What of God? Are questions of free will relevant, or do we live in an infinite deterministic hologram? These profound metaphysical questions are pondered by our protagonist through the fundamental themes of the story; tragedy, resilience, what the lack of love can make us do, and who we might become once we have it.

History changed on December 31st, 1999. Precisely at midnight. With the first tick of Saturday, January 1st, 2000 the lives of one family were forever altered and time-travelling consequences began to manifest from their ancestral past. David Becker is an astrophysicist and an abuse survivor, from a line of violent alcoholics. Deborah Becker is a political scientist and natural-born leader from a line of extraordinary women and dreadnought mothers, each of whom in turn delivered their children safely into the next generation.

The peculiar lives of their predecessors, the epigenetics of a war-torn, alcohol-soaked ancestry, and entangled events from previous life-changing Saturdays seem to connect through cause and effect to two modern-day seminal events that befall first Dave then Deb. With an ominous diagnosis now hanging over their young family, Dave seeks answers in science and medicine. While these ideas are rational and quantifiable, he also finds them deeply impersonal and emotionally barren. Torn between reason and beliefs, he hates the religious indoctrination of his battered youth and loves the metaphysical mysteries he took shelter in as a boy: the infinities in mathematics, probability calculations, emergence and contingency. He must understand what brought this threat to his family forward from the past. Chance? DNA? Fate?

Fearing the inevitable, Dave is forced to consider irrational explanations. Either that or confess to himself his mind is failing and accept catastrophe. Beginning to doubt his own senses, no longer sure of what's real and what's imagined, he encounters his very own personal *Fate*, a being he becomes convinced is real. She comes to him in the dusk of his dreams, rhyming cryptic wisdom and singing malign revelations.

The Greek myth of the Fates; Clotho, Lachesis, and Atropos represent inescapable destiny, spinning the thread, measuring then cutting the length of each human life. Clotho is the spinner of life starting in the womb; today we might say evolution and genetics are her domain. Lachesis is the allotter of time, the length of thread each of us are gifted. Today she might be the Fate of medical science and biology. Atropos translates as "she who cannot be turned" in her assigned task of cutting the threads of each life. Her modern-day domain could be the laws of entropy and our beliefs around death and an afterlife from religious traditions. The ancient Greeks asked what are we at our very core, purely physical and fully explained by reductionist definition or something more? Something that emerges from the cocoon of infinity as if the particles and energies have a will … a quantum butterfly?

Ultimately, Dave must face the tattered ghosts of ancestry, physical abuse, alcoholism, and his simplistic religious upbringing as the everyday events of family life become diabolical. A battle for all the possible futures of the Becker family begins between the rational light of day and the fearsome, fantastical night culminating in a life-and-death *if only* story. "If only" is a common construct born of hope and regret, a daydream we all have from time to time about the events or experiences that suddenly turn our lives in unexpected directions. For his family to survive, Dave must choose what matters most to him—self-preservation at the expense of pride? Status and power over love and vulnerability? Pragmatic and reassuring rationalizations over self-acceptance, forgiveness, and redemption?

What a grand and crooked construction we humans are. These scientific theories, metaphysical mysteries, and soulish questions fill me with melancholy, joy and wonder. That's what I hope you feel as you read this quirky, tragic, funny, surreal, and sometimes shocking tale of abuse, addiction, sexuality, war, genocide, and social change, the old animus of science and religion, the endurance of suffering, and the resilience of family. I hope you find reflections of your own story in this epic of love, chance, choice and the living Fates of our infinite genes.

With thanks,

Kenneth Evren
kenevren@kenevren.com

"We are caged in history with the beast of ancestry and our future is devoured."

Felix Adolphus Becker, 1919–1984

CHAPTER 1

CRIMSON IN OUR CHEMISTRY

I don't remember much, at least not in the "do you remember the time when" sense, of the aptly named in family lore *seminal incident*—my seminal incident. There was a kind of void that followed the crack of his fist's impact with a roar so loud it was silent, save the electric buzz of flowing blood. My concussed memories have been polished by years of water under the family bridge, no doubt conflated beyond all proportion. Viagra'd to swollen purple prose. I can't be entirely sure of anything except maybe the impression left by the stomp of hormones, the body's electrochemical storm troopers, leaving boot prints on the metaphorical asses of neurons everywhere. My recalled senses seemed to perceive on a different time scale the signals damp and smeared out over the vast, churning surface of a silent slow-motion hurricane. The vacuum in my head vibrated. Time outside clicked along smartly, I'm sure, but if Einstein could have measured at this level of subjectivity, he would have grinned like a sugar-crazed child at my embattled neurons blazing in bright but sluggish unison, a bloated sunburst as the floor approached my head.

I remember the metal chair legs and feet, the underside gears of a drop-leaf table furry with dust on grease, the feel of grit on cool linoleum. I remember a stench and the amorphous, dimly lit fear that I can call up even now via that same electro-chemistry. A time-travelling magic carpet. Today the fear is feeble, but in those many bad old days the fear was bright. The stench of his breath blows at intervals, waxing and waning as he screams, inhales, and screams again. It seems as though all of my history lives in that stench. I'm forever connected to that stench.

I have a clear memory of giggling. There's a second impact, but this one is soft and round, nothing like the thunderclap of the first one. Familiar things look different from this vantage point, handles seem backwards, square cupboards are trapezoids, doors and windows aren't obvious. This strange juxtaposition evokes memories that are too specific for invention, which is how I know for sure I was there in that upside-down kingdom that was so often the subject of my father's sermons. Familiarity is usually safe, but not this kind of familiarity. I remember too many upside-down slivers of history. Trauma inspires a molecular memory that bypasses the senses and infects us deep down in the spaces between things—whispered violence, rumours of war. I think that's what lives under my skin: memory like the Old Testament, Sodom and Gomorrah, Job scraping his boils with a shard of pottery.

Outside the windows that look at nothing from down here under the kitchen table there's a neighbourhood: a plum tree in the backyard, the garage where I once saw a gutted deer hanging from the rafters, the across-the-alley Macintyre's back porch where Mrs. Macintyre stood to call her sons Gordon and John home for dinner, the yard next door where I saw up Erica Lundgren's nightgown—all familiar, nothing safe. I feel sleepy and comfortable down here; the table legs make me happy, but I don't remember why. There's a puckered eclipse as my father's fat round face blocks the light, another jet of stench, pre-vomit. I remember remembering, *I'm learning about pulsars in school.*

The stench reminds me of the time our Labrador Hobart rolled in a rotting salmon carcass, which reminds me of the beautiful outgoing tide at the mouth of the Fraser River where I used to walk him, which in turn delivers to me images of silver mercury in flecks streaming, bending around a grassy point—a welder's plume of flashes and sparks sprayed by the sun across the broad shoulders of a dirty brown and blue, broad river.

A river's shoreline always looks different when seen from water level, like the kitchen looks different from under the table. The headland is unfamiliar, not down at your feet but at eye level, new and exciting, something to be admired as you sweep past on your way out to sea. There's history in those rocks, in the grass and reeds. Memory hangs from the stunted crabapple trees and Garry oaks, time and place grow into people, like roots running in reverse, up from the muddy ground, through the soles of work boots or moccasins, into the bloodstream, pumping you full of the land and its history—not the gilded and glossed version from books, but the lived-and-died history of everyone who feeds the soil that once fed them.

Sadly, I can't say which of these beautiful tableaus are me remembering things and which are me remembering things remembered. I guess it doesn't really matter considering that memory is fickle, more story, less chronicle, constructed by an illusion—me, you, us—fictions all. I can't even be sure which illusion is telling you this story—the one I was then, the one I became when I left, the one I am now, some of each like a compilation self, Dave—The Greatest Hits. But even that logic is suspect because much of this story lives in my skull in real time and I can still feel all the hot pain if I allow it. So most probably it's the illusion I believe myself to be, telling you this story—the idealized me—because in reality I'm a long way from ideal, and even though there's no such thing as sin, I believe I should suffer for mine. And I do.

But back to our hero: *No longer aware of his body's orientation in three dimensions, his amygdala has curled him into a defensive ball waiting for higher levels of cognition to boot up and save the ancient reptile within, still and holding fast, vulnerable and unprotected, a fool behind long-ago vanished armour.* I like that description of myself under the kitchen table even though the science is suspect. I think I'll use it in a book one day. The rest of the story is less reptilian, more familial: what I did, what was done to me, what I caused in others, and what was brought down to us all through the generations. I suppose that's just so many noodles spun from a giant ball of family dough, a feast of boiled rationalizations with butter and raisins. To account for what-made-me, what-I-made, and what-will-be-made-from-what-I-leave-behind, you have to see them all as the same person—a multi-generational being born of what ancestor did what to whom and when, and what that caused and such and so on unto the third and fourth generations. Yea and amen, drop the mic.

Apologies, I wandered into the future. Where was I? Oh yes, about to invite you to join me in the asking of that big, common question ... *what if?* A more philosophical, less personal, less potentially pathetic thought than *if only*. If only walks us dangerous down the block into the empty house of *why me?*

Why this family, why this particular year of our Lord, why these particular ancestors, why these eminently measurable degrees of longitude and latitude, why this smell in the air, why this specific microflora in my gut? Well, that last one I might be able to answer. As far back as I can remember and farther still by way of pictures and stories, everyone in my family loved noodles and dumplings. Every culture the world over makes noodles and dumplings in one form or another. They're always peasant foods and my family are the royalty of peasantry, so naturally we're all noodles-and-dumplings people but of the middle European variety. We like bacon, onions, and sauerkraut in our perogies, apples or plums or curds of dry cottage cheese, but not potatoes and cheddar—those are made by the Ukrainians. My grandma made me noodles with brown butter and raisins, sometimes with cinnamon on top, or savoury and sour noodles with onions, vinegar, and fried headcheese. Noodles were always egg noodles and dumplings were always perogies, but they were big rectangular pillows, not the dainty half-moons from the grocery store. The Chinese have chow fun and har gow, the Japanese have gyoza, Africans make semiya or muthiya, Americans make chicken stew with dumplings, Italians make gnocchi in Umbria and frittelle di baccalà in Liguria, Jamaicans make fufu, coxinha comes from Brazil. My family's noodles and dumplings are nothing so emotional, exotic, or sensual as those others. The politics of otherness so easily slides satisfaction down the gullet, don't you think?

Our noodles and dumplings pedigree came from the homogenized mud stuck to the army boots tramping back and forth across the lands traded as war spoils between Austria, Germany, Poland, France, Russia, Ukraine, Hungary, Czechia, Slovakia, Croatia, Serbia, and the Balkans. That tangled mess of central and Eastern Europe flung so many ignorant, desperate, poor, and frightened peoples of all kinds across the world—religious zealots, crafty capitalists, idealistic communists, and farm-calloused dreamers—all landing on the shores of countries soon to be subsumed beneath an avalanche of whiteness. A plague of biblical abortion for the non-whites. Thanks to images from *National Geographic* on Sunday evening TV, I see these European countries as bull hippos posturing, preparing to fight, shitting out a wet stream of dung-people into the path of their propeller tails, and covering the earth in all directions with their invective. Not an auspicious people—we the spewed, the loud, and the grave—landing in sulphurous lumps at the feet of First Nations, fouling their lands, melting deep into their firmament to become the stuff of fetid genocide.

In my family's case, landing in lumps is characterized by the playing of the fiddle, the fucking of close relatives, and the drinking of potato-based alcohol. Such was our legend, my inheritance from Graf-Otto Meier Becker, my great-grandfather, a German-speaking half-Russian from Austria, immortalized in family lore as Grab-Onto-My-Pecker, Gomp for short. My great-grandparents—GG Gomp and GG Zophie—floated down the muddy Fraser River from Harrison Mills on a handmade raft of sturdy, dirty logs lashed together with stolen telephone cable, their shelter on the raft the severed ass end of a rusty logging camp work bus fixed to the logs with chokerman's chain. Can't you just hear the Pecker fiddle accompanied by great-grandma Pecker on a jaw harp? That image is probably too Appalachian, but I don't know what the Russo-Germanic equivalent of the hillbilly is; in the theatre of my mind there's no Golden Pond, no Kerouac, just Chilliwack and a broad, muddy plain fingered by a broad, muddy river on its way to the Pacific.

The world then? According to Gomp? Phone calls from God, bone-bending labour, bootstrap ethics, the edge of starvation, constipated emotions plugged up by bacon fat and black bread, loosed on occasion by the perfumed suction of potato moonshine. I can't imagine him having a dream in his head. Maybe that's naïve or immature, or just the self-enlightened bullshit of subsequent generations, or maybe it's simply the pissed-off reaction of someone living his legacy. I can't really know which it is from here inside my skull, thoroughly trapped in my subjectivity even though I was trained in objectivity—I mentioned I'm a scientist, or at least I was.

Was is a powerful word. Behind it lies many hopes and dreams crushed, many transformations, changes, and lessons learned. *Was* when connected to the subjectivity of *I* is ultimately a personal apocalypse. If we could see ourselves beyond the scale of one lifetime, we would see both our present state and what we will become as inevitable, a chariot race between choice and consequence, swinging low, barrelling down the double helix and bringing forward time-travelling repercussions on the wings of epigenetic avenging angels. Alas, this is a cause-and-effect sermon from the pulpit of science that I have yet to deliver.

But back to the hill*willies*—Willy being a far more Russo-Germanic name than Billy, which recalls the Mississippi rather than the Fraser. So the hillwillies floating down the muddy Fraser are looking for a bend on which to adhere like a virus in the bloodstream. Graf-Otto had recently taken a bride, Zophie Giesla Reinheimer from Tabor, Alberta, daughter of a beet farmer, as his tiny, leathery bride. Family lore says they left Alberta for the coast in hopes of logging money, which was better than farming money, but the reality was that the Reinheimers had too many sons-in-law—they were up to six already. Graf-Otto got the runt of the litter.

In the 1920s, logging in British Columbia was a lucrative profession but also far more dangerous than most ways of earning money. GG Gomp, being a sturdy oaf of farming stock from way back, made for a clumsy logger. This equates to a dangerous logger, which often means probable dead loggers nearby. He didn't last long in the camps. He was not smart. Certainly he was powerful enough, but he lacked the catlike grace needed to dance the booms and the elfin ability to efficiently trip the forest. He lacked the deft hands needed to fell a tree while all others in the vicinity remained upright and breathing.

Apparently, the only thing he did better than almost anyone else in the camp was to predict with unfailing accuracy the worst possible outcome of any set of circumstances presented to his senses. A valuable skill, to be sure, but only if one is not also seen as the most likely cause of the predicted worst possible outcome. Also valuable in this situation would have been the ability to shut up in hope of not only being proven correct but also not responsible. Any asshole can continually predict disaster and be right eventually, but in a logging camp to brag about it with supernatural accuracy is a death sentence one way or another. How do I know this personal quirk was his maladroit superpower? I wasn't there. How can I surmise all this from yellow pictures and family stories told by drunks? The shit doesn't fly far from the bull hippo, my friends—twenty feet or a world away, you're still a dung-person.

The Fraser Valley is filigreed and fertile, with many a good place for a penniless couple to burrow in and sprout potato-eyes from the mud. The fleeing Beckers bumped down the Fraser River delta bend by bend, island by island. Rejected from Matsqui Island by its Indigenous band, they tried Nicomen Island but were chased off by Dutch farmers. Douglas Island spat them back into the current as well. MacMillan Island was claimed, Barnston Island was Katzie Nation territory, and Poplar Island was a quarantine camp for First Nations smallpox victims. Annacis Island and Deas Island had well-established multigenerational farms—no room at those inns. Lulu Island was close to the sea, a near last chance, but most of it had been farmed for generations since colonizers had raped and murdered it clear of First Nations in the latter part of the nineteenth century. However, on its uncleared south shore was a settlement of fishing families, a nest of decrepit boats, listing sheds, and float homes called Finn Slough, moniker courtesy of the English farmers who named it after the hard Finnish fishermen populating it. With no clear owner of that south foreshore of Lulu Island, anyone could attempt to claim an open mud bank, but if you weren't a Finn or at least Norse there wasn't much chance of sticking.

Fast running out of islands, the Beckers tried Finn Slough and briefly stuck—lasting maybe a few days or weeks among the hostile Finns; no one knows for sure—but they adhered long enough to hear about a possible landing spot across the river on the eastern shore of a low-slung island called Westham, the very last one. The Finns were only too happy to tow the unwelcome Russo-German and his beef-jerky bride out into the channel and position them in the current so they'd have no chance of returning. My great-grandparents in their desperation had no choice but to try this last stop on the log-boom highway. If they didn't make it, the currents and swells of the Salish Sea awaited them in deep, unforgiving green.

From the point where the smiling Finns cast off the ropes, the Beckers navigated the outgoing tide through a marshy archipelago of almost-islands—Kirkland, Woodward, Barber, Duck, Rose, Gunn, Williamson—islands in name only, all marsh and waterfowl. They headed toward the only one of the group high enough above the tide line to support farms, Westham Island, where they found the small bay the Finns had told them about, uncleared, on the wrong side of the dike. They manoeuvred in using barge poles, quietly moored their rusty platform in the muddy foreshore, and tied off to a huge willow tree that's still there today. The sliver of land that is my family homestead is barely two hundred feet wide at its widest point, maybe a quarter mile long, most of which is still reeds and rushes, not high enough above sea level to avoid the flood tides. A tenuous refuge discovered on Saturday, April 21, 1922.

The raft was home for the first year. GG Gomp used the time to build a dike and to clear what little land he could while hiring himself out to the local farmers as labour. Luckily for him that besides farmers named Coleman and Parenteau there were also Helmholtzes, Wagners, and Schultzes. My family, as I've said, is the royalty of peasantry—squatters, refugees from a middle-European hell, poor, uneducated bumpkins—but this time they had the right last name. You might think this tale is a rise-above story and it certainly looked that way for a while; after all, there is truth in the old blues tune, "Been down so goddamn long it looks like up to me."

CHAPTER 2

SATURNUS

Parenthood steals your soul with light fingers, deftly replacing who you are with a new person, forcing you to fathom who this new person might become. Staring at the bedroom ceiling while the mother of your infant first child snores softly in your arms can be a revelation—the divine or supernatural disclosure to humans of something previously hidden says the OED. Usually, the circumstances of everyday life do not revelate; they more likely accelerate, truncate, or necessitate. The rising and setting of our daily suns is most like whisky and a lullaby, the hum of white noise or the descent into old age at terminal velocity. Rarely do things revelate. That Saturday, Anno Domini 2005, was unremarkable, the same daily declination as always, in every respect mundane. Nothing was special or set apart, but everything became a turning point, unseen until hindsight revealed a hidden *if only* story. We all have an *if only* story, likely more than one. We've all had that time-travelling thought—*if only* is a deep rabbit hole, Alice.

* * *

"I'm sorry, babe," I said to Deb. "Really wish I could do this. I know hockey's usually a dad duty—"

"Hockey for men, figure skating for women, you mean?" she said, cutting me off. "You just keep telling yourself that, Wayne Gretzky."

I laughed. She had such a quick wit. "He couldn't skate well either."

"You can't skate at all! But you're good for other things."

"Like making babies with you?" I suggested.

"Procreate, recreate, don't fornicate," she sing-songed. "I will happily be Sporty Mom today if you play Nurturing Dad. You stay home with Micah; I'll take Adam for his first skate."

"Happy to," I said.

"What time does it start?"

"Ten," Deb said, "but I need skates so we'll go a bit early. I need a decent pair—it's been a long time."

A public skate took place every Saturday except when the ice was out in summer, and Deb was keen to get Adam his first experience on skates. I loved any one-on-one time I could get with either of our sons. Very early on siblings compete for parental attention, so divide-and-nurture is always a good plan. I especially loved napping with one of them on top of me; having a child asleep on my chest while I snoozed was a reconstruction of sorts for me. It allowed me to dream of being so much more than my own father had ever been. Adam was getting a bit long-limbed to fit nicely on my chest, but baby Micah was still just a big kidney bean.

"Don't forget his feeding schedule. The bottle is in the door; don't use the ones from the back of the fridge. Don't wait for him ask, keep him on schedule, set an alarm."

I knew not to protest her repeating of things I already knew. I could mark my acquisition of this marital wisdom on the calendar, beginning from when Adam was about six months old and ending around his first birthday. *Slow learner*, I hear you think.

"I know you know," she added. "I just need to see it your eyes." She pointed a V of fingers back and forth between her eyes and mine.

I met her gaze and gave her my best dad's-on-duty look. "Love you, my dreadnought wife."

"Love you too."

A public skate is families, kids of all ages, a few grandparents, some teens who have dumped hockey but still like to skate, maybe the odd figure skater—they all become like city traffic and lanes develop, a pace develops. Two-year-old Adam was a swishing eggbeater in the slow lane, holding his mother's hands, dangling between her feet, grinning, enjoying the new sensations. He would become a good skater but not until his muscles caught up to his frame. Same for his baby brother; they were both destined to be big men.

Traffic that morning included a Polish Korean sports car—a speedy six-year-old racing his Polish dad around the rink, only to lose an edge and go spinning off into the other skaters, dutifully obeying Newton's laws of motion. A cause born in both Poland and Korea, an effect consummated in Canada generations later. Deb's feet were taken out from behind, and she got hit full force. Adam spun out, unharmed, but Deb slammed backwards. The rink attendant said she looked like a teeter-totter, skates in the air, head cracked on the ice—straight as a board for an instant before she was knocked nearly unconscious. The attendant helped her sit up and stayed with her until she could gather herself enough to stand and be assisted off the ice. With the attendant under one of Deb's arms and the Polish dad under the other, and with unhurt Adam in tow, they made their way to the benches and sat Deb down. This was her seminal incident on a seminal Saturday, the second such confluence of events in our family history. Mine was the first and both involved concussion. But I found out there were others in our ancestry revealing a daisy chain of seminal Saturdays. We'll get to those revelations later, no 666, no seven headed beast, but an Armageddon none the less.

Deb was fine in no time. She laughed it off and graciously accepted a profusion of apologies from the Polish dad. She went back out on the ice with Adam and finished the public skate. She told me all about it when they got home. When I checked her out, I found a fat bump on the back of her head, but that was it, nothing more. Good thing she'd been wearing a helmet. The next day, and the next, and the days after that were all exceedingly normal, as were the thousands of days that followed.

We carried on through the years, Deb and I, past all the firsts: words, sentences, laughter, rage, sorrow, crawling-walking-running, vaccinations, kindergarten, the elementary grades, new friends, all the many, many milestones, all without event, only joy, satisfaction, exhaustion, and love. I felt like a stranger in my own life. Me, the offspring of addiction and abuse, the progeny of hypocrisy, the downstream of an ancestral shitstorm—me, to be in so perfect a life was like the promise of heaven … unbelievable. Of course I was hopelessly idealistic about what loving families are supposed to be like, thanks to my own history, and of course this naïveté would have to end. Perfection is always a trick of the light; it glows sexy in the night but snaps out of existence with the flip of a switch. I know that now. I accept that now. This is the way the changeable universe works, packets of the possible arriving every day and changing the world one photon at a time. I haven't yet mentioned: I'm a scientist, an astrophysicist, so I'm familiar with the infinitesimally small and the incomprehensibly large as well as the odd glimpse of the infinite. I'm also familiar with the purported simple comforts of a God who knows everything, has a plan, and balances love and justice perfectly, all the time for everyone. You see, I'm a child of the church: both my father and grandfather were evangelical pastors. So I ask your forgiveness in advance for any philosophical vertigo you may experience as you follow me bumbling through my personal hall of mirrors, chasing irreconcilable "ologies."

* * *

That November of 2009 the boys were seven and five. The University of British Columbia's women's basketball team was holding an alumni fundraiser. Deb and a handful of her alumni girlfriends were playing an evening game against the current women's team. The alumni were always a mostly all-star team designed to balance the disadvantage in age. The game began and all was well, the alumni holding their own despite the age difference. In her day, Deb had been a solid shooting guard, five-foot-ten with quick feet, excellent aim, and good vision.

The alumni were using basic triangle offence with weak side rotation. The ball went from the forward to the centre to the shooting guard; Deb, as the shooter, was to take the shot, either three points or two depending on what the defense gave her. When the pass came, head-high and hard, she saw two balls, not one, causing her to hesitate and take the actual ball square in the face. Feeling lucky her nose wasn't broken, she sat out the rest of the game. When she came home I could see the worry on her face beneath the blackening eyes and swollen nose. She told me what had happened. Double vision.

We both knew immediately that the previous diagnosis of her balance issues had just become dangerously wrong. Neither of us had any idea what the diagnosis should have been, but we knew it was serious, nothing as innocuous as crystals of the inner ear. The next day she booked an appointment with our GP, who promptly sent her off to a neurologist. We spent that Christmas and a good part of January in a state of low-grade anxiety as she went for an extensive, rigorous round of tests from vision-related brain function to hunting for tumours and everything in between. Nearing the end of January testing was declared complete, and each of the specialists cloistered themselves to analyse the results. Without the constant reminder of appointments, our anxiety dissipated and life returned to normal.

In June of 2010 I attended a cosmology conference hosted by the University of Portland. Their program wasn't particularly noteworthy, but the conference had a reputation as a good place to meet and party. For participants, the drive down the I-5 from Vancouver and Seattle or up the I-5 from northern California was easy. Flights from southern California were quick and cheap. U of P has a tram connecting the campus to downtown, so Portland's beer and food culture was a big part of the agenda, as was my favourite Portland indulgence, a place called Voodoo Donuts—specifically their Canadian-maple-bacon long john. Their genius motto, "The Magic Is in the Hole," is screen-printed on souvenirs for sale.

I was standing on the sidewalk out front in a small knot of fellow scientists, eating my long john, a pair of pink souvenir panties with the "magic" motto printed on the crotch spilling out of my breast pocket—a gift for Deb. We were talking about beer and neutron stars when my phone rang. I saw it was Deb, told my colleagues it was my wife, and answered. My silence and the look on my face stopped the group's banter cold.

"I'm coming home right away," I said to Deb. Ending the call, I glanced up at the group and said, "My wife has been diagnosed with multiple sclerosis."

I left for the hotel as fast as I could, checked out and started the longest five-hour drive of my life. Deb had been crying softy when we talked on the phone, and that was all I could hear in my head as I drove. Music helped. Talk radio helped a bit more but still my thoughts were slashed and bloodied by this new knowledge that hadn't existed in my brain only a short time ago. Words can burrow between your eyes like a migraine, or punch you in the gut and take your breath away, they can cramp a muscle in the small of your back. The news of trauma is like trauma itself: it changes you physically. Scalding neurochemistry sculpts the soft landscape of your body into new spires and chimneys, into knots of malign memory. You can feel it happening during those first hours as you gradually take in the idea that things will never be the same.

The ancients believed human essence resided in the gut, modern science says consciousness is an emergent property of brain activity, religion says we have a soul, philosophy seeks the self—pick your poison. When you're introduced to trauma through mere words you quickly realize that every cell of your body is an inextricably interpenetrating, self-aware whole. There is no division between body and mind, no borderland between you and your left foot, nowhere to run, and nowhere to hide. In this situation there are only two choices, curl up into a ball under the kitchen table or stand up, feel your feelings, then go looking for answers. Me, I needed answers so natutally I went digging into the genetic past.

CHAPTER 3

PURPLE HELMUT

The 1920's passed into the 1930's and peckers made more Beckers. The 20's and 30's were fertile years for *meine trottel vorfharen*: my bumpkin ancestors. I use the plural—peckers— because lineage is always unclear in hillwilly stories, even if I can't fathom the nakedness of the living mummified corpse that was GG Zophie, let alone the thought of touching her innermost inner-moist however briefly (then again, I can't fathom having to eat pig slop or die, and they did that too). Given the circumstances and the times, the fact that they reproduced at all is an epic victory, even if the easily predictable regular drunken beatings of their unfortunately named firstborn, Helmut ended in tragedy. Because of the beatings he was dubbed Purple Helmut by his younger siblings. The beatings began early enough to make him the family monster, at least on this side of the Atlantic; who knows what extended-family ghouls still lurked in central Europe.

After Helmut came Arnfried, Siegfried, Ekkehardt, Berta, Gerta, and finally my Grandfather Felix, the youngest of seven, a position far enough away from the fucked-up middle to be somewhat safe, out at the fast-spinning extremity of a violent family vortex rotating at full throttle. My Grandpa Felix, by the luck of birth order, could see normal from the kitchen table on which he and his afterbirth landed. He spared me no detail about the sins of his father, as if I were the only one he could to talk to, turning everything into a Bible lesson.

"Exodus 34:7 says God will keep steadfast love for thousands, forgiving iniquity and transgression and sin, but will by no means spare the guilty, visiting the iniquity of the fathers on the children and the children's children, to the third and fourth generation."

"Why, Grandpa?" I asked him. "That's not fair." I was already acutely aware of things unfair.

"The Lord is slow to anger, David. He says he is abounding in steadfast love but he will not pardon the truly guilty, visiting the iniquity of the fathers on their children and their children's children. He's talking about worshipping other Gods, and it's fathers who teach sons who the one true God is. He says God is a jealous God and idol worship won't be forgiven."

"That still doesn't sound fair." I said, unconvinced. "We go to Dad's church. I don't get a choice. Dad went to your church. What if we all chose the wrong church and the wrong God?" Such an inquisitive child, me.

"Ezekiel 18:20 says the soul who sins shall die but the son shall not suffer for the iniquity of the father, nor the father for the iniquity of the son. That means if we are made to sin and it's beyond our power to control, only the person causing the sin is punished."

"I don't get it. They sound like the opposite thing to me."

"They're not, David. In the book of John, in the New Testament, Jesus tells us he once came upon a man who was blind from birth, and one of his disciples asked what sin of this man's father had caused him to be born blind. Jesus said neither of the man's parents had sinned. He was born blind so that God might be glorified in his life."

"So God made the man be born blind so the man could worship him?" My innocent, ten-year-old logic found offense in this divine cruelty, and I was more confused than ever.

"Some things are of heaven and some things are of earth, David. We don't always understand why things happen the way they do, or who gets born in a certain way."

It sounded much like the pablum I would hear my father burble from the pulpit on Sunday mornings in future—and Sunday evenings and Tuesday night Bible study. Insert my father for the blind man in this story. Swap out congenital blindness for generational alcoholism. The Bible is such a flexible book. Like a decades-delayed child, Grandpa Felix took great pains in what I now know was the unburdening of himself to me because of his own abusive father and his abusive son … my father. He and I had somehow fallen into the nonviolent troughs of the familial addiction-and-abuse sine wave. His confessions to me were inappropriate but understandable. I was six when he started sharing our family history with me, or at least that's when my memories begin, starting with the story of Purple Helmut. His story explains everything you need to know about my family.

In 1939, at sixteen Helmut walked the few miles' distance from the Becker family swamp to the train tracks, where the CP Rail freight trains ran from the coast, and he hopped onboard. He rode the rails all the way to southern Ontario, where he volunteered to fight for king and country in the coming conflagration now smouldering again in the dry stooks of central Europe—the gala Second Annual World War. The irony was not lost on later generations of the family that the angry alcoholic oaf Grab-Onto-My-Pecker—assumed to have been driven to that state (the alcohol-induced anger, not the oafishness, which was genetic) by the perpetual mayhem of the incessant warring in Europe—that he, Graf-Otto, would mix such bad chemistry in Purple Helmut that the most well-suited outlet for all the assassin's amperage stored in Helmut's black battery was the gala Second Annual World War. He too was now an angry, violent alcoholic. The sins of the father indeed. I used to think that was nonsense until the events of my own life traced a treasure map leading to cache after cache of weaknesses and transgressions that apparently lurked in my DNA or my psyche or maybe just my nightmares. But I digress, regress, and progress all at the same time.

Grandpa Felix told me that years before D-Day, Purple Helmut was in Europe, behind enemy lines, working for the British Special Operations Executive. A German-speaking Canadian boy who enjoyed fucking people up the way most of us enjoy ice cream was a find not to be squandered. After enlisting, Purple Helmut apparently flew through basic training all aces and was immediately earmarked for greater things. Basic training was very basic, not designed for long-term survival on the battlefield but more for a constant churn of meat-weapons. An army is like a giant tunnelling machine with drill bits made of humans slowly grinding its way through an enemy mountain of stone, barbed wire, bricks, steel, fire, and bullets. The odds are stacked against the meat at the pointy end and the churn never stops, but a naturally violent physical specimen who was not dumb, was fluent in German, was blond of hair and blue of eye—a poster child for the SS had he been born in the Fatherland—was the perfect fake Nazi, much too valuable for the army. The British SOE had been turning out fake Nazis for years by the time Purple Helmut arrived in London. D-Day was still more than two years away and fake Nazis were in high demand in preparation for the invasion of continental Europe. Helmut was further trained for espionage and sabotage until he was ready to be slipped into Europe via Denmark. Grandpa Felix said at first the family would get periodic contact from Helmut via Montreal, then just once from England, and after that all was silence.

The story of what Purple Helmut got up to in Europe was pieced together over the post-war years by the family in what sounded to me like a macabre Saturday night parlour game that helped pass the time and keep what modicum of peace there was in the house each evening. The army provided the official details after the war, and letters came from men Helmut served with as well. Letters from Europe also trickled in until the early 1950s, some from colleagues in the secret service, some from resistance fighters, and two from men who can only be understood to be victims. All the letters from Europe should have been alarming given their contents, but in the steady flow of corrupted current that was the Becker family culture, the things that Purple Helmut got up to, from disconcerting to alarming to outright inhuman, served as an emotional safety valve for the fucked-up family, or so I surmise. There were certainly daring deeds, bravery, and even heroic recklessness but set against a landscape of cruelty, love of violence, torture, sadism, and shades of fatalistic masochism.

The first letter arrived in time for Christmas 1947. It was from a field director in British military intelligence, a Major White, writing to inform the parents of the disappearance and assumed death of Purple Helmut during the sacking of Berlin by the vengeful Russians. Major White explained that Helmut had been smuggled into northern Europe, where he was instrumental in the preparations for D-Day. There were no tears, at least none that Grandpa Felix remembered. The news seemed to get swallowed up in the familial lake of fire. Helmut quickly passed from offspring and sibling—a real person, known and remembered, feared, GG Gomp's favourite knock-down clown—into legend, a legend that, fed by more letters, only grew over the years.

The Book of Helmut morphed into the apocrypha that was his life story. A second letter came, this one from a Polish Jew named Silber telling how he and Helmut had blown up a large cache of Nazi ordinance, killing dozens of Nazi soldiers in the conflagration. The chilling-thrilling part of the tale was how Helmut, in Nazi uniform and having talked his way into the compound, lured the duty officer and his men into an office using American pornography as bait, then excused himself for reasons of personal gratification, which made them all laugh. Purple Helmut had learned to make people laugh before he killed them, and the psychology was foolproof. He barred the back door from the outside, walked around to the front gate, took the .50-calibre machine gun from the guard Silber had killed, walked back to the middle of the compound, sat down, and waited for the explosives he and Silber had planted to detonate. As the charges began to blow and the survivors tried to escape, Helmut methodically shot all that made it out the front door with the .50, which is like shooting a rabbit with a shotgun—the holes are large and anatomy becomes airborne. If the survivor was on fire, however, those he let burn.

Purple Helmut was the original Reservoir Dog, a proto-Tarantino character, a murderous military gangster with a flair for drama and no fear of death. The archetype for the spaghetti Western before the movie-sauce was invented. Silber explained that Helmut had asked him, should he, Silber, survive the war, to write to his family and tell them what he and Silber had done; this was the common theme behind every letter. Silber was fulfilling his promise in telling the tale and Helmut was talking to us all, down the generations and from the grave. There were similar stories of sabotage to come, each with a marked progression in the violence and sadism. And the killing became ever more personal; increasingly, Helmut's own plan seemed to supplant the orders he was assigned by the British SOE.

In 1950 came a letter from a French woman with a German name, Inga.

For almost a year Purple Helmut and Inga had worked together identifying targets for Allied bombers to obliterate, incinerate, and otherwise raze. It was the period of the war when air superiority transferred from the Axis to the Allies. Sorties were flown over Germany proper for the first time, the industrial west being the priority, particularly the Ruhr Valley. Purple Helmut haunted the Ruhr Valley, the Rhineland, and Westphalia, sending information back to Allied bomber command in England through Inga. She explained how successful they were at first with many important targets hit—train stations, factories, power plants, bridges, and dockyards. Over time, however, she became suspicious of Helmut. The quality of his information seemed to deteriorate, more cities were bombed and more civilians killed, more neighbourhoods and fewer military targets were destroyed. She could not say, given the technology of the day and the decisions of the now infamous English Air Marshal, Sir Arthur "Bomber" Harris, where the fault lay, but she wrote candidly of her suspicion that Helmut was doing it on purpose, running his own personal blitzkrieg, revelling in his own personally set firestorms.

After the Inga letter came the Duck letter, the best one for a movie plot, the biggest dog in the reservoir. The trail was picked up again in the heart of occupied France in the city of Bourges. Helmut was making friends and influencing people with the help of the French Resistance. The mission was to photograph maps of Nazi coastal defenses without raising alarms, which meant no killings. The Nazis were not to know information was being stolen, according to the agent writing the letter, still calling himself le Canard though the war was long over. I guess the Vichy weren't all yet vichyssoise; a few bad potatoes and gritty leeks were still around after the war so the Duck was still hiding in the reeds with Moses. He reported Purple Helmut was sullen; he didn't enjoy not killing. The Duck surmised that Helmut used this unhappiness with his real mission to sell himself deeper into cover by complaining to his Nazi friends about a fake mission from Berlin, changing the details of his Allied orders to Nazi orders and emphasizing the disappointment of not being allowed to kill. Of course, the Duck could not say anything with certainty but believed this or something similar to be the case. This Duck apparently loved to quack, and the letter was rich with background, the setting of scenes, cultural detail, and self-aggrandizement.

Helmut decided to throw a poker party on the eve of his alleged departure to comply with his shitty no-killing-and-don't-get-caught orders from Berlin. The party had to be exclusive because of the French hookers and the looted French booze, so only the highest-ranking officers could attend and it had to be in a secure location—the bunker where the maps and other valuable documents were kept was perfect. The Duck thought Helmut must have had the high explosives strapped to his body—both as a track-covering device and a just-in-case measure, perhaps set with a timer he could control, because of course no sane person would create a situation so difficult to emerge alive from. Nevertheless, Helmut's party was top-drawer and went deep into the wee hours, after the cognac was gone, the hookers were used up, and the poker money had become serious. Helmut was winning. Eventually it came down to Helmut and a Colonel named Kieselbach. After a particularly intense hand that Kieselbach won with three queens to Helmut's three jacks, Helmut exploded from his chair cursing, drew his machine pistol, and levelled it between the eyes of Colonel Kieselbach … who was now Colonel of Soiled Undergarments. The room froze. Helmut tensed then feigned coming to his senses, laughed, crowed a back-slapping apology, and sat back down. As the six men around the table exhaled and relaxed, Helmut made a self-deprecatory comment that caused them all to laugh, then he shot them under the table, unstrapped the explosives, and walked out. The hookers ran, the incendiaries detonated at a safe distance, and the bunker blazed up into the night like a funeral pyre. The Nazi maps and papers appeared at the appointed place and time, with Nazis none the wiser, along with a request of the Duck to write a letter to Helmut's family telling them the story. Helmut then disappeared said the Duck, no longer operating under orders.

The penultimate letter was from Strasbourg on the German border, and it was dictated by Helmut, the first written in German, the first one the family called a victim letter. The writer, Major Cornelius Kesler, was staring down the barrel of Purple Helmut's machine pistol. But Major Kesler didn't sound like a military target in his letter, he sounded like a victim. The letter was the only one addressed solely to Graf-Otto. Purple Helmut was dramatizing exactly what Graf-Otto had created and the unfortunate Major Kesler was assumed to be standing in for the abusive father. The letter picked up from the point of Helmut's disappearance after the poker game, across France to the border with Germany, and revealed the deterioration of Helmut's grip on his own humanity. Clearly, he was not sane and perhaps never wholly had been. But whatever oxygen of sanity he did possess had now grown thin. In the war around Helmut, the Allies were closing in on Germany from all sides. In the war within Helmut, his demons were closing in. Helmut said he was heading to the hurricane of hellfire that Berlin would become in only a short time. The letter's last line was chilling and direct.

"He will now kill me," wrote Kesler. There was blood spatter on the paper.

The final letter was very different from all the others; even for Helmut it was gratuitous and merciless. It contained two more letters within the main letter, but those were not from the main letter writer, a Russian intelligence officer writing in perfect English, explaining his duty to forward the two unopened letters to the family. The officer no doubt assumed them to be the heartfelt last communications from a fellow operative to his loved ones from deep undercover, uttered with his dying breath.

The two interior letters were inside envelopes addressed by Purple Helmut's hand. The letters themselves were written in educated German this time and the family had trouble understanding them, which Helmut no doubt anticipated, as if he wanted to give them all an unforgettable lesson by making them work to comprehend his final deeds. The family called them the Two Victims Letters. They tell the story of the rape of Berlin by the Russians. Purple Helmut had been not just a willing participant but a ravening and roaring lion pouring out all of his bile, his insanity, his inhumanity, like so much night soil, arm in bloody arm with the enraged and starving Russian peasant army. All his hate, as well as any love there might have been, had been shriven out of Purple Helmut before he took his own life. The first victim letter was written by a thirteen-year-old girl named Marika who had been spared by Helmut in exchange for taking dictation, recounting a blow-by-blow account of his rape and murder of her older sister and aunt. The second letter was written by a ten-year-old boy named Martin who had been forced to watch Purple Helmut rape, torture, and murder three women, one his mother. After the women's ordeal was mercifully over, the young boy reported that Helmut said he was empty and at peace.

Martin wrote, "He tells me which Russian officer to take the letters to and where to find him. He says that after he seals the letters he will watch me deliver them then kill himself, unless I don't deliver them. In that case he will kill me first. He doesn't tell me how he will kill himself, but he assures me many will die in his act of suicide."

The most vicious of vicious circles was closed. The megalomaniacal soil of Austria grows the weed that flings the seed to Canada, where grows a new but equally noxious weed that flings its seed back onto the soil of Germany to soak it with yet more blood. Had Graf-Otto understood that his son was killing him over and over in a vain attempt at retroactive patricide, like a killer robot from the future in an endless loop of time travel? Or maybe, more likely, Graf-Otto understood nothing, simply believing Purple Helmut was the decider of his own fate.

Fate, however, believes in killer robots from the future. Fate is in fact an expert time traveller, navigating the portals generation by generation, disappearing here, materializing there, visiting and revisiting consequences like a wish-granting Djinn with a blue-water business plan. We mortals tethered to one lifetime can't see its overarching shadow. Time travel is no more a fiction than quantum entanglement; the particle—or wave—only seems to be an effect without a cause. Human generations live on the scale of a super-organism, like plate tectonics, too large and too ancient for any one individual to perceive by many powers of ten. Fates' intergenerational consequences quantum-tunnel their way through a conga line of lives into our personal present, happily fucking us in the ass. We sentient apes are each a fixed quantity, our personal three- or fourscore and whatever only charmed thievery. But our genes, ah yes, our genes, they carry the fate-magic across the generations like currents on a river, each of us taken by the flow to our particular stone, where we crack our heads and sink to the bottom.

Too fatalistic, you think. Your mind revolts, your psyche squirms. I am the master of my own destiny, you say. We have preached this to ourselves on many a psychedelic Sunday. Let me say to you that as a scientist (or former scientist or perhaps heretical scientist): whatever I am now, I say that our problem, everyone's problem, is merely perspective. You, me, we—all of us are masters of only the moment, constrained by our time, restrained in our place, popcorn in the pot. Who would you be if you were born a hundred years from now? Who if born into a Brazilian favela or Palm Beach billions? Who if ten thousand miles away in a different culture with different Gods? Smith or Jones, Hatfield or McCoy, Mohammed or Moses, Graf-Otto or Helmut? Would you still be you or someone else? Do those questions even make sense or are we simply alive and ourselves or nonexistent; either dead or never born? Someone should ask Timothy Leary's ghost and let the rest of us know what he says because these philosophical arguments seem like pointless bullshit when you're sitting in a doctor's office on the third floor of UBC Hospital's neurology building on a sunny summer day in 2010 being presented with the difference between a *cause* and a *precipitating event.* A cause offers a tantilizing glimpse at blame; perhaps a genetic inheritance or an ancestral asshole? On the other hand, there's no smoking gun for precipitating events, nothing in the brain scans, the statistics, the latest medical theory, the latest studies on the mystery of consciousness, or the Ted Talks about free will. None of it will tell you why the person who used to live inside that skull over there, the one on the pillow beside you is gone, replaced by a new person and a "diagnosis." This experience tends to kick the shit out of any theory. The observable universe is less complex than the human brain, and for the universe at least we have the advantage of not using the thing we're studying to study the thing we're studying.

The first floor of the neurology building is outpatient services, labs are on the second floor, administration on the fourth, and classrooms, lecture halls, library, and research archives on the fifth. You don't want to be on the third floor—that's where all the bad news gets delivered: multiple sclerosis, Parkinson's, ALS, Huntington's, cancerous brain tumours, and other murderous diseases. If these walls could talk they might say, "Precipitating event; what does that mean?" Me, I want a good old-fashioned cause, a reason, a definable connection, an explanation. I need little arrows pointing from A to B—I'm used to things like stellar maps and spin diagrams. Compared to cosmology, neuroscience seems lost. Also, have I mentioned I'm weak? For emotional satisfaction I need someone to blame, and forget arrows pointing—I want finger-pointing. Watching someone you love acquire a life-altering label creates a deep desire to find the asshole responsible, to find a reason, to connect some cause in the chain of events that came down the years from some unknown ancestor.

Dr. Alfred Ba, PhD and neurologist, loved unanswerable questions. The larger the scope and complexity of a problem, the more he loved it. I loved unanswerable questions too, just not this one. This one pissed me off. Deb's ownership of her own very personal unanswerable question was what began my friendship with Alfred Ba. Alfred had no ego when it came to problems he couldn't solve; for him this was proof of the infinite, proof of things beyond the understanding of humankind, the eternal mystery always receding from our intellectual grasp. It was no wonder we became friends. His internal universe and my universe out there have many parallels, studying the vault of the heavens and the vault of the human mind are surprisingly similar. Both are embedded, both carry infinite possibility, both are uncountable in their complexity, both are daemon engines chugging into the inevitable future along the furrows of the past. *"We are caged in history with the beast of ancestry and our future is devoured"* to quote my grandfather. We are creatures of our time and place in history, our family and faith, our sex, our culture and language, our political structures, our social rank, our teachers and friends, our pets, our possessions, our names, and the things we call ourselves in the bathroom mirror. Who says? I hear you say. What proof do I have for this fatalistic voodoo, this dehumanizing lionizing of determinist rationalizing? Let me tell you who says: the Swedes, that's who!

CHAPTER 4

ALL THE POSSIBLE FUTURES

Swedish people are not just attractive merchants of melancholy in the guise of knock-together blondes; both people and furniture, nor are they simply a domesticated breed of the formerly fierce Viking; they are also a meticulous people, a northern people of long nights and much patience. They are perfect for science. Think of Celsius, Angstrom, Linneaus, Backlund, Von Euler, Klien, Nobel—so many great scientists bred in cold crystal beneath a far northern sky. They proved fate is carried as the quantum-timed music of chance within our genes; even the subtlest of destinies is a song we are given at birth.

Overkalix is a forlorn hamlet in northern Sweden. Over hundreds of years it housed mobs of monks, up to and including the early twentieth century. They did monkish things like make beer and record history in meticulous detail: the daily graces of God, the who-begat-whoms, farming accountancy, mortality tables, the path of comets, and the count of can-nonballs—all long before the age of data and statistics. Thus was born the Overkalix study, made possible by these zealous geek-priests. Today's mathematicians, statisticians, medical researchers, and geneticists all owe a debt of data to these clerics of many yesterdays. It's a worthy irony don't you think? When clerics and scientists—as like Jews and Arabs or Turks and Greeks—stop fighting and turn around to smile for the camera you can't tell them apart. And what did our modern high priests of science learn from these ancient high priests of the one true and Catholic church? They've found exactly what the Bible said they would find. The rocks and trees do cry out. The sins of the fathers do visit down the generations. Hatfield is always Hatfield, McCoy always McCoy. No God required, just DNA.

it's was found that the average grandfather growing up in times of plenty reliably predicts the premature death of the average grandson while also reliably predicting the not-premature death of the average granddaughter. How is that possible? Verily, verily I say unto you: transgenerational epigenetics! A scientific mouthful of math passing through physical bodies, whispering the history of those bodies, though they may never meet. The Swedes discovered the TARDIS of the human super-organism. And scientists have now done more work, studies of studies, new studies of not just the food supply but of war, imprisonment, and upheaval. The results? More scientific proof of genetic time travel. You see, my friend, there's no mystery here, no magic. This is pure science, math, and statistics: genes know what happened to the genes of all previous generations, back to the very origins of our species—*presto questo*—time travel! Ponder this while you learn more of my history and imagine where my story may lead, where I came from, and where I'm destined to end up, whose genes whispered to me, who relives and relieves themselves down the generations through my daily travails. Please think on this, as I surely don't know.

* * *

So back to the morning of my seminal event—apologies if I'm giving you a temporal nose bleed, we're back in the late 1980's now and about to seal my future. It was a Saturday—no surprise. Saturnus, the ancient God of growth, plenty, wealth, and agriculture, not the God of skating but a busy God, nonetheless. He was also one of the original wielders of lightning, so this is an appropriate place to continue my story because there was often Saturday lightning in the house of my childhood. This Saturday was like no other before it and yet just like every other before it. Sound familiar? The potential was always there for Saturday lightning to set off the powder keg that lived beneath my feet, in the platform shoes of my soul, rocket boots of righteous rage for a young Rocket Man.

Why that specific Saturday? I suspect a scientific answer, of course, but I can only guess. I think a new network was connected up in my prefrontal cortex; areas of my brain that had previously functioned independently had their first conversation that day and decided to say, "Hello, and fuck all this shit!" An image of a new possible me was born, a me of my very own, a me I had not imagined before; maybe an epigenetic ghost had risen from its tomb, opening a new circuit in my brain so lightning could flow, slick and hot, along new paths, chasing the chemistry of new feelings I didn't recognize down unexplored mine shafts of emotion. Who knows? A regular Saturday like no other. That's the miracle of science, or maybe just the explanation of a miracle—they're not the same thing. Regardless, the miracle that is the human self (I'm being deliberately provocative here), the neurological mapping of *me* onto the meat that fills my skull, can't in any way explain my lightning, and neither can a bearded old man in the sky. To this day I don't really understand what happened.

Looking up from the floor as I was from beneath the kitchen table, my world was that upside-down kingdom my father had often preached about. I was the last about to become the first, and all of my own doing, with no actual miracle required. I remember feelings of despair, feelings of help-lessness, hopelessness, obedience, and revolt—all conditioned responses I knew well as I crawled under the table like so many times before. Grandpa Felix came into my thoughts, whom I loved very much, I remember wishing he were my father.

Grandpa Felix was our family's first clergyman. He married young and sired more dead children than live ones. Grandma Evelyn went a touch crazy from all the tragedy. She suffered from polycystic ovary syndrome. She was a barrel-shaped woman with facial hair and sharp, angular fea-tures. She played piano and sang in a deep, reedy alto that came straight from her outsized nose as if the bridge were being bowed like a cello. Back then women with polycystic ovary syndrome usually couldn't get preg-nant, but Grandma Evelyn was one of the unlucky ones who could. The fetus would almost never come to term, and she miscarried seven times in nine pregnancies. When the tragedies hit God's number, with two children safely tucked away in the land of the living, she closed up the coital shop and put Grandpa Felix out to celibate pasture. It was then that he had an affair with the most beautiful woman in his congregation, who bore him a child.

Delores Wilt was trim, beautiful, smart, and feminine with perfect pitch and a soprano voice that floated over the congregation like cherubim. Benno Wilt was a simple, solid man who made furniture. Jesus was a carpenter too. Delores came from money and education; Benno came from the trades. I'm guessing the romance of marrying Jesus wore off for Delores, and although she and Benno had made a fine family that lacked for nothing, something was obviously lacking for Delores. So when Grandpa Felix smote her from the pulpit with his wisdom, intelligence, and soft charisma she gave him what he now lacked and more—she gave him an *illegitimate* child (as if humans have the power to legitimize life). The lovers kept their secret, and the child was raised by the cuckold as his own. Grandpa Felix went to his grave never having acknowledged his illegitimate daughter to anyone, which blew some rather large holes in his emotional barn, and the cows wandered. Wilt family suspicions and Ancestry.com gave him away posthumously.

I was the only person he was ever completely honest with (most of the time, anyway), probably because of his guilt about my father. Like many children, Grandpa Felix rebelled against his own drunken, abusive father and his father's world; also like most of us he didn't understand how utterly and completely the same he was. One of the few escapes available to a child of his era was the clergy, so he took the out. His rebellion was to follow the Prince of Peace. I'm sure he believed he couldn't deviate further from Graf-Otto's violent, drunken raging than by joining the Christian church. (But of course, if Grandpa Felix had been born Grandpa Fu, it would have been a different church with a different God though he would have believed every bit as fervently.) At any rate, Grandpa Felix's lot in life was to be my grandfather and endure what he did, and sire my violent, drunken father so that I could endure what I did, so that I could in turn inflict my own tests of endurance on those that I love. A perfectly logical and understandable cause-and-effect chain of events, except for the inexplicable parts. But most of those come later.

I can see now that Grandpa Felix didn't escape our family bent, his drives and obsessions were just channelled toward the pursuits of a higher spirit and a shorter skirt; after all, isn't it better to thump Bibles on pulpits than to thump empties on bars? Isn't it better to fuck another man's wife than to beat your children? Certainly for the children it is. How my father wound up with such a perfect blend of two often mutually exclusive addictions, the Bible and the bar, is a wonder to me. It seems almost miraculous that my father could hold himself together against the rending forces of what surely must have been a cognitive dissonance that could pull Gs like Tom Cruise in *Top Gun*.

Grandpa Felix and I had only seven years of stories together; he died when I was thirteen. I don't remember anything before the age of six. I do remember how awkward I felt at his funeral— too old to cry, too young to know what to do with all the unfamiliar emotions. I was old enough to know that my family was a sham but not old enough to see that all families are shams in some ways. All of us are gloriously damaged, wondrous creatures capable of such beauty and such cruelty.

The one person in our family who Grandpa Felix would not talk to me about was my father. I think he loved him and loathed him at the same time, something possible only between parents and children. My father, the only male child, hence the one to carry on the expunging of Graf-Otto's legacy through the clergy, gave both the sermon and eulogy at his father's funeral. The funeral rites of the evangelical Christian church in Canada are dry as Saskatchewan dust. Emotions are repressed, even frowned upon, the culture is simplistic, populated by rubes replete with fears of being lured off the *one true path* by movies, pool halls, and long hair. As the old joke goes, no sex please, it may lead to dancing. I think that's why when this ilk, my people, go wrong it's a spectacular crash and burn lighting up the night sky like rockets. My people rejected pressure-valve traditions like Carnival or Mardi Gras so with no hope of release, and if not made of thick enough stuff, we go off like Roman candles. Grandpa Felix was made of thick metal. I'm sure that if Grandma Evelyn's mind hadn't succumbed to grief, he wouldn't have cheated on her, but perhaps that's just me cutting him slack because I loved him. He was, however, very thick metal if you consider the fact that he spoke every Sunday to a congregation containing his third and unacknowledged child, the child's mother, who was his lover, and the child's cuckolded father. Set of brass ones on him.

My father, on the other hand, was made of tin, the original Tin Man flying apart on a regular basis at low PSI, but easy to repair with a few rivets. When you come apart so predictably those who love you will, for a time, try to fix you. They won't stop loving you, or maybe they will, but they will eventually stop trying to fix you. They will lose their empathy at your predictable and repeating pathos. There is no empathy under the kitchen table or in the casket. When I see myself young, vulnerable, and huddled under that table, I can forgive myself. However, I cannot forgive my father. He beat the empathy out of me and so I let it go. The fact that I had to relearn to empathize is no fault of mine. I was bent and so I bend.

Our emotions are the sum of our systems—the endocrine, the nervous, the cardiovascular, the respiratory, the immune, and the digestive. It's all just electrochemistry. On that Saturday I was fully charged by the storm. Saturday is the day before Sunday. Saturday is the last day to get drunk before Sunday comes and you have to face the heavenly music. Carl Samuel Becker, my father the Tin Man, was not thick enough. He failed to hold under the pressure of his double life. If the sermon was not writing itself a small drink would help, sometimes starting on a Friday night or a Wednesday afternoon. The week built toward Sunday like a crooked cathedral, and you never knew when the ribbed vault in my father's resolve would give way. He would rage around the house in the wee hours, but only the doors were in danger at that time of night; he was a slammer. He was what we now call a binge alcoholic, the most pernicious kind of alcoholic. He would go for long stretches without a drink and would, during those times, make up well for his many transgressions. And of course every child wants to have a loving and protective father. And every wife wants to have a husband who doesn't beat the fluids out of her child on a semi-regular and unpredictable basis.

The amount of nonverbal communication that takes place in human relationships is myriad, so with some success I predicted and sometimes escaped the maelstrom. I tried to read the chicken bones and have an exit strategy ready at all times. Sometimes it worked, sometimes it didn't. Sometimes he stopped himself and sometimes he didn't. If you wonder why my mother couldn't protect me, it was precisely this unpredictability that caused her to hope against hope until seventeen years had passed. In that process she became a nonentity; grief and shame consumed her. She became a shadow on the floor, an appliance whirring in the kitchen, the smell of a toilet brush, the sound of paper bags being folded. By the time I was ten or eleven she disappeared from my notice completely, growing into the house like wiring in the walls.

So where *was* I? Oh yes, under the kitchen table at the behest of the Tin Man and his popping rivets—fire in the hole!

"Play that again," he had commanded. "You need more practice."

"I hate playing in church." I had never told him that before.

"You're going to as long as you're living under my roof," said Mr. Breadwinner.

"I'm not your possession, I'm my own person. Why can't you see that?"

"This music is for God! You're his possession. *Why can't you see that!*"

At this point I closed the piano, got up, and went into the kitchen. You can guess what comes next.

"Come back in here, sit down, and practise! Do you want to embarrass me? Disgrace me in front of my congregation!"

"You're a *fucking drunk!* You don't need my help with being disgraced."

It was the first time he'd heard me say *fucking*. It was the first time I'd told him what he already knew about himself.

Crack!

Then came that void I mentioned, that roar, so loud it was silent, the electric buzz of flowing blood, the floor approaching my face, looking up at the underside of the kitchen table.

"Shut up, shut up, *shut up!* You're my son! You *owe me!*" He shouted this over and over, pacing around the kitchen table.

The tumble in my head cleared slowly. Focus began to return to my eyes. My brain was booting up and sensory inputs were starting to register. The stench of my father's pre-vomit breath pooled around me on the floor. I remember thinking how cool it would be if you could get dry-ice fog to stink like this, it would be like a nasty fart cloud you could roll out over the mosh pit. I wanted to be a rock star. I loved piano but hated playing the hymns I was forced to play. I loved to sing too but was never allowed to play and sing anything I wanted to. This was another of the family shams perpetrated by my father. Every pastor needed to have a musical family so they could support his ministry by playing in church. I wanted to play "Superstition" by Stevie Wonder or "Albert Flasher" by The Guess Who; instead, I was forced to play "How Great Thou Art" and "A Mighty Fortress Is Our God." I now realize these are great compositions but then I felt like a musical slave, on my way to becoming a non-person like my mother. It was finally giving voice to that feeling that spawned the seminal moment of my seminal incident on this seminal Saturday.

"I don't owe you anything! *Fuck you! Fuck your music! Fuck your church! Fuck your God!*" I screamed from under the table.

It was as if a wormhole had opened into a parallel universe, and that universe seemed to grow, pulling at me. I slipped through and found myself in a vast unfamiliar place, a new universe of possibilities. My very own big banging. All the barriers surrounding me had vanished. It was a transcendent experience. At seventeen years old, under the kitchen table of my family home, physically and emotionally damaged by the father I hated and loved, I began to cry as I hadn't since I was a young child. What happened next changed everything. I expanded from ice, to water, to steam, to plasma, as my father tried to kick me under the table. I can see it over again anytime, on-demand, like a movie playing in my head, so unlike normal, highly contingent human memory. I have lots of normal memories too, but something very different happened in my brain that day while conducting the family lightning.

I can see his foot coming toward me in stop-time as it approaches frame by frame. I see it, perceive its malicious intent, understand what is meant by it, but it's only a fragment of my sensory experience in that moment. My senses are all around me as well as in me. I'm still very much in my body but awareness is pouring into me from outside of me somewhere, from everywhere.

At what seemed like the appropriate moment, I caught my father's foot and twisted sharply. He screamed in agony and dropped as if shot. I held on, not tightly, not straining—in fact, it was effortless. I held on while he writhed and bounced. Years later I ran over a cat that had darted out into the street. I hit it but didn't kill it outright. I stopped and looked in the rear-view mirror. The cat was bucking and bouncing off the pavement as high as the roof of my car. All of its muscles were firing uncontrollably at full power; the cat's brain didn't yet know it was dead. That's the death dance you hear about in war. I'm sure Purple Helmet had tripped to this light fantastic more than once. That was what my father looked like. He was not in control of his body—his bowels and bladder emptied. He shivered and shook and thumped in violent seizure that stopped the instant I let go. He lay on the floor in front of me, panting, sweating, stinking, spluttering, making incomprehensible sounds. I brought my knees up to my chest and sat up, hunched over, still under the table. I looked out at him, feeling nothing but the vast consciousness of my personal expansion, which was still pouring into me from outside as though I were an empty vessel being filled.

My mother came running into the kitchen, took in the scene, and said nothing. I could see all the years of knowing on her face, all the years of becoming what she was, a non-person. She picked up the phone, called the ambulance, and walked out the back door into the yard, leaving us as she found us, offering neither of us any help or any love. I crawled out from under the table and went to my room. The ambulance arrived while I was packing. I heard them tell my mother his ankle was shattered like glass; they said they couldn't feel anything where the bones were supposed to be. They took him to the hospital, my mother followed in the car. I left and never saw either of them again. The date was Saturday, May 20th, 1989.

CHAPTER 5

INDIFFERENT ANGELS

D eb's family history is studded with men with large question marks floating over their heads—me included. If the women were extraordinary, the men ranged from underwhelming to pathetic—me included. Sometimes the pathos was inflicted, or maybe attracted—history doesn't distinguish. In any case and lucky for me, this family saga is mostly about the women.

Jane Elizabeth Brown née Waggstaff, a.k.a. Ginny, and her husband Albert, with their brood Henry, Glenn, and Princess Agnes the Navigator were farming Upper Canada in the 1920s. Deb's great-grandmother Ginny was born within earshot of Big Ben in London on Saturday, November 30th, 1901. London is farther north than all the major Canadian cities, and the winter of 1901 was particularly harsh in England, with the snow deep and the cold keen. If your people are from the UK and you've done Ancestry.com, you know that the gene pool is mostly Angles, Saxons, Celts, and Nordic peoples, all people starved of sunshine, used to long, cold nights, used to greeting death in the morning. Ginny was the first Waggstaff on Canadian soil, giving birth to my wife's line of strong and smart women born of those winter genes, each in their turn married to a weak, damaged man likely sporting DNA from the emotional south brought by the Normans or Romans…me included.

Waggstaff is Old English for someone who wields a stick as a minor official of some kind. Previously it was a medieval nickname for a male flasher—how appropriate. The Canadian branch of the Waggstaff tree is Anglo-Saxon and Celtic-Nordic, sturdy stuff that pushed its way onto ships bound for North America in the nineteenth and early twentieth centuries. The mix of Celts, Nords, Saxons, Angles, and Gauls, with a dash of Roman for spice, had been burbling in the cast-iron cultural pot of Britain for a thousand years before she became Ruler of the Waves. The Brits are an aggressive, mongrel people, the biggest European pox on the houses of First Nations all around the globe, with the Spanish coming in a close second. The British perfected high-minded, stick-up-the-ass exploitation; barbarism should have been coined Britainism given what was done to all the non-white *savages* in need of *salvation*. The irony is that these inferior non-white citizens of the world were necessary for Britain to build its empire; to lift that tiny island nation up into world dominance required a lot of bodies, a lot of backs that needed breaking. Without savages, there is no salvation. A king's conundrum indeed.

The British Empire was on the downhill side of the bell curve when Deb's ancestors arrived in Canada. Great Britain was draining across the North Atlantic like an oil slick, with people flowing into every port of the Empire. The story of world powers is monotonous—they come, they go, forever pissing down the generations. Of course, it's always a mixed blessing, for with dominion comes money and with money comes technology, education, industry, health and well-being. But if you're not favoured by the right birth the best you can hope for, if you're still alive post-dominion, is access to the rummage sale. Failing that, you're gleaning at the dump.

The starting point in Deb's family story is the top rung on the Ladder of the Low. Anglo-Saxon-Celtic Brits with no name or land who, after earning a little money from bone-bending hard work on stolen land, became the Canadian WASP. The White Anglo-Saxon Protestants of World War I Ontario lorded themselves over the French in Quebec, and of course were superior to all varieties of yellow, brown, black, and red peoples. The Brit-cum-WASP of early Canada, particularly the males, were forged of heavy steel, heated and hammered repeatedly over centuries of ignorance and brutality, a people with their very own home-grown church and virgin queen, genetic *fuck you*s pumping through their bloody hearts.

But the female genes in Deb's Canadian lineage proved to be better than the ignorance and barbarity of their distant past. The story of Deb's family is about the smart extraordinary women—and one very fortunate man. Albert Brown's story, breathtaking and incomprehensible as it is, turned out to be the Saturday cause of every Saturday effect yet to come.

* * *

In 1910 Albert Wolstencroft Henry Brown was a teenager working his father's tobacco farm in York County, Ontario. They had three hundred acres on the shore of Lake Simcoe, near Georgina, a landscape the English found as green and pleasant as their homeland. A place where you could see fertility, a place where the tobacco grew prosperity and the people grew dominion. The Wendat people (the Huron in Canadian history books) are alive in that soil, alive in the names of places, but the actual Wendat Nation is essentially over, functionally subsumed; only a few thousand survived the multi-generational onslaught. What was for the English invaders a beautiful, productive land was a future sealed for the Wendat from the time of their ancestors. The geography is welcoming, prepared by a retreating glacier for its role as the gathering place. Lakes pool on beds of rock, deep and clear. Walk for weeks in any direction and there is a home for people and creatures. It's the ideal convocation of the natural world: sky-woman, beaver, loon, frog, world-turtle, the evil son, the good son, all the green plants, the ferocious animals of our nightmares, the gentle animals of our dreams. A bucolic landscape can conspire to summon future inhabitants, lying in wait, patient and silent, luring people for generations. The Wendat, the Algonquin, the Mohawk—they all know this. Their histories were abducted, their ancestry lost, their well-being murdered, their spirits desiccated, their bones sucked into the rings of trees.

The land was too perfect, too rich, too beautiful. The warring Europeans couldn't resist the spoils. They needed this land, they wanted it, and they had the power and technology to take it. All they needed to do was join the pre-existing fray and make war with the warring First Nations, taking sides and switching sides using skills of duplicity well known to the kings and queens of Europe, only adding state religion to give them all the justification they needed. How better to entirely wipe out a people than to wipe out their great-grandparents, steal and brainwash their children, rape them, brutalize them, murder them, break them, then exile the survivors into a life and culture they don't know. If these nations had not been nearly extinct by the end of the nineteenth century, the Ontario WASPs would have been slaughtered while sleeping for what their ancestors had done. But the worm turns, and worms were readying for the feast to come: 1914 to 1918 were good years for the worms.

Albert Brown was in C Company, 80th Overseas Battalion, Canadian Expeditionary Force. They trained in Nappanee. Because England was at war, so were all the Commonwealth countries, automatically and without debate or protest, the supply chain of fodder. The WASP men and boys of Ontario would have gone regardless; still, the whole debacle was sold as an adventure, heroism, and patriotism, not cataclysm or suffering, not meaningless death, and most assuredly not for what it really was—the folly of regal young cocks and old, rich balls.

Ginny, the future recipient of the decidedly non-regal cock belonging to Albert Brown, could see it all too clearly, but being only a woman of only the colonies her insight didn't count. Albert, on the other hand, cock in hand, ran headlong toward the fight, knowing little, foreseeing nothing. Thousands of young men from Auckland to Aneroid did the same, but I can confidently say that absolutely none of them, none of the hundreds of thousands from Canada, not one of the Commonwealth millions, not one of the global tens of millions who fought and died in World War I had the experience that Albert Wolstencroft Henry Brown did. How can I know this? How can I claim this with such certainty? Math—the tyranny of numbers, specifically probability. Probability calculations are the only way to understand this *if only* story. The probabilities of Albert Brown's fate are sinful math, the fractions involved so microscopic, so precise that it would take trillions of soldiers in millions of wars to produce the same result, especially given the not microscopic, not precise, crude killing technology of the day. That's to say nothing of the conditions of the Third Battle of Ypres, more famously known as Passchendaele, another low country mud pit that swallowed young men whole.

All these factors combined with the weather and the terrain to create an event so vanishingly rare that theoretically it should never have happened to anyone, including Albert Brown. That this freakishly improbable event, which ended with his survival, was the genesis of generational tragedy boggles the mind. What this event set in motion is an epic tale of fate delivered one hundred years and one day in the future. See whether you don't agree by the time you're done lending me your neurons.

He shipped to England in the spring of 1917, unable to stay any longer to help his father with the farm. Winter had been cold, spring was late, and the war was early. The train ride to Halifax was the most pleasant part of the journey for Albert, his idea of adventure having not yet been vomited out into the North Atlantic. After boarding the troop ship, Albert's suffering began almost immediately. Five weeks sealed in a cold metal box pitching and crashing in a rolling sea will take the fun out of anything. His sea legs and naval stomach rounded into form a week from Liverpool, just in time for him to wash out the shit and puke stains, gather his wits, and disembark with a bit of dignity.

Very little information is available about Albert's time in Liverpool. The stories were lost in the happenstance yet to come, which made the experience of Albert's personal tragedy inaccessible even to him and more so to us, his future family. Only bits and pieces were gleaned from official military documents and mumbled phrases. The rest came from doctors. Albert Brown flowed wordlessly around his internal obstacles. He left the farm cocky and garrulous; he came back silent and kind.

In the many musings I had about Albert Brown after learning his story I struggled to find rational ground. Quantum mechanics is built on mysterious events that are fundamentally random, chaos theory says that when you scale up to a macro system the tinniest random perturbation can cause a massive change, complexity theory reveals how little we understand about the physical world. I know and understand these facts. I also know ancestry carries genetic fate in the same way a bucket carries water. Reconciling these realities with what happened to Deb and I claws at my logical mind. Somehow this world is made of random math without meaning and iron-fisted physical destiny born of people fucking at a particular time and place in history creating new and random humans. No matter how hard I try, this logic feels hopeless to me. And once you've lived and died the very real and personal consequences of genetic complexity, chance and choice you can't help but be pulled down by the irrational undertow.

The fall rains came early to Belgium in September 1917. This part of Europe was pastoral and fertile, dotted with small villages, low country with a high-water table, farms covering nearly everything that wasn't village or road. The early rains that year would have spoiled some of the farmers' fall crops had it been peacetime. As it was, there were no crops, there were no farms, and there were no farmers. Most of the soldiers tearing up Europe in the fall of 1917 were former farmers, and Albert Brown was no exception. They all would have recognized snippets of their homelands in the few pieces of terrain still intact.

At this point in Western history, cities hadn't yet bled the countryside of families. Ironically, that future bleeding was a consequence of war, wars, and general international assholery yet to come, not the Industrial Revolution as is so often claimed. Europe in 1917 was an eviscerated belly from the low country to the high country. From Holland to the Swiss border everything was drawn and quartered—churned mud, shell holes, blasted trees, trenches, barbed wire, gas, disease, char, and the grateful dead, no common currency, no folk dances for tourists, no breakfast of coffee, bread, cheese, and jam. This was the glamorous adventure Albert Brown found himself in. Passchendaele was just another regional death zone, one of many.

The morning of Saturday, October 13th, 1917 was rainy and cold. The mutilated terrain erupted in dark, unrecognizable mounds like a skinned corpse. The morning sky was red with sheets of sideways rain and the trenches were an open outhouse, muddy shell holes full of rainwater, jellied blood, and body parts. The Canadians were there to replace the spent Australian and New Zealand Army Corps, a fresh round of fodder for the British officers in command. C Company was going over the top this morning and Albert Brown was shitting himself, as were all the other Canadian replacements. The Aussies and Kiwis being replaced looked like walking, talking hamburger, and they didn't spare the arriving Canadians any detail as they trudged past. They did so not out of spite—though they knew what these Canadian farm boys would have to do to very soon—but out of a kind of soldier's chivalry that they should hear truth from the troops, not sermons from the lying British officers. They gave over what ammunition and supplies they had left to the Canadians, impromptu gifts as the lines of young men flowed past each other like schoolboys on a deadly playground, those Canadian lives possibly depending on what was shared. In a world where most little boys crave the love of their mother, this place was the antithesis, the perfect hell devoid of any mother's love. Many cried out for it with their last breath, and the ANZACs knew this, for they had lived and died it only days before, with fat flies still labouring on the corpses of their mates.

Mothers everywhere were silent. Albert Brown was about to meet his fate in the form of vector calculations. It's a wet, dark dawn, the earth is thick gruel, the trenches are canals of disease, the bottom rungs of the ladders stand knee-deep in fetid water, and thousands of men are poised to fight to the death, which for many will take only seconds. With whistles and shouting they rouse themselves up the ladders out onto the broken landscape, crouching, frightened, pushed to advance quickly though a hobbling trot is the only pace achievable in the slippery gloom.

There's a reluctance to rush into the threat of death that takes years of train-ing and experience to overcome, and the Canadian boys of the 80th had little of either. The smash-and-grab of battle hadn't started yet, the sanctioned crim-inality of waiting for the opportune moment to shred your fellow human—let's call it peak vulnerability, maximum meat grinder—hadn't yet arrived. More yards had to be covered, more fodder needed to be fed out before the Germans opened up. And it wasn't a "rain of bullets" or a "hail of gunfire" as so many hack historians have written. The math is wrong, and that's important to note in order to fully understand the death-dealing geometry of what happened to Albert Brown of York County, Ontario.

The First World War was trench warfare, and trench warfare is geome-try, sometimes based on the parabolic arc, sometimes on trajectory, some-times on linear momentum plus trajectory, but mostly on parallel lines and angles of intersection. Aiming mechanisms were simple, so what a good general wanted was firing positions that created angles of less than 180 degrees (so you couldn't accidentally shoot your general) and more than

30 degrees (so you wouldn't be easy to overrun), with the optimal killing falling between 125 degrees and 45 degrees, roughly speaking. In that zone you could fire at will, parallel to the ground from 18 to 48 inches high. This was not rain or hail; this was laser beams, tiny cruise missiles, ballistic razors, crosshatched destiny at 2,400 feet per second. When the boys of C Company reached the shredding zone, that was what met them—pops and crackles calling out the names of the soon-to-be dead.

As the German positions began to fire, the wavy lines of bodies fell, ran, scattered, rolled, and dove. Any slight divot, incline, shell hole, or corpse could be the difference between life and death. With the Canadians returning fire, the angles of mortality increased exponentially. Albert Brown had dropped flat to his belly behind a tiny mound of earth no more than twelve inches high. As he looked up to find his next point of refuge, a bullet entered him just in front of and slightly above his left temple, grazed the leading edge of his prefrontal cortex, and exited just in front of and slightly above his right temple. It was a perfect prefrontal lobotomy measured in microns. The momentum of the exiting bullet turned his head slightly to the left so that he dropped onto his right cheek and was still able to breathe. Had his head not rotated slightly the mud would have suffocated him.

We don't know exactly how long he lay there, but we know it was hours because that's how long it took the retreating Canadian troops to cross the same ground. Albert Brown looked dead. Angus James Burns was running for his life (more like stumbling, I imagine). At the perfect moment, Albert Brown twitched just as Burns sought shelter behind what he assumed was a corpse. When the moment appeared right, Burns pulled Brown up over his broad back and crawled the final few hundred yards back to the trenches, saving Albert Brown and all his future progeny.

It's surprising how little blood results from a head wound like Albert Brown's. The size of the holes are shockingly small. The exit wound is a bit bigger than the entrance wound from the outward force, but compared to the normal butchery a World War I field hospital saw, Albert was easy to patch up. Once his head was cleaned and bandaged he was loaded onto a transport truck headed to Dunkirk, the closest port to Ypres with Royal Navy hospital ships. He was stable and unconscious for the three-hour drive. The big, rugged army trucks of the era were little more than tractors, hard to stop, hard to gain speed with, and hard to ride in without getting thrown around. Albert's injury, in addition to being relatively bloodless, was also virtually painless. Others suffered and died on the way, loaded in as survivors and loaded out as corpses.

At Dunkirk, HMS *China* took Albert on board, upgraded his field dressings, and shelved him away with the survivors they could do nothing more for. He looked as if he would live, but with a head wound you couldn't be sure. At least he was stable and unconscious; most of the wounded on HMS *China* were not so lucky. If blood burbled through adequately closed wounds, they lived, but if their thumping hearts spurted blood through holes too big to plug, they died.

There was also typhoid fever, gangrene, and the Spanish flu. Somehow, sleeping Albert avoided all these other ways to die. And so the new Albert Brown, incubating in the womb of his unconscious, arrived in Dover, not yet ready for rebirth but safely ferried to his future. New Albert Brown began life at the 16th Canadian Military General Hospital in Orpington, the closest Canadian hospital to Dover. Even the essential environment of military hospitals was segregated by rank and country of origin, with white Canadian privates being one of the fortunate classes. Albert was brought into the enlisted men's ward, cleaned, and had his dressings changed again as he awaited examination by a surgeon. In the process, a nurse had picked all the tiny fragments of skull out of the entry and exit wounds using tweezers and a magnifying glass. The holes were beginning to scab over and the healing looked normal, even vigorous. The windows into new Albert Brown's consciousness were closing, while old Albert Brown was a building without Elvis, but no one knew that yet.

After two days of battlefield medicine, three days on HMS *China*, and two more days in the military hospital, Albert awoke to a pretty nurse sitting on his bed, watching him intently. Mary Hasty was an Irish Canadian from Marystown, Newfoundland. Mary from Marystown—she was twice blessed. Mary smiled as Albert fluttered back up into the conscious world. Again he had twitched at just the right time for a passerby to notice. He looked bewildered, but Mary was a veteran of this coming back to the present, and she spoke softly to him.

"I'm Mary Hasty, a nurse. You're at the Canadian hospital back in England now."

Albert appeared to be watching her lips move, so she continued. "You've had a head wound, but you're fine now. That was seven days ago, at Passchendaele. You boys took the town and won the battle, but it was bloody. You're a lucky one, you are. Lots of boys like you didn't make it."

She studied him carefully. When he showed further signs of comprehension, she went on. "We're going to take good care of you until you're right as rain." After another moment's evaluation, she leaned in and whispered into Albert's ear, "The war is over for you. You'll be going home soon."

The fog in Albert's gaze appeared to lift for a few moments before it settled back in. Perhaps it was the songbird lilt of her words that lulled him back to sleep. Mary tucked him in, kissed her fingers, touched his forehead in ritual and left.

The next day when she came by Albert's bed he was awake, calmly taking in his surroundings, so she sat down to chat him up. He smiled, but when it came his turn to speak nothing came out. His mouthed moved, thoughts seemed to tick over behind his eyes, but the two were disconnected. Unfazed, Mary decided to talk for both of them.

"Don't you worry, me love, your voice will come back when she's good and ready."

Albert cocked his head.

"Oh, you can smell that, can you?" Mary had brought homemade fish stew for lunch. "Well, at least we know your nose is all shipshape, then, don't we?"

She paused, turning to look out the window. "Orpington is a lovely little town. That's where we are."

She smiled at Albert, he smiled back. "We've got lots of strong, handsome boys like you, and we're making them all fit as fiddles. Can't send you home to your mother or your girl all smashed potatoes now, can we?"

She could see Albert searching for words, but still none came.

"I can see what you want to say in your eyes, me love. Don't you worry. Those words will drop down like heaven's rain and come pouring out like God's own flood in no time. You just wait and see."

Albert nodded in agreement.

"You keep your happy countenance and I'll bring you some fish stew next time. It's my family recipe and it's delicious. The fish are different here but

46

they're just as fine. You'll see." She touched Albert's arm and was off again.

The rest of Albert was working just fine. He was soon up and about, taking meals, following instructions, walking the halls, greeting others with a smile and a nod, just without words. Throughout his treatments he was agreeable and amenable, a model patient. The surgeon in charge of head trauma quickly concluded there was nothing physical remaining for him to do: the fragment-picking nurse, HMS *China*, and the battlefield hospital had all done well. Albert Brown was alive but for his words, which seemed to have been left behind at Passchendaele. After ten days at 16th Canadian, he was transferred to Gateshead in Durham, a former asylum partially repurposed for neurological disorders, many of which were what was termed *shell shock* at the time. The rest of Gateshead was a veritable periodic table of mental disorders, many without names or treatment until decades later.

In the turmoil of daily life at Gateshead, Albert quickly distinguished himself for his kindness and agreeable nature. He caused no problems and in fact lightened the mood of the men he spent time with. Gradually, therapy helped him to find words in response to direct questions. Single words first, then simple phrases, mumbled but intelligible enough, and so communication outside the keep of Albert Brown's head was re-established though sparse. Last to return were self-initiated words and phrases. There weren't many of those, and there never would be.

With new Albert Brown essentially complete, his popularity among the patients and inmates grew steadily. His sunny disposition, apparent lack of anything bad to say, and pitiable yet engaging impediment combined to make him a form of damaged not envied by the worse off, so the doctors kept him for an extra six months as a kind of mascot. No one asked him whether he wanted to go home. He seemed happy enough. He made the daily life of a considerable amount of institutional square footage more bearable, and more therapy could always add another word or two to his miniscule vocabulary. The only thing that made them eventually send Albert home was how thoroughly and obviously he understood everything that was said to him. The director thought the war would end soon and someone in Canada might miss him. He was fit and strong and helpful and kind, so of course he must go home.

CHAPTER 6

DREAD NAUGHT, MY CHILDREN

M eanwhile, back on the family farm, the one that came to exist because Albert Brown married Ginny Waggstaff on an August afternoon in 1920 in Lindsay, Ontario, Deb's then six-year-old grandmother Agnes Anne bounded in through the back door, blond ringlets bouncing, Mary Janes gleaming, one buckle undone.

"Buckety-fuckety-fuck-me-fuck, buckety-fuckety-fuck-me-fuck," she rhymed.

Ginny's jaw dropped. Agnes's brothers Glenn and Henry roared with laughter from the backyard. It was just one of the many stories Princess Agnes the Navigator told us about growing up with her mischievous brothers, her enterprising mother, and her kind, silent father.

To say Princess Agnes was an odd child isn't an overstatement. She was preternaturally gifted, almost spookily so given the superstitions of those times. But they didn't have a name for her gift back then. As is often the case, people with gifts are also hyper-intelligent. As a young child, she and her gift seemed more inexplicable than even her precocious verbal skills. At times it could appear as if she knew what was going to happen before it did. People and events arrived for her as anticipated before they arrived in actuality for everyone else. She could appear time-bending or wise beyond her years, her responses often eclipsing the comprehension of the adults in the room. Agnes Anne would have been a problem in old Salem.

Over time, Agnes learned to use her gift of prescience to her advantage. Many of the neighbours were wary, especially the women. Her parents and brothers had grown used to her showing up just before being called or her knowing what you were about to say, answering your question before you asked it. Her abilities also extended to gleaning the emotions of others without the need for words. She always knew the right things to say in the right tone regardless of how much information was unspoken, and so she had to become deft at moving puzzlement to amazement before it shifted to suspicion. If it weren't obviously impossible, you might think the abilities Albert had lost in the war were reborn as an extra sense in Agnes. Fantastical thinking, no doubt. Still, Agnes was openly extraordinary, the perfect antonym to Albert. Within the walls of her family home it was safe to dazzle.

Ginny, however, refused to be dazzled. She accepted her daughter's gift as if it was expected of God in exchange for what he had allowed to happen to Albert.

"Agnes, you know better."

"Yes, Mama."

"You always know better, don't you?"

"Yes, I do Mama."

"Then please don't make me remind you again. You're almost ten years old."

"I won't, Mama."

And she didn't. Agnes never again made a false move with her special power, as Ginny called it, after turning just ten years old.

Agnes's owed her abilities to what today is called hyper-cognitive empathy disorder. Why *disorder*, I don't fully understand. Agnes was just a more sensitive receiver than the rest of us. I like this theory because it's plausible based on published research and it closes the door to less-grounded possibilities, such as that Agnes was connected to some sphere of reality we can't see or measure—or the *Fates* are real—ideas I wasn't yet prepared to entertain. Agnes did cause neck hairs to stand up, but her golden ringlets and child's innocent face meant no one could hold onto their unease for long. After she learned to hold her pixie dust until she could cast it without raising neck hairs, most never knew they had just encountered Princess Agnes the Navigator. Ginny relaxed. Albert and the boys accepted living dimly beside her bright light, and the little town grew very fond of their exceptional princess.

Lindsay, Ontario, is roughly the midpoint between Barrie in the west and Peterborough to the east. To call Lindsay idyllic is to undersell it. This finger of southern Ontario that sticks down into Uncle Sam's eye is as close as the English ever came to the rolling hills, lakes, and rivers of their green and pleasant land. Lindsay grew up a mill town on the Scugog River. The river is Main Street, bisecting the town on its way from Lake Scugog to Sturgeon Lake and then, via the Otonabee and the Trent Rivers, to Lake Ontario. The Kawartha Lakes region is headquartered in Lindsay.

Lindsay was then and still is an ideal summer weekend town, the perfect setting for a lobotomized young man, now the strong, silent type, and a spirited young woman to meet, fall in love, get pregnant, and then get married—only slightly out of the approved order of things. Regardless, both Ginny's people and Albert's people were practical enough to see the wisdom of support versus banishment, so an out-of-order family was honoured by ignoring a so-called loss of honour. Pretense prevailed as it always does. Mutually agreed upon pretense creates solid ground for us all to stand on while justifying our actions. People can justify almost anything inside the fences of sanity, many things at the perimeter, and even a few things out on the tiles of bat-shit crazy, especially when religion gets involved—but that digression is too vast to explore here.

Albert Brown was likely in some ways religious too. After all, he was a man of his rural, God-fearing times. Had he been able to express it, his revelation might have been to believe himself chosen by God to survive and carry on, maybe to greatness, but I doubt marrying greatness would have crossed his mind. Ginny, on the other hand, was sure she could make something out of Albert, with no help from God needed, just her brains, her guile, and some determination, all of which she could manage with only the odd escape in a bottle. That was the formula. She knew they would be fine with her at the helm.

But of course Ginny had no idea the Great Depression was coming—no one did. When Wall Street brought the financial world tumbling down like the walls of Jericho, it was Albert's war pension that saw them through. The Browns had food, clothes, shelter, animals, crops, and tools with no shortage of labour willing to work for a meal and a bed of hay in the barn. Agnes told many stories of hobos being given food on the front porch. It was called the Dirty Thirties for a reason. Ginny never insisted they work, but they always wanted to do something in return, sometimes staying for only hours, sometimes months. Albert seemed to know who was trustworthy and who was not. In the years since the war, he had become thick with muscle and light on his feet. He knew his role was physical work and security. A few words, a grunt here, a growl there did the trick. Ginny employed as many men as she could. Her brains and Albert's brawn made a winning formula. Albert never got angry; perhaps he was incapable of it. Ginny was capable of rage but smart enough to pop the cork before she flew too far up the chimney. When she did need to burn down the metaphorical house, Henry and Glenn were old enough and strong enough to shrug off a beating or two. Big, strapping boys were an acceptable target back then. I can tell you from personal experience they're often the most vulnerable.

One night when Henry was fifteen, he snuck out after dark to drink beer by the river with his friends. But Ginny was far too smart to get past. She waited next to the basement door armed with Albert's heavy leather honing strap. After she had waited hours in ambush, Henry finally stumbled down the stairs to the basement door. Gravel crunched and the door handle turned cautiously, rotating through its squeaks. Ginny widened her stance to get a solid base and enough distance to maximize the swing. Henry stepped in and turned his back to Ginny, both hands on the doorknob, slowly clicking the door shut. Swinging with all her might, hissing like a steam engine, Ginny landed the strap with a sharp crack across Henry's back. Through the beer and his thick leather jacket, Henry barely noticed. He didn't start or jump, instead he turned slowly, looking over his shoulder to see where the noise had come from. Ginny stood staring, hissing, and huffing in rhythm. Drunken Henry needed a few seconds for understanding to settle in. Once he realized he'd been caught and punished he mumbled an apology and poured himself upstairs to bed. That was

Ginny's final attempt at corporal punishment.

Through the Depression the family thrived. Ginny had them making sausages, cold cuts, roasts, bacon, chickens whole or in part, milk, cream, butter, eggs, and cheeses—anything you could sell from dairy cows, pigs, and chickens. In 1932 Ginny bought a store in Lindsay from a family who had been bankrupted. Rather than buying it from the bank at five cents on the dollar she bought it from the family at twenty-five cents on the dollar— the right combination of shrewd and community minded, in Ginny's opinion. She stocked all forms of goods and groceries from the local farms, but all the meat, dairy, and eggs came from Albert Brown's farm, which should have been called Ginny Brown's farm. The store became known as Downtown Brown's. Still, Ginny never viewed herself as the downtown type, and not out of contrived humility but because placing yourself above your neighbours was bad for business.

Agnes helped Ginny run the store. Albert and the boys did the hard work at the farm. Ginny hired two charcutiers, Alois and Jerome, from Lac-des-Loups across the Ottawa River. They came to live above the store for two months every year and made all the cold cuts, sausages, and hams. Ginny learned to speak some French and proposed to Jerome an extension of their business relationship, trading sex for income security. Ginny was the boss so Jerome agreed and fluids were exchanged across religious boundaries, not an arrangement one might expect of the close-your-eyes-and-think-of-England type. Maybe I'm being naïve about the pinched Ontario WASPs, but compared with the reputed joyous French fucking of the Quebecois Catholic they do seem a dour lot, though they did procreate to the point of spillover and so were at least adequate to the task. But like the English with their bland food, woollen emotions, and brown teeth, there is a vast country between the ability to chew and a radiant come-hither smile.

Knowing what her mother was doing from the outset, Agnes learned that women could trade their power for sex just as men often did. She accepted the arrangement, knowing her mother was coping with her father as best she could.

Agnes loved Jerome and Alois and they loved her back, being helpless to resist her otherworldly charms. They had big Catholic families back home in Lac-des-Loups. Working for Ginny Brown was critical income but crossing the river into an English Protestant land was literally a necessary evil. They girded themselves with every form of sacramental that could practically be worn while butchering and grinding. Occasionally they would show them to Agnes, touch her with them, pulling the child under their cloak of protection in a ritual kindness born of ignorant superstition no different from that of the Protestants they loathed.

The Browns travelled on through the 1930s toward the next war; Agnes would later say those were happy years. Henry, Glenn, and Agnes grew, Albert shrank, Ginny ran the show. Europe burst into flames again in 1939, when Henry was seventeen and Glenn was two weeks shy of sixteen. They shot across Southern Ontario to Petawawa to enlist. Although younger Glenn was bigger, they lied themselves up to nineteen and eighteen respectively. The next generation of military Browns was launched. Albert deteriorated physically from the heavy work of the farm after Henry and Glenn left to fight. The war made labour scarce so in his stoic, quiet way he did virtually everything at almost the same pace and volume as the three of them had done together. His body simply wore out. When the war ended, Henry was dead. Glenn had survived.

In 1949 Ginny sold everything and followed the migration to southern British Columbia, the California of Canada, where there was more sunshine, less snow, and more opportunity. Princess Agnes the Navigator finished growing up in the boarding-house bustle of Barclay Manor in Vancouver's West End. She flowered into an exceptional young woman from a line of exceptional women, all of whom had been forced to bloom in a pot, confined by the men they married.

The Browns moved to the West End when it was still middle-class residential. A neighbourhood of pretty Victorian houses, quaint four-storey stone apartment buildings, huge trees—elms and maples, chestnuts and arbutus—victory gardens, neatly trimmed little lawns, neatly trimmed topiary, neatly trimmed white people. The West End was a cornucopia of white: cloud, chalk, and putty, alabaster, swan, and winter. The yellow hordes, wagon-burners, and ragheads, as Ginny would have called them without malice but rife with ignorance, were relegated to the downtown's east side, the industrial waterfront, and the neighbourhoods south and east of the CN train station. Back then, going to the Chinks for milk, commandeering a shuttered Nip business, and hiring Gunga Din or Geronimo to work green chain at the mill were common expressions. "Others" were fair game. These were the attitudes that allowed Indigenous children to be stolen, raped, murdered, and buried in unmarked graves, their trauma still alive and well today in the genes of their people. Race is a fiction by the way, a distinction without a difference, junk science predating the discovery of DNA. The term comes from phrenology. Despite the irrefutable scientific fact of genetics we have ossified this non-fact into truth, just like the billions of deluded people who think they were created by their version of Almighty God and claim absolute truth as solely their possession. It's all utter horseshit from the same parade as the rejection of a round earth orbiting the sun, carbon dating, evolution, and the moon landing. Apologies—the closeted TV anti-preacher in me sometimes breaks out the makeup and hair gel and goes looking for a camera.

The Barclay Manor Rooming House was owned by the Canadian Armed Forces Veterans' Administration. It needed good management and "female skills," said the bureaucrat responsible. Again, Albert's war pension status helped secure the position for the family, and again Ginny's abilities were vested in Albert's name. Agnes went to high school just few a blocks away at King George Secondary. Albert wandered the alleys, construction sites, and yard sales looking for things he thought would be useful to the household. Ginny cooked, cleaned, collected the rent, and managed the books and the banking. At night, as usual, she tippled, though she remained as accomplished as ever. Conversation in the house was cheery. The future looked bright to the men cycling through Barclay Manor. Work was plentiful and manly in 1950s Vancouver: logging, mining, construction, policing. Agnes honed her navigation skills on the wide variety of veterans passing through. She finished high school at the very top of her class—no surprise. Her gift grew in strength through her teen years, surely she must have felt like a Titan among mortals.

Glenn followed the family to Vancouver in 1953. He left the Navy, shaved his long black beard, concealed his now numerous tattoos under a button-down shirt, married Adele Bailey, and joined the Vancouver Police Department, making it all the way to the elite—a homicide detective—before retiring in 1988. Agnes graduated high school in 1951, married in 1952, gave birth to Katherine Elizabeth in 1953, earned her nursing degree in 1956, then went to work at St. Paul's Hospital not many blocks away in 1959.

Agnes Collier née Brown was someone special. Walter Collier, her husband, was not. Despite her gift, Agnes couldn't rise above the Waggstaff genes pulling her to save a lesser man from himself—and thus to be always safely in charge. The DNA dictate had passed through into Agnes as well, from ancestry to progeny, just like all the rest of her clan.

Walter was aggressively pedestrian. He believed strongly in normalcy and practised conformity religiously; had there been a Protestant Church called Normaliterian he would have been the archbishop. The 1950s were Walter Collier's best years. The 1960s were all downhill for him, conformists having become thin on the ground. Agnes, on the other hand, grew steadily toward her zenith. She was the epitome of intelligence and good will, hyper aware, her navigation skills ever deft. She always knew the right thing to say, the best lesson for her children, and the best care for her patients. Honest and kind, she was always so much more than Walter, without effort and without him ever realizing it.

Davie Street began to change like nowhere else in Vancouver. It became the Gay Village, it became boho chic, it became Sodom. Agnes loved it. Walter hated it. They had moved into an apartment building just around the corner from Barclay Manor, a giant old hulk called the Warrington on the corner of Davie and Nicola Streets. The building was decorated like British India, with floral carpets, brass knobs and railings, dark wood panelling, and heavy doors. Agnes loved it. Walter hated it. Agnes loved her short walk to St. Paul's Hospital, a daily stroll up and down Davie. The life of daytime Davie Street was stuck in the 1950s, but nighttime Davie Street had moved on to the 1960s. Walter was at sea with nighttime Davie Street. You couldn't get farther from conformity without dropping off the edge of his flat earth. He could see an impending demise for his wife and child in this environment of rebellious gay men without limits, or so he thought. Limits were important, the guardrails of decency on the highway of life. Walter believed in the signposts of conformity and the white line dividing anarchy from order. No need for God, just good analogies, because

Walter was a committed atheist, which was the only nonconformist thing about him.

In 1957, Agnes gave birth to child number two, Richard, who was nick-named Duffy, and by 1964 Walter was done with the small apartment and the neighbourhood bacchanalia. That was that.

"We're moving," he declared, not giving Agnes a choice.

They moved to the suburbs, to the working-class neighbourhood of Dunbar, into a house bought by Ginny and put in Agnes's name.

"It's her house but you can live in it" was all Ginny ever said. It was Walter's turn to have no choice. If he did harrumph, no one heard it.

The suburb of Dunbar was then an enclave of small, postwar houses originally built for the white working-class civil servants, trades, and labour needed to groom the rich neighbourhoods of Shaughnessy, its most luxurious street simply called The Crescent, and the almost-as-wealthy Southwest Marine Drive. White —but inferior people—were also needed to clean the city's shimmering waterfront homes on West Point Grey Road and the cliffs above Spanish Banks and Jericho Beach, or to staff the private yacht clubs, private golf and tennis clubs, and run the downtown busi-nesses, restaurants and hotels. Segregation by postal code, enforced by a knowing look laced with condescention; a barrier no less if not a colour coded one.

Agnes lost her walk to work, but the drive was just ten minutes over the Burrard Street Bridge, as were Ginny and Albert. On weekends Walter and Agnes visited them with the children. Ginny enjoyed the visits but wasn't grandmotherly in the typical sense; her engine ran hot and the radiator was full of gin. What today passes for engaged parenting Ginny saw as pander-ing. Her school was old, and being heard was far less decorous than being seen. Her mind was still sharp, which made increasing idleness a source of frustration to her. Albert was fast becoming a doddering old man. As the work at Barclay Manor slowed along with its guests, Ginny began to drink earlier in the day. Barclay Manor was in decline, in the winter of its useful life, just like Ginny and Albert. The Veterans' Administration closed it and put the property up for sale in 1974. Albert and Ginny moved into the Warrington, the same apartment Walter and Agnes had outgrown ten years earlier. Albert became well known in the building for his stash of salvage, some of which, surprisingly, was worth a buck or two. Before urban gleaning there was dumpster diving, and before that there was Albert Brown. Albert knew all the spots, had an eye, and was old-man strong. He knew which night clubs had a propensity to shed valuables, which apartment buildings had tenants with a penchant for changing décor, and which converted Victorian houses had gay bohemians with a proclivity for excess. The Davie Street denizens got to know the silent old guy who looked like a stooped rugby player and had two dents on either side of his forehead just above the temples. As Albert aged, Agnes took over some of the management of her father from her mother. Unfortunately, this made Ginny feel even less needed and exacerbated her frustrations. She was accustomed to running everything and everyone in her domain like a benevolent dictator. So she drank wine in months with an *R*, gin and tonic in months without, plus some overlap for the old-fashioneds.

Agnes quietly filled in when needed. Albert kept buggering on, as the English say, until he died on the toilet at age ninety-one. Ever considerate, he finished, flushed, cleaned up and sat back down, stiffening enough to remain perched, pants down at his blue ankles, manhood all a-dangle over the freshly flushed bowl. Ginny found him four hours later when she had to go, thinking he was out junking, as she called it. Ginny followed Albert into the great beyond a few years later, passing away quietly in her sleep as if to cause no fuss, leaving Agnes and Walter next up on the Grim Reaper's front line, which they accepted with the practical outlook of the Canadian WASP. Everyone gets a turn; no use whining about it.

In Dunbar, Agnes became that neighbourhood mother everyone knew. Her home became the one the kids congregated at. She was a nurse so all the mothers trusted her ability to respond to a crisis, from simple scrapes to broken bones. Then there was the way she had of making everyone comfortable, putting an upset child at ease, deflecting the overly interested comments of someone else's husband or winning over a difficult teacher. Everyone always felt good around Agnes. Walter was like solid furniture, unassuming and vaguely reassuring, so he contributed as well in his conformist way. Their home and family were as secure as you could want through the tumult that was the 1960s and '70s.

"Katherine, the world is changing," Agnes said to her daughter. "You'll have so many more choices than I had."

"You mean the world is changing if you're a man," Katherine said with a tinge of acrimony.

It was the summer before her Grade 12 year. "Most of the girls in my class are still being pushed into nursing or teaching, but the boys can do whatever they want."

"That's not true. Look past what people tell you and make your own decisions. You're very smart and very capable—you could do almost anything. The path may be different for you because you're a girl but that won't matter. You'll figure out how to get where you want to go, probably faster than any of the boys, just like you always do."

"Is *this* where you wanted to go?" Katherine waved her arm wanly at the small kitchen.

"Your father is a good man, Katherine."

"I didn't say he wasn't. I just meant you spent half your life raising us, not working in your career."

"That's exactly the kind of choice I mean, one that you'll get to make. I couldn't—it wasn't an option for me. In my day, when you got pregnant your career was over, you weren't going anywhere. Your generation has permission to be both a mother and a career woman."

"How nice. I'd like to talk to the man who gave us that permission. I have some sexual gratification advice for him."

"I can infer that advice, thank you, and it's *men*, plural. You'll have to tell a lot of men to go fuck themselves over your lifetime, so just be prepared."

"Mom, you potty-mouthed rebel," Katherine said with genuine admiration.

"Just remember to cut your own trail, my precocious daughter, because there won't be any men doing it for you. You're beautiful, they'll line up to share your bed but they won't see you as an equal."

"I'm not as beautiful as you."

"You're more beautiful than me, my dear girl, but that doesn't matter. Beauty is just dumb luck and you can't count on luck. Brains and heart are more important than beauty."

"But you can use beauty to intimidate girls and manipulate boys," Katherine countered.

"Beauty can always be used that way," Agnes said. "But beautiful women are usually perceived as dumb. Is that what you want? You're a long way from dumb."

Instead of answering, Katherine continued, "And what about manipulating boys? Is that why you chose Dad?"

"You can be cruel, Katherine. It's going to get you in trouble."

"I'd rather be honest than worry about preserving a man's ego."

"Then you'd better be able catch as well as you pitch."

"Mom, that's a gay sex metaphor. It doesn't mean give-as-good-as-you-get anymore."

Katherine and Agnes were cut from the same cloth; some battles were inevitable. Agnes had lived through the Depression, war, and social upheaval. Katherine was growing up in a stable world she could count on, behind a white picket fence built by Agnes using her otherworldly gift. Katherine was independent, smart, flamboyant, and a bit self-centred. And she sometimes had a tendency to ignore her mother's advice. Agnes had never wanted Katherine to marry Lester Glasscock. She had pegged him as an impending disaster from the start and she was never wrong, literally— well ... except once, when it came to choosing her own husband. Agnes knew all about the beery history of the Glasscocks. She had heard rumours about the other Lester Glasscock—a great-uncle of the same name. Lester the Molester they called him, a man mothers steered their daughters clear of. Despite Agnes's objections, Katherine married Lester and the family Fates rolled on, with the next in a line of gifted women married to yet another damaged man, and the next extraordinary woman, Deborah Jane Glasscock soon to be crafted by the astounding complex mystery that is the combinatorics of genetic chance.

CHAPTER 7

CITY OF TREES

The University of British Columbia campus is a small city in the middle of a massive forest. There are thousands of girls to choose from if you have the chops to be the chooser. I certainly did not. Deb and I met in a lunch line on a rare snowy winter day in February of 1994. Dirty melt water and squeaking boots, cold and damp and grey, snow the consistency of cream cheese, typical for the temperate rainforest. I was wandering the halls of thought, trying to picture the light-years of distance between galaxies that I was learning how to measure. I must have looked melancholy.

"What's up, Earl Grey?" she said.

I crashed into the moment. This beautiful girl talking to *me*? I balked, hesitated, mouth a bit open, not looking directly at her but up and to the left as if checking the part in her hair, obviously flustered.

She assessed me. "Pensive and nonverbal. How charming."

I think my face was twitching.

"Are you a Freudian or a Jungian?"

I was frozen.

"Famous Germanic psychologists?" she said rhetorically, studying me for signs of life.

By luck at that moment the lunch line moved, which caused my brain to drop into gear.

"Presbyterian," I said.

She laughed.

"Rastafarian."

She snorted.

"Kabalarian."

She whistled.

"Scottish, Jamaican, and Jewish," I said. "Not a German in sight."

She smiled. "Hi, I'm Deb."

"Dave Becker," I replied. "Austrian like Freud, at least historically. I'm third-year cosmology. You?"

"First-year poli-sci. My people are very WASPish, from England, also historically, but my last name's Welsh and a real winner—Glasscock." She met my eyes, daring a reaction.

"Isn't that a kind of dildo?"

She exploded in sheets of laughter, so much so that everyone around us gawked.

"Well, Dave Pecker, you have me there, don't you?"

Her confidence was so obvious it made my shoulders slump, like a dog with its tail between its legs. It seems cringe-worthy now, both of us trying so hard to be oh so very smart. It was actually her level-one test for guys she was interested in. How would the subject react when ambushed by an obtuse question that required an answer with at least a modicum of intelligence? I passed, not with the quickest of witty retorts, but what I lacked in speed I made up for in creativity.

My reclamation at Deb's hand had begun. I fell in love with Deb very quickly. She was so much more of a whole person than I was. And I was a perfect project for her, everything she wanted in a man who wasn't anything at all like her father yet utterly undeveloped, incomplete, and uncertain. I was Goeddel and Heisenberg combined in a human theorem, all the stuff she wanted in just the non-form she wanted it, a true son of my mother. She could make me over in her own image.

We eventually bonded deeply over our shared lack of a father figure, but that came later. We began by fucking each other senseless—her term, not mine. I brought the appetite; she did the cooking. She taught me to play at dominance, let my ego run, inflict pleasure, pull hair, pin down, respond to her words, her instructions, her sounds—none of this was me, it was all her. I was her project named Dave. I loved it! Who wouldn't? Not only because it was fun, but because it made me finish growing up—I could finally see myself as a man, not a boy. And for her I was safe. She gave me the opportunity to finish growing up without risk to her dominance. What a gift she gave me! I mean emotionally, not sexually, although I was a virgin when we met. I was to be a man she could respect but control and be safe with, the female version of the male Madonna–whore complex. I might well have been the subject of a book: *How to Build a Good-Boy-Bad-Boy Husband*. How's that for an honest assessment of my own manhood, or lack thereof?

Deb was all the things I knew I wanted and many more things I didn't know I needed. Yes, that's all honesty, no ego, me—another unflattering self-assessment, don't you think? I don't mind all this self-effacing transparency; with Deb I was punching above my weight, and my weight class was not my fault. She made me more than what I was when she found me.

I came to learn that her intellect was the primary attractant for me, a relationship deal-breaker I hadn't even known I had, yet it turned out to be the thing I craved most. Everything started with smart, then went to wise and kind, then other things I didn't know I needed like strong and confident, then to beautiful and sexy. But dirty—I hadn't yet developed a taste for dirty; that was found money. Most of this was opaque to me at the time, though; none of it except for physical attraction was in my conscious awareness during those early days. We dated all through university. I fell for her with velocity, and the power was all hers to begin with.

We did all of our significant firsts together: saying I love you, crying, fighting and apologizing, farting in each other's presence, learning to see your sex partner as a human being with a mind and emotions, feeling the binding gravity of sex, and experiencing vulnerability, a particularly tough lesson for me. Let me tell you about the morning I learned it. Once was all it took. I always found her outline under the sheets so sexy, almost irresistible, and mixed into that was the feeling of being safe with her that I had yet to recognize. I'd thought it was all love and chemistry, but given the circumstances of my childhood, I craved safety and security—I just hadn't realized it yet. In the best relationships you learn things about yourself that only the person you love can teach you, not in the teacher-and-student sense, but in the call-and-response sense. Like a Southern Baptist church choir, you evoke notes in each other; your note needs the harmonic, or the fill, or the run. Hopefully you give good notes back and forth, but it doesn't always work out that way.

We'd had a very sexy weekend with another couple previous to this particular Saturday morning, when all my vulnerabilities gushed forth from a broken sewer pipe of backed-up emotions. The girl was a casual acquaintance of Deb's, from her large circle of friends. The girl's boyfriend was a nice guy, not an asshole—Deb's no-assholes rule was inviolable. Group sex was a campus activity I had only heard about before. This was another way for Deb to control me. I understood but didn't care. She was a goddess in my eyes, and I provided her a reflection that was flawless. Every goddess needs her supplicants.

We got together with them Friday after class and wandered back to Deb's apartment Sunday afternoon as if we had danced around Stonehenge all weekend—emotionally high, physically sated, deeply happy with ourselves. Fast forward to the following Saturday morning. I woke with images of the four of us in my head. I was very hard. At that age I was always hard, every morning. An early-twenties penis is a marvel of hope and persistence. Deb was asleep on her side. That gorgeous shape beside me, luxurious brown hair spilling down the pillow, naked back, ass turned toward me, inviting me. I lubed up and sidled over to her, slipping myself between her cheeks and looking for her to respond as she always did, with a soft, half-awake sigh, a little arch in the small of her back, angling herself to accept me into her. This time I got a startled response.

"*No!*" she barked at me in a voice I hadn't yet heard.

I withered like a parched flower in the Joshua Tree sun, physically but much more so emotionally. I was back under the kitchen table for the first time since the last time I had seen my parents. Deb sat up angrily. I rolled away from her into fetal position and started to cry. I was so distraught and hurt that all my childhood vulnerability flooded back in a tide of shame. I was too small a vessel for this legion of feelings. It felt like a time-tunnel regression into childhood, a sci-fi B movie, me tumbling ass over tea kettle against a black-and-white spiral.

Deb's anger quickly changed to concern and apology. Her period had started the night before; I hadn't known. It took a lot of debriefing for us to get the day back on track, an effort that went well into the following Sunday. We had to plumb the depths of our shared sexuality, her position as leader of that aspect of our relationship, our power dynamic, which was trending from her dominance toward balance, and of course my childhood trauma. Trauma had begun our bonding over our lack of sober fathers, which began our inextricable binding into one, and which also began our march toward the inevitable, irretrievable, and unredeemed future.

Is there loss in the unredeemed? Is paradise inevitably lost? We've all experienced words that can't be taken back, moments of opportunity that slip by unnoticed, or possibilities that wink out of existence because the phone rang, the dog barked, or the baby cried. These almost-were things are whispers of possibility, the corpus of the incorporeal, dust in the wind, to quote a famous progressive rock band from the monocropped, chemical-soaked American prairie. A life with Deb was my chance to be retrieved and redeemed, to avoid being dust in the wind. My second redemption was still many years in the future.

* * *

"Any ideas where to go for lunch?" Deb was lounging on the bed, reading a magazine about Napa Valley wine.

We were staying at a two-star hotel called the Post about halfway up Nob Hill in downtown San Francisco. Deb and I loved San Francisco. So much of it is similar to Vancouver, and we felt at home there.

"Let's splurge." I was standing at the window looking down at the street, enjoying the bustle. "Why don't we go to the St. Francis? We can have a fancy lunch, then explore Union Square."

"I think we should find a local place in the same neighbourhood," was her reply, downsizing my ambitions. "I like the idea of exploring Union Square, I don't like spending that much on lunch."

"Okay. I'm up for a food adventure."

We walked out onto Post Street, went down Stockton to Geary, and headed west, toward the ocean. We connected up with Market Street and found Maison de Tolérance, an inviting little French bistro not far from the French embassy building. She thought the name was very San Francisco: it means *brothel* in English. Deb knew that. I didn't.

We were seated at a window table. The waiter was either French or he was faking it well. "What would beautiful *madame* enjoy?"

She glanced at me suppressing a giggle. "Tomato bisque and croque madame."

"*Très bien.*" He looked at me, staying with French to test me. "*Et pour monsieur?*"

And the role of Asshole in our production will be played by Jean-Guy the-Fuck's-His-Name, I thought it, but I didn't say it.

"What will you have, Dave?" Deb interjected a bit too quickly, probably because I'd paused.

I understood what he had said but it was too late to protest without sounding whiny. Slightly annoyed, I just said, "The same, please."

"*Bisque de tomate et croque monsieur.*" He couldn't resist correcting the gender of my sandwich. *Asshole de deux.*

After my accidental emasculation, Deb waited for Napoleon to leave before explaining that a croque madame comes with a poached egg on top and you eat it with a knife and fork. Croque monsieur is dipped in egg and fried like French toast, and you eat it with your hands. I knew they were both essentially ham and cheese sandwiches. I didn't know there was a gender difference. I wondered how, in this gender-bending city, sandwich naming was navigated.

I had learned that if I made Deb laugh she didn't feel as guilty about being too bossy or controlling. "Is there a *croque transgenre?*" I said.

"*Croque bisexuels*," she quipped.

I came back with "*croque lesbiennes.*"

She lowered her voice. "You're going to get us in trouble. We sound like homophobes."

"Those could all be delicious sandwiches," I protested. "No phobias intended."

Lunch was over the top. I had never had a soup and sandwich that good, another example of Deb adding new vistas to my view.

We had driven our little truck down the I-5 from Vancouver, sleeping in the back. I'd marked the Walmart in Medford, Oregon, in our map book, which was the pinnacle of analog nav-tech in 1998. It was a little past the halfway point. We spent the night in the parking lot, left early the next morning and made it to Fisherman's Wharf by 2:00 p.m. It was August, we had been married that spring and spent our honeymoon on Salt Spring Island. Going to San Francisco was a spur-of-the-moment decision. A sixteen-hour drive was easily doable and gas was cheap, plus two nights at the Post Hotel with parking and it wasn't going to cost much more than two hundred Canadian. We walked all over downtown and the waterfront. The sidewalks and streets were crowded, with more traffic than we were used to, lots of one-way streets and oddly shaped intersections, the chaos was a bit intimidating. I remember feeling as though I was constantly being squeezed off the sidewalk into traffic. Deb's shoulder bag kept bumping me. I was trying to be chivalrous, walking on the curb side. As people streamed past us she kept drifting into me, bumping me toward the street on the old broken sidewalks. With lampposts and newspaper boxes materializing at irregular intervals, I dodged and danced to keep up with her—she had always walked like three people in a hurry. She hadn't noticed her leftwards drift but she did say it felt as if the streets were tilted. At the time, I thought nothing of it.

* * *

Deb knew nothing about physics or astronomy when we met, but she picked up the material quickly. She became my quiz master, sometimes not even needing the text book but for the mind-bending math—for that I was on my own. I took exoplanets and astrobiology, biophysics and galaxies in third year, and in fourth year I took cosmology, high-energy astrophysics, and planetary science. I was fascinated by the possible physical conditions on other planets or extra-solar bodies, the surface conditions—if there even was a surface—and the weather conditions. Did it rain methane or diamonds? Were the winds so strong there weren't any mountains? What life forms might evolve? Carbon like us? Silicon? How big or small would creatures be?

All of this had lived in my boyhood imagination. I had been warned by my Grade 12 physics teacher that if I decided to pursue astronomy, I'd have to be willing to climb up to some pretty high places. Telescopes and observatories are usually high up, often with many flights of outdoor stairs. I hadn't considered that when I confessed my fear of heights to him. My fascination with the cosmos had developed closer to the ground, in parks, backyards, and on the odd garage roof. I had the marks for a scholarship. When you need to stay away from home as much as possible, school is a good alternative. I didn't have the courage for gangs and was never good enough at sports to make the school teams that travelled. When I left home, Social Services found me a place to live so I could finish the final month of Grade 12, and through them I was connected to a scholarship at UBC.

The next fall I moved onto campus, and thus began a new life for me. After first year I found a cheap apartment a long bus ride away, but I had a rent subsidy and a full-time summer job on campus—another subsidy. I elbow-greased my way through the first four years, after which my marks got me research assistant work so I could specialize in astrophysics and earn my degree. Deb and her family helped out a lot. I didn't pay for a meal for five years, and working in construction for Deb's father Lester was a valuable source of odd jobs paying good money.

The only other person who knew how fortunate I was to have been found by Deb was her neighbour's son, One-Legged Norm Junior, son of One-Legged Norm Senior. Twelve years older than Deb, OLN Jr. had long kept a not-so-secret flame for her. I doubt the one-legged thing would have fazed her, but he was just too familiar, a fixture of her growing-up years, and he wasn't a project. OLN Jr. lost his left leg in a motorcycle accident when he was twenty-one. OLN Sr. had lost his right leg many years before in a heavy machinery accident. They enjoyed standing side by side. Mrs. OLN Sr., Judy—who was often a stand-in for Deb's grandmother Agnes— was a veteran caregiver of one-legged men, her story was an epic of the neighbourhood. Deb said Judy inspired her, that everyone needed a Judy regardless of their limb count.

The One-Legged Norms, as they were called (a great band name, don't you think?), lived two houses west of the Glasscocks. Sandwiched between them was the widow Mrs. Rain, a perfect emblem of Vancouver in name and disposition. Mrs. Rain was apparently born aged sixty-five and only got older from there. Back when OLN Jr. had two legs he would play with and supervise Deb and her brothers Anthony and John. Between their two front yards was the iron curtain of Mrs. Rain's front lawn, grown from imported seed cut with an imported English reel mower sporting imported Japanese steel blades. The lawn was a perfect, weedless putting green that was off-limits to all dogs and children. If Mrs. Rain could have figured out how to banish cats, birds, flies, and beetles, she would have done that too. Street hockey was no solution—as in East Berlin, things always seemed to find a way over the wall. OLN Jr. would play goal, and inevitably the ball would end up on Mrs. Rain's lawn. Sometimes it was retrieved, sometimes not.

OLN Jr. told me Mrs. Rain sat at her front window most of the time on most days. When they were playing street hockey she wouldn't leave. She looked a lot like the Queen—smallish, greyish, mustelid. You wouldn't picture her as being nimble, but back in the day she was a gymnast, according to neighbourhood legend, a tumbler for England in the Olympics. This tiny woman with a steel-grey, pin-cushion perm was like the OG of parkour. From her front window, out the door, down six cement steps, and onto the front lawn, depending on where the ball had landed—it was an even money bet as to who would get there first, geriatric Mrs. Rain versus the teenaged, two-legged OLN Jr. in goalie pads. Deb, Anthony, and John were too small and without a hope against Her Ninja-Majesty. When the supply of hockey balls ran low, Deb's father Lester or OLN Sr. had to go visit Her Majesty, cap in hand, to get the balls back. OLN Sr. took advantage of his one-leggedness to instill guilt. Lester appealed to their shared Empire roots, his being Welsh, the seat of the Prince of Wales. Neither man would speak of the exchanges to their wives, likely for fear of either Katherine or Judy getting involved and no doubt seeing how things could go very wrong. Peace across front lawns through obsequious gestures and the clandestine purchase of extra hockey balls was the diplomatic brief. At least that was how Deb told the story after the demise of Her Ninja Majesty, when OLN Sr. and Lester were free to confess their duplicity.

I ensconced myself in Deb's family and the neighbourhood goings-on from the start, but our life on campus and our life at her family home were kept separate. I would have left my cigarette-butt apartment and moved in with Deb if she lived at home, but that was never going to happen. Deb wouldn't have it. Her family home was only ten minutes from UBC, but she wouldn't live off-campus during the school year. I couldn't see why, but they weren't my family, and any family was better than mine. I was born without eyes.

* * *

A 1976 Pontiac Grand Safari station wagon is a perfect student's car—cheap, virtually indestructible, DIY fixable, massive capacity for friends, teammates, gear, furniture, dogs, large goats, small horses, the cast and crew of a modest movie. If you've never experienced the cavernous interior of a North American station wagon dated anywhere from the late 1950s all the way through to the mid-'90s, whose last leviathan standing was the perfectly named Buick Roadmaster, you have missed the last industrial propaganda tool of the American dream, pure and incarnate. It was the last warship of an idealized colonialism, reduced in scope to rolling the asphalt sea of landlocked towns, buccaneering the pedestrian iniquities of the average working family.

When Deb needed a car, she got to drive the Grand Safari. I had never been in one before. I had certainly been in many other giant scows of the '70s and '80s: the Lincoln Continental, the Chrysler Imperial, the Mercury Montcalm, the Cadillac Seville, the Buick Riviera, even the now extinct AMC Matador Barcelona with its appalling vinyl landau roof. I knew these cars because my father traded in vehicular status, he bought and sold automotive assumptions. He loved the appearance of wealth, and since he couldn't afford new he used his congregants like street dealers, swooping in on newly widowed seniors and wealthy car aficionados to get lightly worn, low-mileage, slightly diminished status symbols, new to him, and deeply discounted because Jesus said so.

Lester Glasscock, on the other hand, was of the opposite persuasion when it came to cars. He bought himself only brand new Ford F-150 pickups, no options, at the lowest price he could find, even if he had to drive two hours to save two bucks. However, when it came to buying for Katherine (because buying a car for the little woman was a man's job), he displayed the same tightwad penchant but with used cars. There had to be a deal involved—the vehicle itself was secondary—so the white woody Pontiac for Katherine had come from Kelowna, five hours away, from an old Dutch couple. Lester proudly floated the Grand Safari back home, down and around Highway 97 and the serpentine Hope-Princeton, rolling the old springs like drunks in a rowboat, docking in Dunbar, taking up nearly half the width of a house on the street out front.

It was Easter Sunday 1995, about 4:45 a.m. Deb was nineteen and I was twenty-two. She had borrowed the station wagon and we were high on acid with six friends. Deb was at the wheel and driving much too slowly, as stoned people do, through Stanley Park as the darkness creamed toward first light. We rounded a curve to see a small group of pigeons roosting in the road. Do pigeons really do this? Sleep in the middle of a road, even a quiet one through the woods? I don't know, but they did that night. We all thought they would fly away, but we were going so slowly that they didn't hear the car until the very last second when most exploded skyward. But it was too late for a few who thumped and bumped the underside of the car, bursting up past the side windows, which was trippy and surprising to our drug-addled senses.

Deb rolled to a stop slowly, and we all turned and looked back. "Do you see that?" she asked no one in particular.

A lone pigeon sat crooked in the middle of the road at a forty-five-degree angle, motionless. We all got out and circled around the dead-but-alive Lazarus-bird, which is what someone whispered that Easter morning—I don't remember who. This would have made a great absurdist movie scene: a giant station wagon, all four doors open, engine running, eight stoned and silent people standing, sitting, squatting in an unkempt circle around a concussed, cock-eyed pigeon, all deeply enthralled by the unlikely circumstance of the angular avian.

How long did we remain immersed in this experience? I have no way of knowing. I've gone on at length about the fickle nature of memory, even without the use of psychedelics; add them and you have Fellini, not memory. Maybe it was all a group hallucination, an intersubjective imagining—such is the nature of drugged neurons. Regardless, we eventually did move on and drive away, still slowly, still silent, until someone snickered, then another, and another, until we were all braying uncontrollably to the point of tears. Deb had to pull over or risk slowly driving off the road.

As we gradually calmed down to snorts and chuckles, someone noticed God's very own Salvation Army up ahead. In a field by the sea, a Salvation Army Band was gathered, brass and banners glinting in the sunrise. The faithful were singing, giving the impression of the ultimate scene from *How the Grinch Stole Christmas* with all the Whos from Whoville harmonizing around the levitating Christmas star.

There looked to be around fifty souls all told. What we did next is the stuff of legend, both embarrassing and awesome, something only the young would do given that peculiar combination of innocence, ignorance, daring, and stupidity, before our more boring and mature sensibilities aged into place. Deb pulled away from the curb and drove past them, parking again just beyond the field where the woods resumed, out of sight. No words were exchanged. There was no plan, no premeditation; everything was spontaneous, a kind of group consciousness. We were eight chemically altered self-aware blobs of polymers suspended in salt water acting as one.

We all got out, unsure of what we were doing, happily tripping but with a tinge of mischief in the air. Why, I can't say, but I started to take my clothes off. It just seemed like a good thing to do. No prompt to the others was necessary, and in moments we were all naked. I put my sneakers back on, everyone else did the same.

I said, "Follow me," and they did.

I turned and walked toward the woods, toward God's Own People. It felt so good, walking naked in the forest at dawn. I felt my skin as a single organ, the air like a thin liquid. We slipped into the woods, approaching the band from behind. Something about being nude in the woods felt ancient, free, natural—and dangerous.

"We're the pagans, they're the Christians, we're the pagans, they're the Christians," I chanted in a whisper.

Deb and the others joined me softly. "We're the pagans, they're the Christians, we're the pagans, they're the Christians, we're the pagans, they're the Christians."

It was *Lord of the Flies* without the malice. We were on the cusp of an attack with unspoken intent. We slowed then crouched in silence at the edge of the woods. I held up my hand for a brief moment to indicate standby, like the special-ops teams do in the movies, then sliced it downward with a war whoop. We bolted from the woods onto the field toward the startled, slack-jawed congregation, screaming obscenities, like naked, howling wolves falling on a herd of sheep.

The Sally Ann band members sputtered, the music fumbled, and the fearful faithful began making involuntary movements, striking odd poses, and making strange gestures of attitude. Some cowered, some scowled, some stretched up or craned around to see better, some froze in place. Some even smiled. All were unsure of what was happening. We were transported, a screaming pack of pagan barbarians from the tenth century. We ran, encircling the now silent band and bewildered faithful as they struggled to process the information flooding their senses like fouled water. They closed ranks but didn't run even as we began to chant again.

"We're the pagans, we're the pagans, we're the pagans," we yelled.

As we flaunted our naked bodies at them—tits bouncing, cocks banging from side to side, young, beautiful, nubile, sensual—an ancient battle played out again that morning, near the close of the twentieth century in a giant urban park within a city approaching a population of two million. Victory for the naked pagans hung cool in the April dawn until the band leader shook himself into the moment, appeared to mouth a silent *fuck you*, and rallied the band.

The tuba farted into life first, then the drummers began to punch as the cymbals clanged a call to arms, the trombones wobbled up, and a few baritone voices chimed in with muscular support as their ranks fell back into formation. They began an aggressive version of "Onward Christian Soldiers," the full band and all the voices now ascending in unison, calling the very saints from the clouds above. The battle was joined!

They burst forth into a holy mushroom cloud of ebullient song. We chanted louder, we jeered, we lathered the morning in profanities. The band blew a hurricane as the faithful rose to heaven on the lungs of angels. Cacophony battled harmony until spit flew like machine gunfire arching in frothy silhouette against the rising sun.

Then we pagans started to laugh. We began to lose coherence, we stumbled, our formation broke, we laughed harder. The band, seizing the opportunity, blew like the rapture was at hand. At the peak of all possible verve, the congregation began to jeer and laugh as it sang. With our ranks now shattered we made for the woods, the faithful cheering and jeering ever louder at our retreating asses. The band degenerated into lobbing aggressive honks of derision, blaring brass, and cutting percussion launched at us like mortar shells. This was the legendary battle of the Salvation Army's Annual Easter Sunrise Service of April 16th, 1995, versus the beautiful and tragic Naked Pagans. The Attack of the Naked Pagans. I'm sure what began as eight of us grew to eighteen or eighty over the years as the Sally Ann's faithful warriors retold their heroic tales over tea and cake. As for us pagans, we eventually came down from our high, though it took half a day and lots of orange juice.

As for me, I hadn't intended to become the pagan chieftain that morning. Intention to do anything when high on acid is a milky concept anyway, but there was no question Deb had opened something up in me, a confidence and sense of belonging, to her, to her family, even to her neighbourhood, a belonging I had lacked all my life.

No one can say with certainty what significance will accrue from their youthful misadventures, but for me this was the beginning of the completion of me at the hands of my beloved. How could I not fall in love with her? How could anyone not fall in love with a person who gifted them with confidence and a sense of belonging by their mere presence? If I wasn't already helpless and hopeless when it came to Deborah Jane Glasscock, my decimation was complete as I chased her, stoned and naked, through the woods of Stanley Park while all the Christian world was singing.

CHAPTER 8

A THEFT OF GRIEF

Deb and I had a backyard wedding on Saturday, June 20th, 1998, held at a family friend's house. The yard looked north over Jericho Hill and Spanish Banks to Burrard Inlet and the West Vancouver waterfront. The setting was beautiful, the weather a perfect day in June, sunny and warm but not too hot. The guest list was small, and everyone brought their own drinks. I had no money, and although Deb's family had some, the focus was on cheap and fun, both of which were well managed. We were in our fourth year as a couple. University had just ended for me. Our plan was a quick honeymoon close by, and then back to work. Deb had landed a job with a big ad agency when she graduated, at the top of her class, of course, in a department specializing in political messaging and campaign strategy. There were bills to pay, loans to service, and I had a dissertation to write. We chose Salt Spring Island for our honeymoon because it was cheap, close, and we loved it there.

The Glasscocks knew how to drink at a wedding; they had been marinated in alcohol and baked into a boozy fruitcake of abuse. A people similar to my own minus the violence. Despite that fact Lester had never liked me. I think his dislike sprang from envy: he saw in me someone who had overcome what he couldn't. And the impending PhD intimidated him. Katherine, on the other hand, saw me straight through as if I were transparent: she saw a victim of abuse who chose not to become an abuser, a survivor who wouldn't create more survivors. She was right, and she was kind to me. Katherine the Great was a good mother. Lester was a too-often drunk father, but he wasn't abusive. He didn't physically hurt anyone, but he wasn't warm, loving, or accessible. Deb got what she needed from Katherine; her brothers suffered for the void that lived where their father was supposed to be. The youngest, John—I refused to ever call him Dewey—carried on the family tradition of alcoholism. Anthony did too but eventually put it behind him.

The Southern Gulf Islands ferry leaves for Salt Spring from Tsawwassen terminal, well south of Vancouver, close to the American border. It services all the tiny island harbours as it winds its way through the channels between Galiano, Mayne, Saturna, and North Pender on its way to Salt Spring Island. Deb and I had made this trip many times before. Even today, the West Coast hippie vibe of the 1960s is alive and well on Salt Spring—people making jewellery, gardening, playing guitars, growing pot, and sewing clothes. There are old-time farmers, artisan cheese makers, multi-generational fishing families, starving artists, dreadlocked and tie-dyed young moms, and house boaters. The music scene in the pubs is eclectic and the local chefs are pretty good, as are the coffee roasters. Every Saturday from late spring to harvest there's a huge public market next to Centennial Park on the Ganges waterfront.

"Let's do the Naked Hippie Lesbian Stoned Farmers' Market and Craft Boutique on Saturday," That was Deb's favourite mouthful-of-a-moniker for the weekend market. She loved the authentic, unpretentious people building a life of their own choosing, and she loved the intellectual romance of that idea, as long as one didn't mind a little poverty with their romance—and on Salt Spring no one seemed to. Summer brought the rich sailing and yachting people, the float-plane people, tourists from Vancouver and Seattle, and day-tripping families from Victoria. We knew all this, so a honeymoon in June before school let out was our plan.

The ferry docks at Long Harbour, a short drive into Ganges. We had booked the Salt Spring Inn—tiny, old, full of character, and in need of a little love. It had creaky stairs, a restaurant usually full of locals, and rooms that overlooked the harbour—just seven rooms in total. Three "deluxe" rooms actually have a private bathroom as well as a fireplace and view of the harbour, while the four at the back all share one large bathroom. Booking in January would always get you a deluxe room at the front with a private bathroom, obviously essential on a honeymoon. The suffusion of love that comes with a public declaration of life together is a powerful aphrodisiac. "Till death do us part" is a profound thing—sex seems better, easy optimism greets you in the morning, the most mundane conversation enhances the bond. Time shared grows new people, each modified by the nurturing of the other. Love, simply put, is what we humans want and need most. Those of us who grew up without it know this acutely.

Three hours on the ferry is a joy if you bring the right attitude and put schedules out of your mind. We read magazines, drank tea, walked the deck, and sat in silence watching island shorelines pass by. Gazing at houses high up on rocky crags or down at the water's edge with long piers on stilts mooring boats of all description. Seabirds, seals, the occasional pod of orcas, fishing boats, and kayaks entertained our lazy senses. Everything was blue, everything was warm sun, salty breeze, and the sound of water being cut by the bow plane. I don't think we were ever not touching each other, holding hands, embracing, kissing, rubbing against each other, fondling each other when no one could see. There are lots of private places for private moments on the deck of a large ferry that's only half full. By the time we docked we were hound horny. We had each learned how to satisfy the other and took equal pleasure in trying to outdo past delicious tortures. Deb would have made me come in my pants had I not stopped her in the nick of time; what drove her over the edge was me fondling her breasts and rubbing her nipples. We were each armed with the knowledge of the other's luscious vulnerabilities. Youth is a dream come true before morning.

Driving off the ferry into town was excruciating. Deb had her hand in my pants the whole way. I hid the bulge while we checked in, but on this island you can have sex in the park, in public, if you're just a bit discreet and no kids are around. When we got to the room we were more than ready. Experience had taught us that slow and deliberate was the way to start. Early on in our relationship we'd torn each other's clothes off ravenously, but now we knew how to take our time and slowly build to ravenous.

Love is a psychedelic, a hallucinogen, a spiritual awakening. Sex is not love, but in the moment love can be sex. "Love is Love," sang a boy named George once upon a time. I don't know how but I seem to have been prepared, against all odds, for a future where I was loved despite a past where I was not. Perhaps my people had some of that same tooth and claw that Deb's people had, that never-surrender attitude they were so famous for. Love is as much a decision to persevere as it is the bliss of sweat and dopamine. The ability to persevere is an asset in an uphill life.

I rolled over and exhaled; "God, I love you."

"Love you right back," she said, slowing her breathing. "Do you think anyone heard us?" She sounded a bit sheepish.

"I don't care. If they did I hope they're jealous."

"Maybe we turned them on? My commentary was pretty hot—at least *you* certainly thought so."

"'Take my heart, oh please be true,'" I warbled, "'it's a gift for only you, I am your willing plaything, you can do anything to me.'"

"Where do you get this stuff from? Your head should be completely full of cosmology by now. How can there be any room for song lyrics from before we were born?"

"My mother loved all those old '50s crooners. She played them incessantly. I think they were her escape."

"My Grandpa Walter loved Slim Whitman, I'm emotionally scarred by falsetto yodelling."

I chuckled a snort. She liked to tease me about how I laughed.

"He was Welsh. His real name was Otis, but Dewey was his middle name," she continued, "I'm surrounded by Deweys."

"You poor thing. I promise I'll never sing a Slim Whitman song to you, even if I could, which I can't."

"I'm sleepy, darling. Curl up with me."

She rolled onto her side. We spooned and began to drift off into a contented, postcoital haze. Birds sang outside, the sheets felt like a safe childhood, the sunlight dimmed, and the old-fashioned wallpaper began to dance as I slowly sank into the half-sleep of an afternoon nap. Indistinct music floated up under my awareness, the wallpaper became musical notations, the room swayed gentley as the ocean lapped against the window panes.

You're my magic, you spark me …

I felt the warmth of her skin next to mine.

… fearsome, fiercely into flame.

A song began to form. It was exciting and new; in my dream I strained to hear it. The singer sounded Irish; she had a pure soprano voice.

Your deep cadence calls to me,
I'm helpless, I'm hopeless, you are spinal-final,
so beautiful, so beautiful, I can hardly breathe.

Images turned, tumbled, and repeated in my dreaming, like an Escher drawing set to motion; indistinct people and abstract buildings flowed across a wallpaper screen; shards of someone else's memory, events from lives past.

You were made for me, Terpsichore,
shelter, shade for me, Terpsichore,
a welcomed blade through me, Terpsichore,
you're my dree-eee-eam,
you're my dreeeeeeam.

The aroma of baking came to me—bread, maybe buns—and I saw my mother's back turned, the strings of her apron knotted around her waist.

You're my willow to weep, my pillow to sleep,
you're the chills that run up and down my spine,
you're my willow to weep, my pillow to sleep,
my cross, my empty veins, my funeral wine,
you're my willow to weep, my pillow to sleep,
you're a thief of grief, my refuge, my divine,
and your eyes hold the shine of my crimes.

Then the music faded but the singer kept going acapela; changing the tune to what sounded like an old Celtic song.

Softly sang the girl in the willow tree,
gently floated her voice on the glen.
Came the wind asking her why she sang sadly.
Answered the girl, I was hung here by men.

They wanted my sweetness each one at a time,
and when I refused them they beat me,
and raped me and left me here hanging.
The girl in the willow tree,
sadly singing,
a corpse on the glen.

I burst awake as a vision of her corpse winked out like a distant star against the sunrise, instantly alert, not moving. The dream had frightened me, the voice sounding as though it were in the room with us, singing to us as we slept. I had the impression something ominous had taken a seat in the corner, but of course no one was there. The birds still sang, the wallpaper was motionless, and I could smell the ocean—it all seemed like nothing but a bad dream.

* * *

It was trees that first started my reclamation. Forest canopy, parks, boulevards—trees began to open me up and help me make acquaintance with myself. Even before I fell in love with Deb I fell in love with her Vancouver neighbourhood because of the arbutus trees. And they're all over Salt Spring. If you've never seen one, I feel sorry for you. They naturally lose their bark, exposing a light-brown, Polynesian-girl skin beneath, tones of creamy brown in swirls like clouds, smooth to the touch, almost varnished, glossy with patches of bark curled over like rolls of burnished paper. Their curvy limbs undulate upward, opening out into a canopy of fat, mottled, succulent leaves. Arbutus trees stand out in the temperate rainforest like a drag queen in church. I had never seen a tree so beautiful before, so exotic, so fittingly set on wealthy lawns in front of grand houses. In those days there were still lots of arbutus all over Vancouver's West Side, all the way out to UBC and into Pacific Spirit Park.

I was smitten. Just a forty-minute bus ride from my dark basement apartment in the ironically named Mount Pleasant district lived the West Side people and their West Side trees. The university people. The beach people. Deb and her part of the city filled me with desire. I was longing for a better life but had no idea what that life should be. I had a grinding conviction of the need to find a better shell for my hermit-crab self.

When Deb arrived in my life, she seemed wonderful and exotic too, like an arbutus. A beautiful girl from the rich part of town. Why shouldn't I have a girl like that? I remember thinking that when I first met her on campus that day. Such an immature, pathetic, and needy way to see another human being—in terms of personal acquisition, but I was mostly hermit crab then, not much of a young man yet. You can't have lived my experience without being stunted. Who would think that things as common as trees and family would give me all and everything I lacked, common yet so precious, like water. You no doubt see who Deb was to me and why I fell in love with her, so right after I fell for Deb I fell for her mother, then the rest of her family—Agnes, her grandfather Walter, Katherine, and even Lester, who never requited my love, unspoken as it was. These three women gave me all the love I so desperately needed. Agnes, Katherine, and Deb, grandmother, mother, and wife, generations of love all in one package deal. My cavernous need for female affection was met in these women. Mother love is the juice of the world; without it everything dries out, seizes up, and breaks down. I was so fortunate for a time because of these three women. Never underestimate the power of a brilliant, kind, and strong woman to balm what ails you. Unfortunately, to be fixed one must first face what's broken, something I hadn't yet done in my scant few years of malnourished manhood, and that was also the reason I was safe for Deb to love. She could see what was broken, and being brilliant and kind and strong, she was confident she could fix me.

* * *

We went downstairs to the restaurant for dinner that evening and sat on the deck, watching the harbour. I didn't mention the dream but the image of the singing corpse stayed with me. As the sun set behind the hotel the little town red-shifted in the dimming light, with the yellow moonrise soon reflecting off the water. We took it all in, listening to the waves gently lapping.

The following morning, we walked to the Tree House Café for coffee and breakfast, then strolled to the park and sat on a bench, holding hands as we watched the boats in the harbour and kids playing. All was idyllic, a dream for dreaming. It was a Friday; the market was Saturday, so that day we decided to drive to Ruckle Park at the other end of the island. We made stops for a bottle of pinot gris at Gary Oaks Winery, goat cheese at the Salt Spring Cheese Company, and a focaccia with tomato, cheese, and black pepper from Morningside Bakery. On we went to Ruckle for a picnic, with a final quick stop at the Ruckle Farm stand for mustard pickles.

The park itself covers many acres with lots of trails leading into the woods or down to the ocean. We had our favourite little cove down and away from the picnic area. We packed our feast down the steep trail and spread out on a huge log that had been there for decades. The tide was at mid-point. With waves lapping, ferries going past, and trees overhanging the steep cliffs, it was the perfect secluded beach except at high tide when crabs and starfish took over for a few hours. After our meal we stripped and swam in the cool bay under the warm June sunshine. There are days that should be preserved in amber; if only we could remember to step back and receive them deeply, tune ourselves to the experience. It's a hard thing to do for youth and beauty, so entangled in our own heads as we are in those gilded years. Perfection was that day. I am thankful I can still feel it alive in me. The weekend of our honeymoon was, to that point, the best Deb and I had shared. Thankfully there were more and better days to come, but we didn't know that then. I didn't think any of these thoughts that day as we floated naked in the pristine, salty blue, on my back, eyes closed, the sun a pink kaleidoscope on the inside of my eyelids.

We were up early the next morning for the Saturday market. In June the crush was still manageable, but by the Canada Day long weekend it would be like Times Square on New Year's Eve. The top of the market runs across the top of the park, which is where most of the crafts are—then it turns right and heads toward the harbour, all food and farm stands on that leg before turning again and heading back up to the top of the park. The stores and galleries of Ganges surround the park: the grocery store, Salt Spring Island Coffee, the bookstore, the Tree House Café, West of the Moon, kayak rentals, some art galleries and yoga studios, the pizza place— the whole area maybe twenty square blocks. We strolled and shopped for hours. Strolling was hard for Deb; me, I could stroll. But as the morning progressed she slowed to my pace, which prompted me to ask whether she was okay. She was just tired, she said. But something about it didn't sit right with me; I usually had to work to keep up with her. Still, I decided she knew best and put it out of my mind.

We had what was for Salt Spring a fancy dinner that night at Hastings House, our one splurge that weekend. Drinks, a bottle of wine, and dinner for two almost two hundred bucks, a gift from Agnes and Walter. Sunday was the ferry home, eggs Benedict, and mimosas at the inn before we left. I could see our future from the deck of that ferry, reflected on shimmering water, an assurance of all that was surely to come. We sat nested, wrapped together, watching the Salish Sea swish by, fixed in the flow of scenery, too fed and full of ourselves to move.

* * *

Lester introduced me to Scotch that Christmas; high and holy Christian holidays were the only time he would elevate from beer. Deb, Katherine, and Agnes made the feast. Walter, Lester, and I took on the traditional male holiday role of sit-eat-drink, not quite eat-pray-love but meaningful in a working-class-man kind of way, though I doubt it would make for a good book. I looked at them, Walter and Lester, and did not see myself as the anchors they were. Polite though I always was, inside I judged. I was a meteor rocketing the night sky compared with what they had brought to their wives and children. I would be better, better than them, better than my father, better than anyone I saw around me. I would be the lone male who lived up to one of these Waggstaff women and their annoyingly extraordinary gifts.

New Year's Eve 1998 was a frosty, open-air rager in our little bungalow neighbourhood. Since all of us Burkevillians were frozen in situ by weather from the Arctic because the jet stream had slipped south that winter, the obvious thing to do was to turn our little enclave into a giant progressive party. Every Christmas outdoor train sets hooted and tooted, one house even had a model alpine tram running from the front lawn to the crest of the roof and back. Another had a miniature Ferris wheel in red and green, still others had Santas, Grinches, Rudolphs and assorted other reindeer, every form of lighted Christmas icon you could think of was represented.

On New Year's Eve the indoor parties started around nine, after the little kids were asleep and the older kids were watching movies. Deb and

I circled the neighbourhood several times. The tradition was to take an empty glass with you from house to house and at each stop, someone would fill it with something. We were relatively new to the neighbourhood then, and without kids, which left us free to visit rather than host.

The evening poured on into night, and the streets slowly emptied; kids and families, friends and relations went indoors to eat, drink, dance, and watch the festivities from around the world on TV. We were just two people with multiple invitations so we did a circuit, starting with the Stewarts. Owen and Daisy were about ten years older than us. Their little house was full to spilling, with every light on, every appliance working, and food on every surface. We talked, we grazed, we drank.

From the Stewarts' we went to the Wong's for one of my all-time favourites, *xiaolongbao*, a steamed pork dumpling—no surprise. Traditionally it was served with a dipping sauce of red wine vinegar and minced ginger, but Grandma Wong added green onion, a dash of hot sauce, and toasted sesame oil to her dipping sauce. My noodles-and-dumplings gene was ecstatic.

After a few more drop-ins we ended our rounds next door at the Bandis'. Bruno and Sarah were a Swiss couple originally from an Italian canton on Lake Maggiore bordering the two countries. Bruno was one of just a few pilots left in Burkeville. The Bandi household was the same as all the others in Burkeville that night, full to overflowing with people food and drink, humming with music and conversation. We had an hour to go before midnight when the main transformer for the entire neighbourhood blew off the telephone pole with a thunderous boom that cannoned across the nearby runways, echoing off the hangars. Everything went dark. Everything stopped working. All the movies and TVs stopped, ovens began to cool, and fridges began to warm, but the candles and barbecues started up in mere minutes. People went out into the street to see what had happened. One of the advantages of being close to the airport is emergency services, and we had a BC Hydro works yard close by. The crew was there in under ten minutes, with an appreciative audience singing Christmas carols while they worked. Wisely, none of them accepted the numerous offers of a cup of cheer.

Twenty minutes later, Burkeville had a brand-new transformer. They flipped the connection and we all powered up. New Year's Eve 1998 was back in business before the food had time to get cold. We piled back into the Bandis' house and watched the ball drop from Times Square. Deb and I got home about 2:00 a.m. I was too full and very drunk. Deb tucked me in, then crawled into bed beside me. As the bed spun I heard that beautiful, clear lilting voice again, the one from my honeymoon nightmare, she sang: *Should old acquaintance be forgot and never brought to mind, we'll drink a cup of kindness then for days of auld lang syne.* Her tone was again enchanting. After the song, through the rotating delirium, I heard her say something that sounded like a fragment of poem:

It will always arrive, that thing, whatever it may be,
dizzying down from all the possible futures,
like games of chance tumble-dumped from a bright celestial box,
ringing with notes of joy, pink with pathos,
singing with sighs of sweet, bluesy sex.

What thing? I remember thinking as the words melted into a drunken slumber.

* * *

What is a bad Canadian? Someone who isn't polite? Someone who doesn't use *eh* as an exclamatory interrogative—"How's she goin', eh?" Someone who can't drive in the snow, doesn't like hockey, can't skate? I never learned to skate. I blame God for my inability to skate, not my father. It's almost the only thing I don't blame my father for.

Unlike the rest of the country, in the southwest corner of British Columbia, rarely does winter arrive in your backyard of its own accord; usually you have to go find it. The winter of 1998 was the exception. Most years mild Pacific winds dominate, winter storms come from the west rather than the north, from Hawaii and the Philippines—the Pineapple Express. Spruce, fir, and cedars grow thick and tall in the temperate rainforest. Frozen blue-sky days and starry winter nights, so common on the northern Prairies, are exceedingly rare. The Salish Sea is chilly but unfreezing year round. Moderate temperatures push inland for miles until a mountain or two gets in the way. A moderate climate for a moderate people.

To find reliable winter ice you have to go indoors. Vancouver was still small in the 1970s when I was a child, without a lot of rinks and even less ice time. There was just one rink close to my house—at Sunset Park, and it serviced most of South Vancouver. I remember only one visit to that rink, although we frequented the park, the community centre, and the pool a lot—those activities we could do without parents. The one important thing my formless mother did was to make sure I learned to swim—credit where credit's due. But a trip to the rink? That single visit was a public skate on a Saturday morning with my mother and the Tin Man, a one-off because we were in church every Sunday so Saturday was busy for my parents. On Saturdays, when I wasn't busy being abused, I was left to my own devices. That's why I blame God for my inability to skate.

Vancouver comes by its blue-green reputation honestly. Parks and trees are ubiquitous, and the ocean is never very far away. I grew up under a canopy of trees and a canopy of parents, a neighbourhood busy being a leafy village. I wasn't the only one being beaten or abused. I had friends living a similar life, but the don't-ask-don't-tell times settled a circumspect silence outside those prideful, working-class front doors. I wondered who knew, who could see the signs? As an adult, I now realize others surely did.

I remember going up Fraser Street with my grandmother Evelyn to get bread and doughnuts from the konditorei—the German bakery, and meats and cheeses from the German delicatessen. I remember the cooler in her basement—the urban version of a root cellar. It was a cement room troved with pickled herring, sauerkraut, dill pickles, jams, preserved fruits, sausage and pickled yellow beans. Carrots were buried in sand in a hole cut into the concrete floor, as fresh in February as when they came out of the garden in October. I remember noodles and dumplings in her kitchen, the windows slick with condensation from the exhaling pots, the massive gas range squatting in the corner, dominant and brooding, a hulking spectre on lion's feet, burner plates that lifted off to expose the molten core of the earth. The fridge was like an Oldsmobile stood on its end, bright white and chrome, art deco. Cross-shaped silver handles flanked the graceful spout over the white enamel sink. Sitting at Grandma Evelyn's chrome and Arborite table in the warm kitchen, my skin squeaking on the vinyl chair, I looked out the wobbly Edwardian glass to the wider world, to the back alley and its back entrances—the lumberyard, the rear entrance of the bicycle shop, the back door of the doctor's office with its appended paperboys' shack in the parking lot where we collected the bundled *Vancouver Sun* for our paper routes.

It seems as though everything about my growing up was a scene outside a window, a witnessed world, an alley, a basement, a back door. I was never able to walk through a front door, in full light, in confidence and knowledge, in acceptance and love, all the things I thought a young boy was supposed to feel. I was a prisoner of insecurity and immaturity, blind to possibilities, born to use back doors. But as I've said, my people are noodles and-dumplings people, so why should I have been anything other than simple and backward? Sure, by the time I came along the dirt had been washed off and the poverty attenuated, but the peasantry persisted like drunks on the porch with a fiddle and washtub, caterwauling in a foreign tongue. Nothing to be done, no way to shut them up.

I'm not looking for sympathy. I'm merely trying to express how it felt to be me when I was a boy. I overcame, I moved past—beyond the mudline-bloodline. We all shoulder baggage regardless of how thoroughly we never go home. So no tears for young Davie, please—just bear all this in mind when it comes time to judge my future failings and how my never having learned to skate as a boy opened the door to our family demon. You see, rental skates in a working-class neighbourhood are a cheap and well-used commodity, so when a timid child of six, wearing worn out, ill-fitting skates, finds himself Bambi-ing his way around the rink, struggling like the two-year-olds he sees beside him, amusement in the eyes of the adults, derision in the eyes of the older kids—well, it's just too easy to leave by the back door. Had I learned to skate, everything might have been different.

CHAPTER 9

MY WILLOW TO WEEP

Deb was happy to trade Glasscock for Becker. Deb and Dave Becker. Has a bit of musicality to it, wouldn't you say? Princess Agnes the Navigator certainly thought so. It was unfortunate that she didn't live long enough to meet her great-grandsons. Nothing that year—1999—turned out as anyone expected. It was as if some cosmic debt had to be paid to some unknown ancestor, as if the army of the dead just showed up out of nowhere, old as bones, bringing calamity ringing forward from forgotten battles long ago fallen silent.

Agnes may have been at a loss too, had she lived to see it all, but maybe not. She came from a long line of those-who-showed-up. When the shitstorms blew hard and long, well equipped or ill equipped, regardless of circumstance or distance, Deb's people showed up—a strong suit of theirs akin to their famous work ethic. You could count on the WASP to arrive, invited or not, needed or not, always capable and never requiring reciprocity or even thanks. While that may sound like a mixed blessing, and it is, unless you've gone through the meat grinder of daily, incremental, unceasing suffering and loss measured by the inch, you will have no idea how welcome this unwelcomed strength can be. There's something about farm people—a recognition of practicality, a plodding relentlessness, an understanding of cycles and interdependence—that gets lost in the big-city streets, like car exhaust filtered through the leaves of Vancouver's arbutus trees I love so much.

* * *

"Two hundred and twenty-nine pounds is huge for a hockey player," Deb said.

"Get that mass moving at forty clicks per hour and watch out," I replied.

We were watching a Canucks game. Todd Bertuzzi's stats came up.

"I need to pee," she said, struggling to her feet and waddling to the bathroom. Among her many complaints was having to pee hourly. "Oh my God, I weigh almost the same as he does!" she yelled from the bathroom.

"Please don't beat the shit out of me," I yelled back.

"Shut up or I'll roll over and crush you in your sleep. No wonder I'm so exhausted all the time and can't walk two blocks without sitting down. Thank God for spandex. Who gains fifty-eight pounds being pregnant? Is the kid gonna be born five years old?"

She thumped back down on the couch beside me with a grunt, and I felt the sofa cushions lift a little. Tenderly, I put my arm around her shoulders and pulled her close. At nine months pregnant, Deb indeed weighed nearly the same as the Canucks' first-line power forward. She was horrified. It was spring 2002, and Adam would soon be born. We were so connected, so in love. The years since we'd first met had only gotten better. We were married now and embarking on making our own family. We were invincible. I looked at her on the couch beside me, my gorgeous, glowing power forward, and knew beyond all doubt if something happened to me, the kids we had decided to make together would be perfectly fine. She would be another dreadnought mother from a line of dreadnought mothers and I could be a good father because she wouldn't allow anything less.

It would've been better if Princess Agnes was with us for the ride. Deb and her grandmother had been close, and long after she died Deb still felt the loss. I could see it on her face occasionally. But I could also see that the anticipation of motherhood filled her with power—Deb was what a female superhero should look like. Deb Becker 2002 edition, nine months pregnant, two hundred and twelve pounds of life-giving girth, a Dreadnought peeling the ocean, bristling with heavy guns.

It made me think of my own mother, a nonentity, the opposite of Deb. I understood that because of my own mother my hopelessly idealized view of Deb, her mother Katherine the Great, her grandmother Princess Agnes the Navigator, and her legendary great-grandmother Ginny Brown was inevitable. I just couldn't help it. Any family would have been better than my family, any mother better than my mother. Try as I might, I felt nothing for my mother, her memory having been paved over and the potholes all filled in long ago. I remember being amazed at how completely Deb, Katherine, and Agnes had replaced the emptiness with belonging, how despite testing for them, like pinching myself, I couldn't summon up the old feelings of loneliness. They had vanished like a thief in the night (sometimes there is no better turn of phrase than in King James English).

After the winter of 1998 and the experience of being snowed in for three days, which never happens in Vancouver, we made the decision.

"If we have one, then I want two," she said. "After that we'll see, but it's important to be prepared for the idea of two before we go down this road."

Two kids sounded great to me. Maybe one of each, maybe not, either was okay. I had grown up alone, and I sometimes wondered whether a sibling would have made things easier or just created a second victim. "I'm good with that—and not too far apart."

"That depends on my eggs and your sperm, but we can have lots of fun trying. You're such an easy target."

"You trained me well."

"And you never once complained, did you?"

"No, but I remember being a little intimidated at first."

"You mean when I popped your cherry?"

"Thirty seconds isn't long enough to get intimidated," I replied, which made her laugh. "I meant the triathlon training you put me through after."

"You were such a good boy, only too willing to please."

"And I never heard you complain either—kind of the opposite, actually."

"Men need to be mind-fucked before they're actually fucked. You enjoy being told what to do. Narrative turns you on."

"Do you think our kids will grow up to be as potty-mouthed as you?"

"I predict that in the day-to-day they'll learn the word *shit* from me and the word *fuck* from you," she said.

"If they don't learn them from their friends first."

"Or by lip-reading hockey players on TV."

"Are you completely sure you want to be a mother?"

"As sure as anyone can be. I've thought about it a lot. And about you," she added, which made me a bit trepidatious but I kept silent and let her go on. "I don't think I would do this on my own. I could but I wouldn't. I doubt my parents had any deep discussion before they had me and my brothers. You and I have dissected our family histories enough times for me to be sure. What about you?"

The first time the possibility of fatherhood had entered my imagination, it felt like an emotional leeching. I hadn't shared that with Deb—not yet anyway. She was the only reason I could consider the possibility of becoming a dad, the only reason I could imagine I might make a good father.

"I was terrified at first," I said, "for obvious reasons. And I wouldn't do this with anyone else but once I let myself dream about doing it with you, the fear went away … at least the terror did. I'm still afraid, but not of being a father. The things that scare me now are the things I'm sure everyone worries about. Will the pregnancy go well? What about the act of giving birth and those first months when they're so tiny and vulnerable? Then you think how long they're actually vulnerable for, how many years they need you to protect them. If I go down that road too far, my father's waiting for me, so I have to be careful not to psyche myself out. But as long as it's you and me, I can do it."

She looked at me thoughtfully. "I can understand that. The things that'll happen to my body are intimidating, but I'm okay to face whatever happens as long as we're together. And don't worry, we won't turn into our parents. We can see their mistakes and make different choices."

"We'll make different mistakes, Deb," I said. "We just have to make sure they're small."

"We will. We'll make sure they're small and done out of love, not some idea of how things are supposed to be, or worse, out of ignorance. We'll let them be who they are. Gay, straight, creative, nerdy, sporty—whoever they turn out to be will be fine as long as they're good people."

"I can do that if you can," I said, "and I'm sure you can so I'll just follow your lead. You had a real family growing up even if some things were fucked up. You know how to be a family, you guys are all fine."

"Almost." She rolled her eyes slightly. "But you're right, I had both examples, one from Mom's side of the family and the other from Dad's. That's how I know you're going to be a great father, because you've totally rejected everything about your father. I can see it on your face when you look at my dad. You know he's an alcoholic like your dad was, but at least he doesn't abuse anyone. When I see that look on your face, I know I was right about you as a husband and I'm right about how you'll be as a father."

"I didn't know I had a *look* for your dad. I hope it's not obvious."

"Don't worry, it's not. I've seen it on your face briefly in predictable situations. I was watching for your reaction. I noticed, but he didn't. He doesn't notice anything. Mom notices, though, and so does Grandma, and they feel the same way about you as I do."

"Thanks. That's a relief." I chuckled to myself. "Okay, I'm all in if you're all in."

"All in, babe. We're going to be formidable!" She pronounced it *en Français*.

And thus began our parental journey. But before we had kids we decided to practise on a cat. In retrospect it wasn't such a smart decision; cats are independent and little real-world caregiving happens. We had thought a dog might be too much, though in hindsight a rabbit or a guinea pig would have been smarter.

* * *

"Dave, I'm going to help Mom with the canning. I'll bring dinner back with me. If I'm not back in time, please feed Rafael."

"Will do, babe," I answered by rote.

"Dave, you won't let our future children starve, will you?"

"I'll be the best future father ever. I stand like a mountain, our children will thrive on my ramparts. I dominate the landscape; many creatures find shelter and sustenance on my slopes, I stand in all weather, and I lift those I love closer to the sun."

"Hey, self-help Dave? You'll feed the cat, right? If you can't look after a cat, I won't have babies with you."

"Our babies will not be evil. This cat is evil, but I'll feed this cat in order to pass your parental fitness test."

"Dave?"

"Yes, Deb?"

"I love you."

"Love you too, darling."

Lots of places offered lots of cats to choose from for adoption, but Deb had fallen in love with Rafael because as a kitten he looked much grumpier than any future social media Grumpy Cat. He looked more like Pissed-Off Cat, which was such a cute incongruence. Even I had to admit that malevolence on such a tiny, adorable face was hilarious. Had social media been a thing back then we would have made a fortune.

"Can we have this one?" She asked the woman, holding up a tiny black, white, and marmalade kitten.

"Fill out your information and agree to an unscheduled home inspection," the woman replied, pushing a form at us. "Once we've reviewed your application, we'll call you."

I thought Rafael looked like Joe Pesci in *Goodfellas*. Dangerous. That should have been enough of a warning, but I wasn't prepared to challenge Deb's maternal instincts based on resemblance to a movie villain so I went along with it and we adopted Rafael. His nickname would soon take hold, courtesy of me: Cunty the Cat. Surprise! Cunty was not a nice cat. His vulgar nickname may sound ridiculous to you, a gross overstatement, perhaps. Trust me, though, it's not.

Rafael became thoroughly Deb's cat on the ride home the following week. As soon as we got around the corner she made me stop the truck so she could take him out of the carrier—our first instance of bad parenting. As she held him on her lap, I thought the ride might freak him out or maybe he would have the opposite reaction and curl up and go to sleep— but not Rafael. Standing on her lap with his hind legs, he stretched himself up between her breasts and stared out the window. Cradled in voluptuousness, softly braced against the movement of the truck, he planned his criminal acts. We got him home to our bungalow in Burkeville, made sure all the doors and windows were closed, and Deb placed him on the floor. He looked out of sorts for less than half an hour. Once he had explored his surroundings—the living room, the kitchen, the hallway and bedrooms—he went back to looking like Joe Pesci.

Rafael was a playful kitten; even I admit he was entertaining and lots of fun to play with. I thought control of his claws would come in time. Deb didn't seem to notice how sharp they were. We bought a scratching post for him and he loved it. He would sit on the platform like a bird of prey—when he wasn't disembowelling it, that is. The thing was shredded within weeks, and I had to keep replacing the carpet wrapping. Whenever we had company over he'd crawl under people's chairs and harass the backs of their feet. There was no pattern in who he picked, and it wasn't always the same person. He was still a kitten, so this seemed cute and only cost the occasional sock. He kept at it until his victim finally gave him an adequate reaction, picking him up or moving to a different chair, which didn't always work, or putting shoes on, which never worked. It was kicking back at him with the targeted foot that was the reaction he was looking for. He wanted his prey to move so he could attack and kill. While most of our friends found this funny, I found it embarrassing. Deb found everything Rafael did adorable.

Things went mostly fine as the cat became part of our life. His comings and goings harmonized with ours. He continued to ignore me and nestle himself between Deb's breasts every chance he got, though he never once curled up on her lap like you might have expected. I'm surprised Deb didn't start to lactate. If Rafael had been able to figure out how to make that happen, I guarantee you he would've suckled. As he grew he became more beautiful, his calico colours blooming. Lucifer couldn't have been more gorgeous as he fell. You see, almost all calico cats are female. A male calico is a genetic rarity—more proof that Cunty was a demon.

Our little bungalow in Burkeville was an old house, built in the 1940s for wartime housing of air-force personnel. Stanley Burke was the president of Boeing Canada at the time. The street names are aeronautical and the street design is aerodynamic, with flowing curves and cul-de-sacs; it was the first subdivision in the city to spurn a grid pattern. Bungalows of that era had some very specific design elements: the room locations, door placements, number of outlets and switches, counter heights, and cabinet sizes were all very different from today. People are taller, appliances are larger, and we need more outlets and switches. Our particular Burkeville bungalow had a 1980s fridge that fit under the upper cabinet but just barely, with only about a four-inch gap. Most of our neighbours had removed the upper cabinet to accommodate a modern fridge if they hadn't renovated the kitchen entirely. I discovered too late that this gap between the fridge and the cabinet became the cat's hiding place.

The day Rafael earned his nickname, blood was shed. I had made a snack and was crossing the kitchen with a plate of food and a cup of green tea. As I moved toward the living room, the cat leaped from his lair between the fridge and the cabinet and landed on my back, claws digging into my shoulders, hind legs spinning like a teenager smoking tires, shredding my lower back. I exploded like a piñata—food, tea, plate, cup, cutlery—and screamed, "You *cunt!*" (we'd been watching early-career Ricky Gervais). I reached back and tried to grab him by the scruff of his neck, but he let go and dropped like an elite paratrooper. Before I could turn around, he was gone. I was livid, roaring like a maniac, screaming, "You cunt!" over and over. I hunted that cat, throwing furniture around, turning over chairs, throwing the sofa on its face. He was fast. He darted from cover to cover and I couldn't catch him. If I did, his cunty days were over, and he knew it. Sweating, yelling, threatening him as if he understood every word, I finally opened the back door and he bolted outside to safety. I slammed the door shut and that was the end of Cunty the Cat, at least in our house.

Deb got home in time to dress my wounds and help me clean up. I went to the doctor for a tetanus shot. She loved that cat but couldn't bring herself to argue for clemency, and she knew exile was better than what I had in mind. I saw Cunty in the backyard a couple of times after and threw things at him or turned the hose on him. I never made good contact, but the message was clear. I think he must have become a stray. I hoped he would get eaten by one of the eagles that hunted at the river nearby. Deb occasionally scanned the backyard for him. We agreed our next pet would be a dog.

* * *

Adam was a reluctant baby. He wouldn't drop, and doctors wanted to do a C-section. Deb had hired a wonderful doula, a retired hippie nurse named Rose. She had seen it all.

"No home birth," Deb told her up front. "I want a modern hospital."

"No problem," Rose said. "Bathtub or birthing suite, either way I've got you covered."

As the due date passed, Adam still clung to the rafters. A C-section became more of a possibility, but it wasn't what we wanted. A surgical appointment to give birth seemed like such a clinical, unromantic thing to do. But it was also the safest option. Rose endorsed our decision.

Adam's head was huge and he looked to be approaching ten pounds. Even now, thinking about the first half of that day makes me squeamish. Deb endured it. The experience was antiseptic and technological. The surgeon offered to sit me below the equator where I could see Adam emerge from the incision, but my stomach quailed. I declined and stayed up in the cool, blue north, safely seated … just in case. Deb was frozen from the waist down and lightly anesthetized, high but aware. I sat near her head. As I recall, I didn't say much, but I admit to purging these memories. I played brave but my stomach was in knots. Women are strong, men are weak. I forced myself to get through it. By late afternoon the worst was over and we were back in the room with brand new Adam. Rose had swaddled him expertly; he looked like a loaf of French bread with a face.

Evening came and Deb slept as I sat with Adam in my arms. He slept too. I felt like the great protector on watch. The engine of fatherhood turned over and I started to become who I would become, to leave my immature, broken self behind. The next iteration of me began, fully a grown man charged with the well-being of his family. Macho bullshit, you say? No, it's not. It's the most profound expansion of personhood any man can experience. It's the perfection of self-sacrifice and the revelation of unconditional love. All limits disappear, circumstance and conditions become meaningless; all you need to do is accept the beginning of your personal ending and the joy is boundless. That's what I say. That's what I never had. That's what I felt. And there are no wrong feelings, so I'm told.

I was surprised at how much there was to learn, or maybe *to experience* is a better term. We had taken all the prenatal classes, but there were hurdles to clear before we were allowed to take Adam home, the main one being latching on and breastfeeding. Rose was there the next morning to help, the specialist nurse came in, and the process began. It was a bit difficult for mother and child at first. I had to look away. I was feeling too much. Adam eventually got the hang of it and Deb breastfed him for the first time.

The next hurdle was Deb's post-surgery recovery. She was sore and weak. As long as she was in bed she was fine, but getting up and moving around was too painful. We weren't going home that day, but by the next morning it was obvious we were. She was up and around, albeit gingerly. Adam continued to do well at his one task.

The final hurdle was a psychological one for both of us—having a newborn in the house. I can't tell you how profoundly Adam's presence changed the spirit of our little Burkeville bungalow. The nursery was no longer anticipatory, it was occupied. There were new sounds, new routines, new smells, new items on the shopping list, expectations of safety within the physical space, to say nothing of a new polarity in the energy between Deb and me.

There was also the growing reality of parental love. For me this was a test to see if I could maintain the attitude I had sent up into the universe: acceptance of loss of control, acceptance of the possibility of catastrophe, acceptance of being vulnerable to utter decimation, acceptance of unspeakable joy, acceptance of my inevitable failure at some things, acceptance of playing a supporting role. All of it amounted to the same experiences of previous generations of flawed humans. Given the profoundly flawed humans of my family line, though, I felt like Superman, more than up to the task and completely comfortable with the list of things I needed to accept. The physical reality of Adam's presence in the house had only reinforced my commitment to the universe. I had passed my own psychological test. I would be razed to the ground but survive should anything happen to him.

Six months of sleep deprivation is a grind. The duration is different for everyone, but ours was six months, like clockwork, for both boys. But with Adam, every experience was new so of course time stretched, similar to when you drive somewhere for the first time. But there's no GPS for parenthood. The second time seems to take half as long because you recognize the landmarks. Adam's first six months of sleep schedule was no schedule at all. The surprising thing was how quickly he learned to wail at the top of his tiny lungs when one of us walked past his open door and dared to not go in. We had to steel ourselves to listen to his piercing, indignant screaming for ten or twenty minutes before he conked out—an eternity of parental suffering.

"Should we go in?" I asked, always the first to crater.

"No." She was adamant. "We can't fold like a cheap tent every time he cries. He has to learn he can go to sleep on his own or we'll have four years of sharing our bed."

"Aren't we being cruel?"

"No, we're not being cruel. We're doing what's best for him, not what we want in the moment."

"Lots of bad things are rationalized that way."

"Jesus, Dave, we're not talking about Mayan child sacrifice. This is what Rose and almost all the books say. Our job is to teach him all the necessary life lessons, here, with us, where it's safe. He has to be smart and good and kind and independent by the time he's a young man, but now all he needs to know is that he can fall asleep on his own."

"Sorry. You're the dreadnought, I'm the dinghy."

"Your favourite 212-pound analogy. Maybe I *should* have rolled over and crushed you."

"I would have died happy by your girth," I taunted. "And you were born a dreadnought mother from a line of dreadnought mothers, it has nothing to do with size, it's how formidable you all are."

"A perfect wife and a powerful mother with heavy guns and long-range missiles. Lucky for me your expectations aren't that high."

Babies become toddlers, a new and wicked form of fascist dictator but now with expanded powers. So of course we ratified our agreement to have another. After enough time passes and the memories of pain, frustration, and fatigue dip below the horizon, mothers everywhere turn to fathers everywhere and say, "One more time with feeling, Bert."

Micah was conceived and born on roughly the same schedule as Adam. He also clung to the rafters, was recalcitrant and late. Rose was our doula again, same hospital, same ob-gyn team, different delivery surgeon this time, but another C-section because, as certain potato-chip brands say, you can't have just one.

Bringing Micah home was not scary. This time it was all peace and contentment. Everything is easier with the second one. Sadly, there are also fewer pictures, fewer mementos, less focus on milestones, and less fuss in general. I can't imagine what happens to a number seven—like my Grandpa Felix—but in a normal, non-abusive, loving family. What form does the benign neglect of number seven take? Do the parents even remember the kid's name?

Our first home, the Burkeville bungalow, was now full. It was an ideal home in so many ways, and I wanted ideal for us. Deb was more practical because her childhood had been more realistic. We worked things out in the way families do—evolving dynamics, adjusted expectations, accommodation, and expansion, making room for the development of two new humans who would become themselves over time, within our jurisdiction and under our watch. Flexibility and easy adaptation are the keys to a happy bungalow short on square footage. Six months of fresh new hell ensued with Micah's appearance, sometimes dampened by Adam's toddlerhood, sometimes made worse. It was especially fascinating to watch the dynamic between the two of them grow and change.

We soldiered through the sleepless nights a second time, needing less discussion as the territory was familiar, our handoffs more innate. Neither boy walked until about fourteen months so we had a little time before double mayhem erupted. Constant vigilance is exhausting, and thankfully the backyard had a good fence and the neighbourhood had lots of eyes.

After Deb's second stint of maternity leave was over, she declined to return to her big ad agency job. "My kids, my choice," she told them. That was her stance. She didn't care if that wasn't feminist enough for some of her colleagues. The scope of our lives changed: the breadth narrowed but the depth became bottomless. We were so happy it was borderline absurd. Why is familial happiness seen as shallow by so many very earnest young adults? We had been of this camp once, quietly derisive of so-called middle-class values, silently stack-ranking other people's life choices. The word *hubris* was coined for twenty-somethings. Contentment is a learned skill. We were content with our little family and our choice to shrink our lives down to the scale of small children, and excited to expand back up with them as they grew. Once Micah crossed over the six-month Rubicon, we were almost giggly, trying hard not to be smug, with the next generation safely delivered into the twenty-first century. But our smugness was fated not to last.

Motherhood is the most powerful state to which a human being can ascend, bar none. Men think they rule the world but that's a fantasy. When you marry you learn. When you have children with the woman you love you learn more, you learn voluntary subjugation. Children are born happy vassals to their mothers and eventually they're released, but not so for fathers. Forget the clichés about the continuance of the species; drill down into the psychology of the family and you'll find that mother love and motherfucker share a pillow. There's a reason for the *MOM* tattoo—notice very few *DAD*s get inked? Maybe I'll be one of the few.

Over the course of events yet to come I had little choice but to become a urine-stain savant, a laundry lothario, an excrement expert, and an amateur child psychologist—all things I expected. What I didn't expect was how sharply life can turn while everyone around you just keeps on going. Besides becoming a dad-mom, I also became a porn addict, a debt whore, a yeller-at-clouds, and an enemy of a God I didn't believe in—all new skills acquired when the suffering began. Lots of people experience suffering, you say, and it comes in many flavours. Yes, I agree. I could see it in the eyes of the young women watching us in the many waiting rooms we came to know—suffering and fear—fear of a future about to be stolen.

CHAPTER 10

NAMED LIKE SHAKESPEARE

Names have power and the act of naming something is a claim to that power. Names are like a war where hearts and minds are the battle-field—choose the right one, say Fat Man or Little Boy and you're Shiva, destroyer of worlds. I guess you could be Brahma or Vishnu, but my family was never very good at happy stories. The ability to name something or someone is an act of the imagination—it's also the ability to falsely accuse or murder with a word. Some say language is what makes us human. I say language is the effect, not the cause. Imagine one of our ancestors imagining hot cave woman Doris over there, wondering whether she will fuck him quietly so they don't get caught by that giant asshole Slagathor, who will kill them both. Without the ability to imagine there would be no homo sapiens and consequently no language, no music, no dance, no storytelling around the fire. The ability to imagine the *what if* scenario, or in the case of Deb's female progenitors the *why not* scenario, is what lets us run wild outside our skulls. And wild we do run! Cruise missiles, chastity belts, and Caesar salad are all children of the very same sentient bag of meat wielding the ability to imagine. Human essence is blind and timeless; flashes and sparks in the bloodless dark.

The extraordinary women of Deb's family were all blessed with powerful imaginations. They each imagined a world that didn't constrain them just because they sported vaginas. Ginny conjured material prosperity through two world wars and one depression, Agnes spoke security, harmony, and wisdom into her home as walls fell and cities around the globe burned with revolution, and Katherine was the first to face down the old boys' club as well as the failures of her father, her husband and her sons. And although Agnes was nicknamed as a princess, Deb's mother, Katherine the Great most closely resembled the empress after whom she was named.

Princess Sophie von Anhalt-Zerbst was a Prussian princess, the stuff of fairy tales. What kind of story do those words conjure? What kind of music do you imagine? Harpsichord and privilege, violins and stockings, political intrigue and powdered wigs—the story could be interesting or it could be as boring as Sunday school. After Sophie von Anhalt-Zerbst, whose name sounds like a tractor engine coughing to life on a frozen prairie morning, married Peter III of Russia, her half-German second cousin, she participated in and maybe even orchestrated his coup d'état, becoming empress of Russia in the bargain, so Sophie became Ekaterina. She chose a quintessentially Russian first name to add to her new Russian last name, Romanova, thereby shedding her Germanic skin in favour of rebirth between the sturdy thighs of Mother Russia. Her new name was a way to sell herself to the Russian people. Slick politics.

So what's in a name asks the Bard? I mentioned that Albert Brown's story built a rat's nest in my imagination, it connected so obviously to our story, mine and Deb's that I couldn't help myself, I named his *Fate* as if "he" were real. This act of the imagination gave me such relief that I did it again and named my own personal *Fate*. I'll accept your judgment now and hope for reconsideration later, once you've seen the full landscape of our diabolical destiny.

War is a decidedly masculine pursuit so Albert Brown's personal Fate is obviously male, and for context I gave "him" one of those compound German words for a name: *der Feinschmecker*—the Gourmet—so appropriate in his case because of the delicious impossibility employed in dishing up Albert Brown's small-f fate, delivered as it was with the Germanic precision of the Kaiser.

Through the painful years, as my imagination was bent by experience, I came to believe *der Feinschmecker* had an accomplice, my personal Fate: Mrs. Bleatwobble—though I hadn't yet named her. That would come later, once she and I got to know each other better. And why not name her too? We humans anthropomorphize everything. I came to see Mrs. Bleatwobble as a wicked old harpy, sitting in the corner, glasses perched on the slope of her nose, calm and patient, knitting the future in soft, colourful prison stripes. We time-bound mortals, daily coiled as we are around the future's whipping post without a valent thought in our pretty heads, stand waiting for our flesh to be split open. How very tragically Greek of me, you say? How apropos, I answer. The original myth of the Fates says there are three of them—Clotho, Lachesis, and Atropos—assigned to all humanity for all time, spinning and weaving then cutting the threads of each individual life but I say we each have our own Fate waiting to be named. So what's in a name, asks the Bard? Life and death, I answer.

* * *

Katherine the Great was a straight-A student. Her brother Duffy was a C+ jock who played soccer and rugby, rowed and played tennis. They were classic working-class Vancouver kids of their West Side times. Sadly, Duffy got caught up in the cocaine culture of the 1980s. He was a *playa* with the Hell's Angels' circle of dealers. He and his girlfriend-of-the-week were tied to the bed and burned alive, either for an unpaid debt, for infringing on territory, or for some other gangland bullshit—no one ever found out.

In 1982, when the murders happened, Glenn Brown was the senior homicide detective assigned to the case. The bodies were positively identified through dental records—it was that bad but Glenn knew immediately it was his nephew Richard from personal effects belonging to "Duffy"—there aren't too many Richards with that alias. He broke the bad news to his sister Agnes and brother-in-law Walter. It was something he had done dozens of times before with strangers. He knew the murderers would never be found and the facts would never become public so it was kinder to spare his sister and brother-in-law the scorching details. He told them it was a deliberately set house fire causing death by smoke inhalation. He didn't say the bedding had been set alight around them.

Katherine Elizabeth Glasscock née Collier, named after an empress and a queen, was to be the future of the family, then, but first there were a few hurdles to clear. After realizing Lester was a mistake, she still gave him children to fuck up—Deb and her brothers, Anthony and John. This arguably wasn't so great, but she did put Lester out to metaphorical sea in the metaphorical royal dinghy, forever to bob irrelevantly in her royal yacht wake. Or so she had hoped, all while underestimating her children's need for a functioning father. Glasscock alcoholism wasn't Katherine's fault, but she had been warned by Agnes. Lester was a simple man's man, what the English call "a bit of a lad." He played rugby, wore the Welsh dragon proudly, and drank beer constantly—only beer, nothing else, not even water. He believed strongly in the health and hydration properties of beer. He was a construction site foreman who worked his way up through almost every trade without any formal training. He was a typical alcoholic in that his real identity was buried beneath the empties. He couldn't bear to look in the mirror and he wouldn't talk about it.

As soon as the youngest, John, a.k.a. Dewey (Dewey Glasscock—poor kid), was in school, Katherine ran for school board, won easily, and quickly became known for her smarts, her strength, and her many smoke breaks. She used to take just two or three drags, butt out, update her cup of bad coffee, and get back to whatever meeting she was dominating or argument she was winning. Whereas Agnes's *navigation* skills were used in reaction to people and events, Katherine used her powers for rhetorical combat, as if she had her own little army of jack-booted storm troopers stomping around inside her head, always spoiling for a fight. While Agnes's legendary ability to decode any situation was like counterpunching, Katherine was a knock-out artist. Opponents went down! But she could be subtle if she wanted to; not everyone needed to be knocked out. Machiavelli was a rank amateur compared to Katherine. Her opponents learned to stay on her good side and out of her way as much as possible. Even just the presence of her giant old station wagon in the parking lot was enough to make her foes duck and run. That Pontiac became her political flagship, an emblem of how unstoppable she was. If you wanted to avoid her, you checked the parking lot; if it was there, you hid, left, or got ready for a fight. It wasn't so much that she was mean—well, maybe a little—she was also smart, well spoken, and gifted with a nose for weakness. She was the antithesis of my mother, and it was no wonder I admired her so much.

Katherine was a born politician. Part of her political brand was the alcoholic husband and the murdered drug-dealing brother. Everyone knew her story, and she carried the burden publicly so it added to her well-known empathy for the underdog, for those who knew what living with loss felt like. Even in the supposedly more progressive politics of her day, a woman still had to fight twice as hard as a man for every inch of ground, so a sympathetic story was good politics.

After just one term on the Vancouver School Board, in 1986 Katherine was elected to city council. She made it her business to know every administrator and principal in every school in the city. She knew every teacher on the union executive, all the new school board members, and a good number of provincial politicians in government and opposition. She was connected.

Katherine never smoked indoors, even back when that was acceptable. She claimed to do her best work on smoke break, outside with the other smokers. Smoking and swearing were signs of authenticity, people you could trust, while drinking made you suspect. To Katherine, getting tipsy meant you were weak and getting outright drunk meant you couldn't be trusted (no surprise there, eh Lester?).

Yes, Katherine was smart, strong willed, astute, kind, and a bit mean—depending on who was talking—and very beautiful. Another Waggstaff woman who could have run a large country had *she* been born a *he*. Deb got her love of politics from Katherine. She enjoyed hearing about Katherine's day, about policy decisions, how people postured for the media, or what went on behind closed doors. Deb saw the talent her mother had and with the hubris of youth decided she would do better.

Deb was going to follow in her mother's footsteps when our kids were old enough, but she was going to go further, much further; the sky was the limit.

"Why didn't you go into politics, Grandma?" Deb asked Agnes. The three women were at the family home in Dunbar, outside on the deck, enjoying a glass of wine in the August sunshine. It was the summer before Deb entered university.

"Nursing was acceptable for women then. Politics was still just for men." Agnes summed up three decades of women's struggle for equality in two sentences.

"There were women in politics during the war," Katherine interjected, "but when the men came back things went back to the way they were before, worse in some ways. Your grandmother's choices disappeared almost overnight."

"A war? Which one?" Deb asked her mother.

"World War II," her grandmother answered.

"Great-Grandma Ginny was tough enough for politics," Katherine said. "She was fierce but her choices were nonexistent."

"She had no choice but to work the farm business," Agnes added. "All Great-Grandpa Albert could do was manual labour, so without her we might have lost everything in the Depression, even with his war pension."

"Which war?" Deb asked her grandmother.

"World War I," her mother answered.

"Was Great-Grandpa Albert totally unable to speak?" Deb asked her glass of wine, directing the question at neither her mother nor her grandmother, deciding not to referee who answered.

"Yes," said Katherine as Agnes's mouth began to open. "Your great-grandmother Ginny did all the talking. No wonder she drank." Ginny was the only person Katherine could pardon for needing a liquid crutch.

"My mother had an affair," Agnes said, knowing full well she was throwing a grenade into the conversation.

"*What*?" Katherine was incredulous. Deb looked at her grandmother in bewilderment.

Agnes smiled as if remembering Ginny's affair fondly. "With Jerome the charcutier."

They all fell silent for a moment. Agnes picked at her plate of fruit and cheese, waiting for more reaction. Katherine was dumbfounded. "I don't know what to think," she said. It wasn't like Katherine the Great to be without an opinion. "Grandma really had an affair?"

Deb said nothing, watching the dynamic between her mother and grandmother unfold.

"She coped, she drank," Agnes said, as though that explained everything, obliquely defending her damaged father. "She was tough but she wasn't superhuman. She hit Henry sometimes, Glenn too, a couple of times."

"Why are you telling me this now?" Katherine said.

"I'm telling you both," Agnes replied flatly.

"Okay, so you're telling us both, but why now?"

"Because alcoholics can be just as absent as someone who's been lobotomized by a bullet."

"So you're saying it's okay if I decide to have an affair, that I have an understandable excuse?"

Agnes skirted the question. "Powerful women can find themselves alone. Other women resent power in a woman more than they do a in a man. Your grandmother was a powerful woman in her town, and she was smart too. She picked Jerome because he was from somewhere else."

Katherine looked away for a moment, thinking, watching a humming-bird buzz around the feeder. "When did this happen?"

"I was ten or eleven, so 1936 or '37 I think, a few years before we moved west." Agnes closed her eyes and sat back. "The farm and the store were doing well, things were very busy, and there was a lot of pressure on your grandmother to keep everyone fed. At least twenty families depended on her for jobs and food on the table, maybe more, not including us. She saw plenty of men using their power to extort sex from desperate women during the Depression. I doubt she felt any guilt about doing the same."

"How did you find out?" Katherine asked.

"I just knew."

"How do you know it wasn't this Jerome's idea? There's always a sexual toll women have to pay, a power imbalance that requires a coy smile when really you're repulsed or a sexual put-down you're forced to fire back at some cat-calling group of assholes so they don't see you as prey. They add up, but you have to keep showing you're tough, you can't be intimidated, even though you shouldn't have to deal with the bullshit. And you never know who's going to suddenly switch from seeing you as a person to being blinded by their dick—one minute you're having a conversation the next minute they're staring at your tits."

"Your grandmother had all the power, Katherine. No one could make her do anything she didn't want to do."

"We're not all victims," Deb said. "I like flirting, I enjoy a little tension, I like the not knowing and the anticipation. I can shut it down or deflect it if I want without having to be a victim."

"Some can, some can't," Agnes said. "My mother decided it was better if she controlled the situation. She was used to being in control, she was good at it, and she was never a victim."

Katherine chuckled. "We're all like that, the women of this family. We're much better at control than taking a back seat to anyone."

"I don't want to control anyone," Deb said. "I want an equal, I don't want to have to play games."

"There're always games, Deborah," her mother said. It's the rules of the game that make the difference, and very few women get to make the rules—that's what makes women vulnerable. It's always better to be the one making the rules."

"And settling for someone like Dad so you can?"

Katherine winced. "People change. You can't know how someone you marry is going to change, so you can still wake up next to the inevitable even when you thought you'd dodged that bullet," she offered in her own defense.

"We all got married with our eyes wide open," Agnes said. "Each of us knew we were trading certain things for control."

"The problem is you don't know what you're trading until ten years and three kids later." Katherine mused for a moment before carrying on. "The political competition for me wasn't particularly tough, the barrier to entry was pretty low, Lester's drinking didn't cause any problems, and the way I handled it actually helped my profile."

"I always knew what my father wanted to say," Agnes said, returning to the past. "But it was hard for my mother because she was all alone in a way—so who can blame her for her decisions? If my father knew, he said nothing. If anything, he was even kinder."

"A silent, kind man that takes direction is a unicorn. If you find one, pinch yourself because you might be in a fairy tale," Katherine quipped. They all laughed at that and thus the topic of Ginny's affair was de-escalated to something less threatening. Katherine picked up the Chardonnay and topped up their glasses.

"Your father is always kind, but he does have some idiosyncrasies," Agnes said to Katherine.

Deb looked straight at her mother. "Better than being drunk all the time."

Katherine sat down. "People judge women by the men they choose; other women can be especially cruel. Don't forget that Deborah, and yes, Mom, you warned me, but the patterns repeat if we don't see them. You couldn't see it with Dad and I couldn't see it with Lester until it was too late. I thought he'd choose me over beer."

"Deborah is right," Agnes declared as if not listening to her daughter. Deb and Katherine stared at her. Again Agnes returned to the past. "He was able to communicate at a very basic level. He answered questions well enough but had a hard time initiating a conversation. He could communicate the point he was trying to make with body language, mostly for specific things like jobs around the farm; for complex things he'd look at me and I'd speak for him."

"Who gave you the Navigator nickname, Grandma?

"My older brother Henry."

"He died in the war."

"Which war?" Deb asked again.

"Oh for Christ's sake, Deborah, keep up!" Katherine interjected with a grin.

"Henry died at Dunkirk in World War II. He was reading about Prince Henry the Navigator in school—that's where he got the idea."

"My nickname was more obvious," Katherine said.

"I thought she was an important woman," Agnes said. "I read about her in high school, I liked her name, and we didn't have a Katherine in the family—everyone was an Elizabeth, a Jane, or some other English queen."

"Never trust a woman in power. They're more devious than men by a long shot, and better at getting what they want." Katherine's advice wasn't a surprise. Both Deb and Agnes had heard it before.

Agnes leaned forward in her chair, looking over her glasses at her granddaughter. "When you have fewer choices, you have to work harder to get where you want to go. Your mother is a fighter, Deborah. Ginny would have been proud." Agnes spoke to Deb but her remark was clearly intended for Katherine's benefit.

Katherine took a sip of wine and considered the petunias spilling from the hanging baskets. "Don't make the same mistake with men that your grandmother and I did."

"Children need help to see their parents as merely human," Agnes said, as though offering a quote for posterity but subtly revealing the point behind her revelation of Ginny's affair.

"Birth control changed everything for women," Katherine said to Deb. "We don't have to get married before twenty anymore. You can have sex with impunity because of the pill."

"To sex with impunity," Deb replied, raising her glass in a toast.

"So don't get forced to make a choice before you're ready, Deborah Jane." Deb's middle name was added only when Katherine wanted her point to sink in deeply. "You're so beautiful they're going to line up if they're not already."

"Hopefully a longer line than your mother had—" Agnes allowed a pause to nestle an unspoken name into the conversation. "—or I had," she added in consolation.

"Beauty is just dumb luck and you can't count on dumb luck," Katherine said, quoting Agnes to Agnes.

"I wish you would quit smoking," Agnes said in retort.

* * *

Nothing much happened the night of December 31st, 1999, in the context of global events Y2K was a non-event. But in the context of my world, that night was an unprecedented massacre. The death of Katherine the Great was not a surprise. She had been diagnosed with stage 4 lung cancer seven months earlier and was in palliative care at St. Paul's, the very hospital where Agnes had spent her career. We were all there on death watch that night—me, Deb, her brothers Anthony and John, Lester, Walter, and Agnes. The TV was on in background as the new century approached. Islands of conversation floated in an ocean of silence. Checking on Katherine as her breathing ebbed and flowed had been going on for roughly forty hours. She was indeed a fighter. Attending the deathbed of a loved one is a marathon. The human body, no matter how sick, doesn't give up the ghost easily. The autonomic functions of human life are a freight train that doesn't stop until all the track is gone.

Agnes was asleep on a reclining chair in the corner under a knitted blanket, the kind volunteers make for fundraisers. Walter was seated beside her. The rest of the family was scattered about the room. Deb was on Katherine's bed, holding her hand as machines beeped, gurgled, and whooshed—the music of the Fates, now synonymous with modern medical technology, their ancient ways so easily adaptable.

I was napping fitfully on a cot in the other corner, dreaming of stars and galaxies, the vacuum of space and humanity's fragile existence. I saw images of a pinwheel galaxy, like fireworks spinning, and words began to bubble up. Out of a low, droning rumble came the thumping stomp of a ponderous bass line, like the Soprano's theme song—"Woke Up This Morning". A voice began …

The pinwheel galaxy spins and spits its spangled load, rhythmic, regular, fantastic, it goes 'round pounding.

In my dream I said something but to no one; I was alone, the seat beside me was vacant. From behind me someone whispered "*shush*" into my ear. The voice was female, her breath was warm and scented with wine. I was in an ornate theatre, sitting in a gilded balcony on soft leather, surrounded by velvet drapes the colour of oxblood. On stage was a figure dressed like a griffin in flowing saffron robes looking like a character from Wagner; the bassline rumbled beneath him as he spoke his lines in a declamatory baritone.

Alone in the silver night we dart from snippet to flash,
quantum-timed to saxophones and Epiphones and unknowns.
We are augmented minors, perpetually passing chords, born to blend in come-'round resolution,
to harmonize church-organ fat in tasty four-part: thick-bottomed bass, creamy middle, high thirds keening up sharp,
a chill-the-spine purple magic only the vow-takers can't feel.
Da Vinci vanished in strokes of holy oil.
Mandelbrot made drunken cats.
Sky Church sustains then fades, Jimi stratocasts the stratosphere.
All ancient beasts that stalk our soul-barrens,

an alchemy of star stuff and winter night,
rock-a-bye below the incandescent arcs of meteor tails,
wet-electric, alive and alone.

The woman behind me leaned forward and whispered again, saying "*Listen carefully, David.*" The performance continued.

There is a certain voice in the strings' vibrating whine,
calling way-far, drawing dust from the Belt of Orion,
blowing hot plasma from black-hole jets,
heavenly harps slaving to the draw and blow of God's sloppy old black lips.
It will always arrive, that thing, whatever it may be,
dizzying down from all the possible futures
like games of chance tumble-dumped from a bright celestial box,
ringing with notes of joy pink with pathos,
singing with sighs of sweet, bluesy sex.
Hammer-on and snap-off, Jimi,
let's hear it licked like every woman wants to be,
slicker than any spin doctor's harlot tongue.
It's 3:00 a.m. on a winter's night and the pinwheel galaxy needs no spin doctor.

I awoke with a start, remembering the fragment of poetry that I'd heard before in a previous dream: it was Mrs. Bleatwobble whispering to me, crafting her manipulations, but I didn't know that then. I looked at the clock and saw midnight approaching. Everyone in that room was prepared for the final breath of Katherine the Great. Deb was watching her intently as the interval between breaths grew longer and the macabre game of counting the seconds began. The room gradually became silent in anticipation. All of us were watching Katherine's face, her hollow eyes closed, her mouth gaping, her beauty now sunken into the death mask we will all wear one day. This phase dragged on for almost an hour. New centuries had begun ringing in across the globe, and ours was only moments away when Katherine the Great sucked her last breath through her clenched teeth and stopped breathing. The seconds passed, growing to minutes as the year 2000 rang in on the West coast. The heart monitor flatlined, the beeping became constant, and the gurgle and hiss stopped. "Auld Lang Syne" emanated from a speaker in the now softly sobbing room.

A nurse had entered, unnoticed, to switch off the technology. She stood behind us as we gathered around the deathbed, then suddenly burst though us, hit the alarm on the wall, ran to the doorway, and yelled, "Code blue!" She rushed back in the room and, again slicing through us, ran over to Agnes on the chair. Slamming the chair flat, she started pumping her chest, but it was far too late. While the twenty-first century came to be, Princess Agnes the Navigator had died peacefully in her sleep during her daughter's death watch in the very hospital where she had spent her entire working life—and no one had noticed. Katherine was just forty-eight. Agnes was seventy-one. Ginny had been gone for sixteen years. The last of the extraordinary Waggstaff women, Deborah Jane Becker, sat in silent shock at the loss of her mother and grandmother on the same night. The date on both death certificates was Saturday, January 1st, 2000.

CHAPTER 11

PAPER ARMS

Words never lose their power. Why is that? Because we can't turn off our ability to imagine what it's like to inhabit those words. Swords pierce the body but pens fly the battlefield, leaving the bodies where they fell. Leaving the woman who saved you from yourself where she fell is excruciating but I had no choice, at least not if I wanted to face my sons in their adult future and tell them I did everything in my power to save us all. The fact that I couldn't do for Deb what Angus Burns had done for Albert Brown is the biggest failure of my life. This is my life's most profound regret which is utterly irrational. Could I have reorganized the atoms of her body by fiat? Could I have healed her by an act of will? Could I have done anything at all that would have changed the past, present or the future?

I found her diary when I was almost seventy years old, in a box of cookbooks I had ignored since foodies went online. The thing about age is that, unlike words, you lose your power. While standing in your pain your legs begin to tremble, and eventually you can't stand up any longer, slowly buckling beneath the weight of the years.

* * *

Monday, June 21st, 2010

It took over a year for them to diagnose me. Who is "them"? All of them. My GP, the ear/nose/throat doctor (*otolaryngologist*, not a word I knew before), the chiropractor, the ophthalmologist, the naturopath, the neurologist, the neuro-oncologist. Seeing her was scary. In the end it was Dave's friend who got me out of the swirl and in to see Dr. Ba. The swirl is all the ideas of what might be wrong with you while you sit in yet another consult after a bunch more tests and listen to the latest theory based on the latest results. None of it's very reassuring. I almost had to go see an infectious disease specialist, and then, OMFG, someone thought it might be Lyme disease. Can't remember which one that was, probably the naturopath.

Tuesday, July 6th, 2010

I've never been asked so many lifestyle questions. I'm sure they were thinking substance abuse, mental illness, hypochondria—if sluttiness was a syndrome someone would have mentioned that too. Basically, it had to be my fault somehow—WTF? There were so many questions about possible environmental toxins it made me wonder how dangerous our house was. Radon gas? Toxic fumes from carpet? Gas leaking from the furnace? I couldn't sleep through the night for weeks, had to keep checking on the boys, which I hadn't done since they were babies. In the end the diagnosis was just as bad, just as many unknowns. You have this disease called MS but it's a complete mystery. They say no one gets it if they live between the tropics so vitamin D might be involved, three times as many women get it as men so sluttiness might be involved. What if you're an arctic slut? If you were raised on a farm you're more likely to get it, possibly caused by a pastoral lifestyle and church every Sunday. The Amish are so screwed, doubly if you're Viking/Amish. Is there such a thing? Hypervigilance is considered a factor too—if you grew up in a home that wasn't safe or with constant conflict you're eight times more likely to get it because of overproduction of cortisol as a child. Gee, thanks, Dad. All this searching for a cause feels like being turned inside out. I went from baffling a small army of medical professionals to one medical professional diagnosing me with a baffling disease. Me, personally, my body—first a bafflement then the proud owner of one, after almost a year spent being low-grade pissed off or low-grade scared. More cortisol.

Thursday, July 29th, 2010

Dave doesn't understand. He can't, and I don't blame him. I just wish he could, which is possibly stupid. He certainly gets the father thing. It's a miracle he doesn't have MS too, given how much pain he's had in his life. He's not good at putting things into perspective, which isn't surprising, so this disease seems scarier to him than to me. He thinks I'm his partner in this little adventure we have going, but really I'm his boss, which is why it scares him so much, which is why I love him so much. I just don't want him to worry. I can handle this.

Saturday, August 28th, 2010

Sometimes I feel the drudgery of everything. Maybe it isn't that different from before—vacuuming, laundry, what to make for dinner—but before it felt easy to laugh off and now not so much. I can't tell him. I have to be strong for the three of them. I'm stronger than all three of them put together, even without Mom and Grandma. I bet if they were here I'd have this beat by now.

Sunday, September 4th, 2010

Things I used to do without thinking are getting harder, I can feel it, have to plan based on how much energy I have at different times of the day, when I need to rest. That's why I need to write this all down, so I can track things, record the little details before I forget, get them laid out chronologically so I can deal with them when I get moments to myself. I'm sure he's starting to notice, he always teases me about my RFN gene—Right Fucking Now—how I just plow through stuff. I always had physical strength—thank God for sports, it gave me a base. Physical strength will help keep the disease at bay until I can kill it.

Monday, September 21st, 2010

Having this foreign presence in my body is like an anti-pregnancy. I loved being hijacked by my boys but I hate being hijacked by MS. There's always fear at the back of my throat that I can't quite swallow, I'm always on pins and needles wondering what's going to change next. The fear is so subtle sometimes even I forget, but only for a few minutes, usually when I'm watching the boys—gives me resolve to protect them.

Tuesday, September 22nd, 2010

I've been thinking a lot about what I dreamed my life would be like, before Dave and the boys, and I'm a bit surprised. It's been mostly what I wanted up to this point, but now I can't see past this disease to after they're all grown up. I can't see past them as little kids. They're so vulnerable! Shit, I wish they would grow faster. I used to relish these ages, before high school and jerking off, now I'm watching them for every little bit of growth, every new ability. I need it to go faster. I love to see those little glimmers of who they're going to be next, hoping I won't change too much too fast, have to keep pace with them. If I can just get through these next five years I'll feel less stress and I can turn my mind to beating this disease, to getting back what I'm losing. I won't accept defeat. I won't accept losing myself to a "diagnosis."

Wednesday, October 13th, 2010

The doctors don't understand this disease, don't know where it comes from, why it flares up, or why it goes away, which means they don't know why some people beat it. I'll be one of those people. No way I'll end up in a wheelchair, no chance! Norm Sr. and Norm Jr. have started to look at me differently, like I'm about to join their club. No, I am not—just the thought of it scares me.

Thursday, November 18th, 2010

Today I noticed a kind of washed-out spot in my left eye. It went away in a few minutes so maybe it was nothing. I'm hyper aware of every little thing my body does, paranoid of another incident of double vision. Dr. Ba says my brain was overheated by the exertion of playing basketball. He pointed out the tiny spots on my brain scan, the scleroti. Dave was fascinated, but I couldn't see anything. Supposedly the trained eye you get from looking at thousands of scans makes them easy to see, so Dr. Ba says. I understand the symptoms come from my brain but something is changing. I feel it inside my body, I don't buy the inscrutable brain thing. I hate it! There must be things I can do—eat clean, exercise, meditate, do yoga, do breathing exercises. My body can heal itself!

Friday, December 10th, 2010
Have mild balance issues most days now, today was a little worse than usual. Dr. Ba says this means the kind of MS I have is called primary progressive, not relapsing-remitting. Great, the rarest form of a rare disease. With PPMS, symptoms don't go away, which I can live with for now. It's not that bad. It'll go away when I can get somewhere warm for a while and focus my energy on healing. I'll be fine. Grandma lived thru much tougher circumstances, Mom lived with Dad, she was a great mother despite him, despite Anthony and John, so this is nothing. I can beat it. Dave and I talk a lot about how he's overcome his past—if he can do that, then I can overcome this.

Saturday, January 15th, 2011
Judy's been a big help, been there for the boys after school when I have appointments. Too many appointments. The doctors want me to feel "cared for," especially Dr. Ba, he says with brain disease it's critical to address things holistically, not just the body. Believe me, I get that, and I plan on using my mind to heal my body so I try not to get frustrated with whichever doctor or clinic wants to see me for whatever reason. I'm using their energy to build mine, trying to focus on their good intentions, not the intrusion.

Sunday, February 6th, 2011
Strangely, I don't feel as alone as I used to. When Dave's at work and the boys are at school, sometimes it feels like there's another person in the house with me. I got that feeling again today, not sure if it's scary or not? The disease feels like a presence, something that wasn't there before, like

unwanted company sitting in the corner watching me. It's probably just good old-fashioned paranoia, I don't notice it when everyone is home. It's another good reason for getting Rhombus. The boys always wanted a dog and he's good company during the day. I take him to Pacific Spirit Park when I have the energy and the weather isn't terrible—I can't get too chilled. The forest fills me with life energy, even just a walk with him and Judy thru the neighbourhood is good mental health. We told the boys he's a family member, that dogs are like another brother that's perpetually three years old. Adam and Micah are almost nine and seven, they're getting better equipped to look after themselves, so it's good they have to look after Rhombus now too. All good lessons except, LOL, they're both still too squeamish to pick up poop with their hand in bag, they say it feels gross! They love to take him to the park in the station wagon, which is big enough for him to do laps in the back. The boys love Mom's old Pontiac as much as I do. They call it the Fortress, could fit themselves and nine friends into the back seat. I could never sell it, reminds me of her too much. It still smells like cigarettes a bit, which I love, which is so wrong. Not that anyone would buy it anyway—no one drives cars like that anymore, especially not in Dunbar. Maybe in Burkeville, but definitely not Dunbar.

Saturday, February 26th, 2011

I took them to hockey this morning—I love doing that. It's my best time of the day, before I get tired, before the symptoms get noticeable. Sometimes the scorekeepers can't read my writing. I can write simple names just fine, but the odd names can be tough, I mangle those some-times. I'm assistant manager for just Micah's team this year. Adam's team is fine without me—I've done my share of double duty anyway. For sure no scorekeeping for me. Ba says not to overtax myself. Too much cold makes me shiver, the space heaters aren't enough anymore. I now know what chilled to the bone feels like. The chill can last a long time after we get home and into a warm house, even then I have to have a hot bath. I know it's the disease, makes me nervous. Soccer is worse, tho, because it's outside. God forbid we should disrupt summer beer-league slow pitch with kids' soccer, so it's spring and fall outside no matter what the weather. Stupid shit I'll change when I'm on council.

Tuesday, March 8th, 2011

I'm on the lookout for pain but there doesn't seem to be any. It's supposed to be one of the symptoms, so guess I should count myself lucky? That's a laugh. I sleep like the dead, but then I've always slept well. I'm just getting tired earlier, which I tend to ignore, so I'm more ready for bed than I used to be. Libido is strong, no change there, good for me and good for Dave. He's a lucky man and he knows it. His fortieth is a few months away, I'm going to throw him a surprise party—but the day before the actual day, that'll get him. I'll invite some of the couples we used to play with so he can compare. It'll be fun to remind him of when I put him in training back in university.

Wednesday, March 9th, 2011

He's such a great dad, so determined to be the opposite of his father in everything. The boys adore him, Rhombus adores him, I adore him. Wish my dad had been half that attentive when I was growing up.

Saturday, April 2nd, 2011

Today I feel like an imposter, a completely healthy person taking up all this time and attention, wasting all these medical resources, as if I'm faking the whole thing. Then I think thinking that is some kind of weird denial, that I'm inventing imposter syndrome so I don't have to admit I'm sick. What a mind F! Then I get a wave of fatigue out of nowhere or I notice my hand shaking and that's that, the bubble pops.

Sunday, April 24th, 2011

Lately I'm noticing my vision gets blurry when I'm tired, and I get a bit of a tremor too. Used to love to read, now it's tough. Hope that's just the wine talking. At least now everyone can see my symptoms are real. Sometimes it seems better if I'm the one who doesn't believe I'm a "sick person." I couldn't remember where I'd hidden all the easter eggs this year, nothing new tho, done that before, maybe Rhombus will find them.

Tuesday, May 10th, 2011

In the waiting room today, I couldn't help but notice the new patients, mostly women, glancing at me. I could see the look on their faces—fear, they looked frightened. I feel for them. My symptoms are obvious now, must have looked like their future.

Wednesday, May 18th, 2011

MS is life altering. Life altering ... not a phrase anyone wants to hear.

Thursday, June 9th, 2011

I prefer my imposter-person self to this other stranger, this sick person. Actually, I'd prefer to call myself an MS imposter. Women usually get imposter feelings about things like being too smart, too good at something, too highly paid, bullshit like that, but Mom taught me better. I never had those, but I'd be okay being an MS imposter. I'm okay with too much wine being a problem. I like my sexy jock, smart girl, uber-functioning self, or maybe *liked* is the right tense for the jock part, haven't been that since having kids. I'm a MILF now, worried about my uber function, feels like it's fading. I'm foggy sometimes.

Friday, June 10th, 2011

Dave says how beautiful I am—yeah, I've always known that—at least as an adult. But Mom always said beauty is just dumb luck (and she was really beautiful!). It's a bad idea to count on luck for much, getting this shitty disease eliminates any idea of me being lucky. What good is beauty when your brain and body can't function? I'd be super happy looking like Mrs. Shrek if I could be free of MS, could have played rugby instead of basketball, could have beat up all the pretty girls, knocked them on their pretty asses.

Sunday, June 26th, 2011

I couldn't do Dave's surprise party, too much for me. This disease makes me so angry! It's all I can do to keep it bottled up, not dump all over Dave; if Mom and Grandma were still here I could dump all over them, but they're not, and I can't. So I vent and dump in this damn journal but the tremor in my right hand is getting worse, it's not going away as much now, it's getting harder to write. The tremor's heading the same direction as the vertigo, persistent, same as the brain fog. I have to be careful how much wine's in the glass, it's hard to remember to use my left hand. Hot tea is dangerous—about the only thing easier is giving Dave a hand job—LOL!

Monday, July 11th, 2011

Today there's intrusion, which pisses me off. Symptoms are pushing into the day-to-day because they're combining—mild vertigo plus a slight tremor plus blurry vision plus brain fog. When they combine like that it gets tough, and they don't let up. It's getting tougher. Usually late afternoon is the worst, when I'm tired. I'm not as sharp, but that's a busy time. I usually walk the boys home from school with Rhombus and do a quick grocery grab. I love the catch-up conversation with them, what happened at school that day, then it's make dinner, serve dinner, clean up dinner, Dave does homework with them, wine and TV for me, which usually puts me to sleep. Dave does reading and bedtime, by that time I'm done. If I'm still awake at nine o'clock it's bath and bed, my faves—don't know what I'd do without a hot bath. I used to like my vibrator more than a hot bath, not anymore, makes me sad, but sometimes an orgasm takes energy I don't have.

Tuesday, July 19th, 2011

I'm so tired. This disease is a bitch! The symptoms are always running in combination by bedtime, going up the stairs is getting harder. Don't talk to me while I'm going up the stairs, have to concentrate. Imagine having to concentrate on walking up a flight of stairs! WTF! I could just fricking scream! Once I hit the hot water, tho, everything softens up. I used to be more sensitive to a very hot bath, but now it seems the water can't be hot enough. Then I find out from that asshole Ba that loss of sensation is another symptom—jeez, he even intrudes on my bath time.

Sunday, July 24th, 2011

Yesterday I had a brief stumble, had to use the couch to get to the kitchen. That made me curious about "furniture surfing" so I did a YouTube search. OMFG, what a mistake! Those poor women looked like they were leg-humping the furniture, faces all screwed up tight, concentrating hard, huffing and puffing, mouths wide open. Please God, don't let that be me—ever! I'm so scared!

Saturday, August 13th, 2011

The only one I can talk to is Judy, not holding back with her. She thinks I should ask Ba for a counsellor, which I'm going to do, means yet another appointment but I need an outlet who isn't someone I have to count on for help with the boys. Everyone has limits. I can't unload on Dave cause I'm afraid of what I might say, afraid he might get even more scared. I don't want to treat him even a tiny bit like his dad did. I'm so scared. Every fricking day now.

Sunday, August 14th, 2011

Driving is getting dicey—another thing I can't tell Dave. Mostly I'm fine but crowded parking lots are tough, too much movement from all different directions. I'm trying to back up into spots now so I don't have to back out, but I've grazed a few cars and now I'm paranoid about both directions. No matter what, I have to back up, coming or going. Basically it feels like I have to run a gauntlet just to finish normal tasks like shopping. The station wagon feels huge, I know it always was, but I never noticed before. I never drive fast anyway, no one will get hurt, but I'm afraid of the damage I could do. The boys are bit nervous with me driving the car now. I'd walk with them more but that's becoming tougher too. I have to lean on Judy a bit more, but her car is small and the kids are getting bigger—Micah doesn't use a booster anymore. Dave is noticing my reluctance to drive, I'm telling him it's the dizziness. I can't tell him about my vision, caught him watching me alternate closing my eyes to compare so he probably knows. Nothing gets past him—he pisses me off that way.

Wednesday, August 31st, 2011

Today for the first time I had all four symptoms for most of day. I found myself touching things for balance—the countertop, a bar chair, a door jamb, not furniture surfing but not *not* surfing. I'm concentrating on keeping my posture upright and my mouth closed, I remember what those YouTube women looked like. That's not going to be me, I'm younger, fitter, and meaner, don't fuck with me, MS! This is a grind and I can grind. Dave can't really help, the boys get in the way sometimes. Sometimes I just wish I could be alone for this fight, but then one of them melts my heart. I won't give up, I won't quit!

Thursday, September 8th, 2011

There's only so much energy I have in the day, they all have to suck it up and deal. Dave's cousins Annie and Maye showed up for a visit the other day, which annoyed me at first but after a bit I enjoyed it. They took over without asking, without being obtrusive—not sure I would know how to do that, LOL. They made tea, did some cleanup, talked, I think they even cleaned a toilet or two while I wasn't paying attention. They're salt of the earth, Dave says, and he's right—they know what real work is. The boys and I always enjoyed helping out on Farm Day. If it wasn't such a drive I'd buy more groceries from them, but that's not changing now, no way I can drive that far. Going to take them up on their offer to teach the boys how to work when they're old enough. I like the idea of them being farm strong. We talked about it. They made me laugh, hadn't in a long time. How sad is that to suddenly realize you haven't laughed in forever? It's all I can do not to be pissed off all day every day.

Friday, September 16th, 2011

Every little thing annoys me. I never noticed how stupid people can be, not paying attention in parking lots, how fast they fly down a side street like kids and dogs don't exist, stupid shit on the news, people complaining about everything. Try walking a mile in my shoes, whiners! No matter what, there's always somebody ready to criticize something, as if they could do any better, never mind having a better idea. I'd like to see any of them accomplish anything close to what Mom did. Once I'm done this disease I'm going to run for office, kick some ass, educate some ignorant people. I always had the best ideas at the agency, the owner almost cried when I said I wasn't coming back after Micah. I wasn't going to tell him my plan, that once the boys were old enough I was going to be his boss, run my own campaign. Now I can't plan anything, not until I beat this MF'ing disease.

Sunday, September 18th, 2011

Anthony came for a visit. He's been sober for a while now, looks like it's going to stick this time. The boys like to see Uncle Anthony, but they don't know him well, maybe now they'll get the chance. Wish I could have stayed up later but I get so damn tired. I could feel him watching me as I struggled up the stairs, using my grip to stay steady. I liked it better when I judged him. Jeez, fuck him anyway, he has no right to judge me given the things he's done. He should judge Dad, he's the one who taught them both to be alcoholics. Dewey's a lost cause.

Monday, September 26th, 2011

I'm grateful Dad gave us the house. I'm sure he's afraid to come and see what this disease is doing to his daughter. I hardly ever see him. I'm pretty sure he's got some stipulation in the will about how things get divvied up when he's gone. I should ask him but he never comes around, like his job was done when he gave us the house, like now that Mom is gone he's off the hook. Man's got all the emotional savvy of a brick. Dave should step up and set him straight, he's been disrespected by my father so many times, he's just not capable of it anymore. Grow some balls, Dave, have it out. Men are so weak. Damn. I have to be there for Adam and Micah or they'll end up the same.

Tuesday, September 22nd, 2011

The tremor is getting worse and my head shakes too. Was watching myself in the mirror and could see that it's slight but it's there—so weird when you can see your own head shake involuntarily and your eyes correct for the movement—at least that part of my brain still works.

Wednesday, September 23rd, 2011

I like the weight loss. I'm lean in all the right places again and still have my T&A. Dave hasn't noticed, tho. We haven't had sex in months, which is the longest we've gone ever—even with the boys in the way we always found time. We're in bed at such different times, mornings are impossible with school during the week, and weekends are sports. I'll get an after-noon boyfriend to service me, LOL—that'll get his attention back. Sleep feels better than sex anyway. The last time we did it I got so hot I had to push him off me, the thought of another incident of heat-induced double vision scared the hell out of me, bit of a buzz kill, didn't have the energy to explain myself.

Thursday, October 6th, 2011

Yeah, sex. Energy is an issue—my brain wants to, but the body's not sure what it can still do. This is what men take Viagra for. Not so thrilled about this window of understanding into erectile dysfunction. Maybe I should just bend over and let Dave do all the work, not my style but I might have to adjust. Dave would wonder what happened. Sex was Olympic with us in uni, it slowed down after the boys but not much. MS is a bitch!

Friday, October 7th, 2011

I'm getting deep brain stimulation surgery. They're going to drill holes in my skull while I'm wide awake and implant electrodes. I thought I was afraid before, but this is off the charts. It's like science fiction. Ba said they can fix the tremor, same as for Parkinson's. Parkinson's patients get this all the time. The rest of my symptoms will still be there, tho. My vision is fucked but I'm hiding it from everyone. Ba thinks it's mostly balance issues, but it's just as much that I can't see where the fuck I'm going until it's too late!

Saturday, November 26th, 2011

Yesterday wasn't a bad day, but not a good one either, the implant helps the tremor, doesn't do anything for my vision. I came out of London Drugs at 2:00, got in the Fortress, drove out onto the street, and was pulled over. Cop thought I was drunk, and I had to do the walk. I argued with him, finally started to cry, and screamed at him to call my fucking doctor Alfred Ba at UBC Hospital. I spat the number out at him from memory, which was actually harder than the walk. Showed him the DBS remote under my skin, pulled half my tit out. He apologized and let me go. Thanks a ton, Officer Friendly, for a fabulous afternoon. I went home and hid in the bedroom for two hours with a bottle of wine. Judy walked Rhombus with the boys. I went downstairs to say hi, stumbled on the last step and fell, probably because I was a bit drunk. The boys were scared. I sat up and told them I was okay, then pissed my pants. I could smell it. They could smell it. They could see it. I had no idea how to react. Judy took over in a flash so I could go back upstairs and shower. I put my PJs on and went to bed at 5:30, and that was the end of Saturday. I'm afraid to drive again but I probably will anyway.

Sunday, November 27th, 2011

I live in fear. It's constant, a knot in my stomach that never goes away, a dry swallow at the back of my throat that never goes away. My mind won't shut off, sleep is the only relief. I fall asleep instantly, not gentle and normal tho, like falling off a cliff. I cry spontaneously all the time now too, at the drop of a hat, can't control myself. At least the boys find it funny. At their ages crying is no big deal, so when I cry over stories on the news or Serena Williams interviews, they laugh. I don't mind. I'd rather make them laugh than scare them driving.

Monday, December 5th, 2011

I cry without the aid of wine. I cry in bed at night. Worse, I cried after sex, the first time we've had sex in months. Dave was dumbfounded. Afterward I wet the bed—a wild night for the Beckers. Crying then pissing the bed. He offered to pee the bed too. LMAO, very sweet. MS is the C-word, like that stupid cat we had.

Tuesday, December 20th, 2011

I can't pee when I want, I pee when it wants, anytime, anywhere. It's old hat to the boys now, same as watching me fall down. Mom peed herself again. Mom fell down again. The ambulance had to come and get Mom again.

Wednesday, January 25th, 2012

My idea to keep driving turned out to be not so smart, didn't last long. This month so far I've had three low-speed "accidents," one at the grocery store, two at UBC Hospital. Insurance is going to hell, had to tell Dave, turned out he already knew. The boys told him they were afraid to drive with me, said I was raging behind the wheel, screaming at other drivers, it scared them. They don't like the new aggressive me, the take-no-shit me. Who's going to drive them to all their stuff? Scary Mom, that's who. I'm also Wine Mom, which makes me an even worse driver. Can't believe I'm losing my ability to drive! Who loses their driver's license at thirty-six, what the fuck! How am I supposed to function! How is the family supposed to function! I can't drive but I can drink wine, piss my pants, and cry. I could kill myself.

Friday, February 3rd, 2012

Feels like ten years of hell and it's only been two, I think. LOL, my short-term memory is fried. I can remember things from when I was six, like when Dad was drunk and dropped Dewey on the floor. "Oops," he said, "spilled the ball." Mom could have killed him. I didn't understand him growing up, don't understand him now. I hate him sometimes. I wish Mom was here. I miss her so much, miss her strength. She would hold me and I would cry for days—I could stop being the strong one for a few hours. I'm falling apart in front of my boys and I can't stop it, don't know what to do, can't do anything.

Saturday, February 4th, 2012

Adam and Micah barely understand what I say anymore, guess I mumble, my mouth doesn't work properly, instead they ignore me. No one understands. The doctors, emergency room nurses, ambulance drivers, firemen, everyone is *sooooo* nice. I want to throat-punch them all! Ba is an asshole—I never see him anymore. The house is a prison. My body is a prison. I dream about what I'll do on the first day I don't have MS anymore. Dance in front of Ba, pee on his desk, throat-punch him.

Sunday, February 12th, 2012
The DBS implant is helping, and my tremor is almost gone. I'm going to get my driver's license back, then I'm going to walk again. I'm a fighter, I'm a survivor.

Tuesday, February 15th, 2012
My useless husband is useless. Rhombus likes wine. He also likes coffee, tea, juice, milk, and eats anything I drop except lettuce. Some squeezed out of my burger onto the floor, it was the only thing he wouldn't clean-up for me. He follows me everywhere now. He's getting fat. Made the boys roar once when he grabbed pizza right out of my hand. I gave up and just threw a whole piece on the floor for him. The tremor was bad that day, the DBS device wasn't working, I cried for fat Rhombus while the boys laughed, made me happy.

Thursday, March 1st, 2012
Dave bought no-spill plastic wine glasses at the dollar store. I yelled in his face; the boys cried. I can still feed myself, me and Rhombus. I'm not drinking from a fucking sippy cup! I'm going to beat this fucking disease!

Friday, April 6th, 2012
I like going up the stairs to bed, leaving my fucking wheelchair behind. Dave wanted to bring it upstairs, I yelled in his face. I hate him.

Sunday, April 8th, 2012
I now own a wheelchair, a walker, a cane, a shower stool, grip handles on the walls. I don't want to own any of those things, I think I deserve more clothes, makeup, and shoes. Dave and the boys take me shopping on weekends, when they're not at hockey or baseball or soccer or when Dave's not at a meeting or conference. Sometimes Judy takes me, sometimes Annie and Maye take me when the farm is closed. Buying stuff is the only break I get, my only gain, everything else is loss.

Monday, May 13th 2012, Mother's Day
The boys like to push me in the wheelchair. They argue about whose turn

it is—I guess that's good. Annie and Maye take me for coffee too. We're getting me a scooter so I can go out on my own. Whoopee! Judy is over lots. Someone she knows just died of cancer, but I get scooter out of it, Judy's sad about her friend, she tries not to show it around me. Dave got a bunch of tulips, used to be my faves, they're going to wilt like me. How's that for the state of my fucking life on Mother's Day?

Friday, May 25th, 2012
Dave takes the boys and Rhombus out for walks after dinner, I'm not allowed to come. I screamed at all three of them tonight. Now I just go to bed right after dinner. It's their fault for leaving me alone.

Monday, June 4th, 2012
Good thing they take me shopping a lot, I need new clothes—my old ones are too big. Made my last meal ever last night, does microwave chicken count? Dave can have that job, good riddance, laundry too, everything, have to focus on me, they'll be fine without me. I'm always mad or sad, no one needs me, no one wants me. Fuck this disease!

Tuesday, June 19th, 2012
The boys are getting so big, they're strong enough now for me to hold on to. I like when they help me walk. Better day today. I'll be walking on my own soon.

Wednesday, June 20th, 2012
Sometimes I leave my wheelchair and surf. Dave says I leave handprints everywhere. I make sure to surf after Rhombus and I have some food. Fuck him, he can clean it up—he's not the one with the disease. He still has a life, he has *my* life!

Saturday, June 30th, 2012
Adam yelled at me, told me I had to stop doing something, can't remember what it was. I yelled back, "Or what? What the fuck are you going to do?" He's twelve, what can he do about anything? He yelled at Dave, "Why don't you divorce that bitch!" Bitch? My own son called me a bitch!

My heart is breaking into a billion pieces and I'm furious at them. What can *I* do about anything? I'm so helpless in this fucked up body! I'm losing my grip on reality. I can feel it.

Monday, July 2nd, 2012

Dave and I don't have sex anymore. It's been half a year, since just after the DBS surgery. The surgery has helped a lot—my tremor is almost gone, next walking will come back, then soon maybe even driving. After that, fuck him—I'm gone.

Wednesday, July 18th, 2012

I hate the wheelchair; can't wait to ditch that fucking thing. I won't have it in the house, Dave has to leave it in the garage. I can still use my walker and I can still crawl up the stairs. A wheelchair was part of the DBS deal—they wouldn't do the surgery unless I agreed, but it's temporary.

Friday, July 27th, 2012

I can't save my marriage. He's an ungrateful prick, he makes me so angry. I have no family anymore, my mother and grandmother are dead, my father may as well be dead, my one brother is useless like my useless husband, and the other brother is who knows where, and my two sons want nothing to do with me. I have only men in my life, and they're all weak. I told my rehab counsellor all of it, after the DBS surgery when they were teaching me how to walk again. I was away from Dave and the boys for three weeks, was good for me to be away from all the stress they cause. I'll bet they partied. Surgery was a waste of time! It worked for a maybe six months, that was it, have to learn to live with this disease.

Sunday, August 12th, 2012

I'm moving out. I'll get my own apartment and live my life the way I used to. I used to be a size ten, now I'm a five and sexy AF, Dave can't see it, that's his problem, I'm not waiting around for him, told the counsellor Dave was frigid, his face went white, the counsellor looked at him and smiled. WTF! Men are all the same—they can't stand hearing about how weak and useless they are.

Thursday, August 23rd, 2012
Judy doesn't say much to me anymore, not even to humour me. The only ones who treat me normal are Annie and Maye, they know I'll be better soon. I tell them all my plans—divorce Dave, move out, leave him to look after the boys, get a young stud with money, be treated properly, move to Arizona for the desert heat—we laugh our asses off. We talk about my celebrity friends, Serena Williams, Don Cherry, Kobe Bryant, The Rock, Michael Strahan, Ellen, Dr. Oz. They're like my friends, one day I'll meet them all, I'll be on TV too.

Friday, September 7th, 2012
I called the premier and gave her some advice, called the mayor too but he didn't listen—he's a weak man, like Dave, like all men, wish we had girls. When I get elected the premier and I will fix all the mistakes the men made.

Tuesday, September 18th, 2012
I think I have a hundred scarves, maybe more. They're the perfect accessory for any outfit.

Wednesday, October 10th, 2012
Firemen always get here first, then the ambulance. They're all so handsome, wish I could change before they show up, better yet take all my clothes off. I'd rather be carried but they always use a stretcher.

Saturday, October 27th, 2012
I fell again, this time across the edge of the bathtub, bruised my ribs. Judy called 911. Dr. Ba came to see me at Vancouver General, he doesn't work at VGH so I don't know why he showed up, I know the doctor's there, don't need him, told him some days I know what's happening, other days I just check out, too much effort. I'm back home now.

Tuesday, November 19th, 2012
I fell again, down the stairs, missed the railing, my grip is strong but sometimes I miss, can't see anymore, hard to see what I'm writing here.

Friday, December 21st, 2012

I fell again, cracked a rib across the bathtub. They won't let me go home yet, writing this on a note pad at VGH so I won't forget to enter it, might be here for Christmas.

Friday, December 28th, 2012

I missed Christmas. Hospital turkey is awful. Home now, they saved all my presents and some Christmas dinner leftovers too. Jeez I missed them.

Thursday, February 14th, 2013, Valentine's Day

I yelled in Dave's face, "I'm not going into a home with a bunch of fucking old people!" I hate him. He doesn't give a shit!!! I want to die. I should die, then they'd all be happy. Fuck them all! I DON'T GIVE A SHIT!!!!!!

Friday, March 22nd, 2013

I have no life.

Tuesday, May 14th, 2013

I can't see. I can't do anything anymore.

Thursday, July 4th, 2013

Serena wouldn't put up with this shit.

Monday, September 2nd, 2013

I like the firemen. I'll leave him for a fireman.

Thursday, September 26th, 2013

Judy was here, don't know why.

Friday, October 4th, 2013

I like the show *Alaskan Bush People*. I could be one, get out of here, live out in the bush on my own. Fuck the cold, fuck them all.

Tuesday, October 22nd, 2013

Looking out the window at the leaves falling. I like the fall, our street is beautiful.

Wednesday, October 30th, 2013

What do I have left to say. Nothing. Can't read my own writing, fuck it.

Friday, December 6th, 2013

At VGH again. Dave brought my stuff this time, they won't let me go home. Ba said I'm going into the care home. Fuck him! My life is over.

CHAPTER 12

THE PURCHASE OF GRAVITY

Fuck this, really, just fuck this! It's so hard, so slow, so relentless, and so utterly cruel. I don't know how to do this, what to say to her, how to be with her. I'm lost all the fucking time—and I'm never lost! There's no manual, map, guide, synopsis, report, white paper, theory, thesis, story, or even a fucking nursery rhyme about this. And I can't talk to her about any of it because she's not there! We used to be able to talk about anything and everything. How do you talk to the person who used to be your partner about the person who used to be your partner? She's so thoroughly devoured by her own losses—which are of course my losses too, our losses, that she can't help me with my losses because she's not there anymore. And of course I can't help her with her losses because I'm not fucking Jesus!

Do you know what it's like to watch your wife hunch and grapple her way across the living room, clutching furniture, holding onto corners and edges, crawling across a room like Gollum, shaking, shuddering, wavering, her face screwed up in effort, contorted in anger, eyes bulging, straining to focus, spluttering, fuming, and cursing? Of course you fucking don't! She used to be so beautiful! She used to be able to do everything. Now she can't do anything and at times, when the fog clears for a millisecond, I can see she knows it. Soon I'll be wiping her ass and putting in her tampons. Cruelty is a concept I now fully understand. She can't relate to what's happening around her anymore, doesn't get the gist of a situation, says the wrong thing all the time, reacts the wrong way, cries over tennis on TV, gets nasty when the boys need kindness, laughs at her children's mistakes, screams "I don't know!" in my face like a crazy person in answer to every question about what she wants or needs in any given moment, and she gets spitting mad because I can't be intimate anymore. Yeah, my dick has gone AWOL. Excuse the fuck out of me if I can't get it up to fuck a stumbling, slow-witted, perpetually nasty bitch with a tremor, slurred speech, food stains all over her clothes, food in her hair, shit under her fingernails. And she's the love of my life and the mother of my children … square that fucking circle!

The damage I've had to try and fix, the love I've had to try to replace in our boys so they can be full like they're supposed to be is nearly impossible to quantify. I'm so lucky we made those little assholes together, but I still have to make up for the love she can't give them anymore. God, I love those boys. God, I miss her—we all miss her. Oh yeah, but she's still here, at least her shell is. And on rare occasions, the shell occasionally sounds like her and for a split second even looks like her—*if* she's having a good day, *and* the tremor is mild, *and* she's sitting, *and* she's smiling—or maybe her expression is just neutral. And in that vanishingly unlikely confluence of events, for those brief shimmering nanoseconds, I might just forget how she's being dissolved in acid every day. But she never gets to forget, diminished capacities notwithstanding. She still knows she has a disease, a cruel motherfucking disease that is taking her apart daily, a handful of crucial neurons at a time. MS melts the brain from the outside in, and the outside is where all our humanity is. We're a thin layer of meat like the thin layer of atmosphere around the earth. Who would have thought that a human being can be rendered down, boiled apart like an animal being deconstructed for its economic outputs, just a few hundred neurons at a time among billions, every day derailing trillions of reactions? And in that process she becomes a completely different person, nothing like she was before, fundamentally changed, fundamentally fucked over, a new person you never would have had children with, never would have given a second look but out of pity. And the kicker? Most of the time that person has no fucking idea they've changed at all! t's so fucking unfair. She did nothing to deserve this. She should be a MILF by now, a great mom and a hot middle-aged wife, but instead she looks and acts more like a permanently scarred holocaust survivor in her eighties!

Children have different cries for different occasions, and parents recognize them instantly. We know the category before we need the details; hunger, pain, dispute, loss, anger, sadness, or righteous indignation, the cries of a child run the gamut of human emotions. During the dark, dark days, on only two occasions, one for each boy, I heard a cry I had never heard before, and mercifully have never heard again. This cry was so deep, so heart rending, so visceral that even the act of writing it down is painful. First Micah, then Adam. Each crossed the threshold of endurance into a deluge of emotion. Both incidents happened within a few weeks of each other, and each boy used the same language between bouts of uncontrollable sobbing.

"I just want her back … I just want her back … I just want her back."

The only way I could think of to cope was to name the spectre haunting our future. I talked to the boys about my idea. I told them that to name something is to take power for yourself, to know something about what you're naming, to have some control, even just a little. That's when we christened our *Fate* Mrs. Bleatwobble. We used the sights and sounds of the two most prominent symptoms Deb had for our portmanteau. The idea was to name the things that were least like their mother and most like the disease. From then on when things got bad we could wink or nod or whisper *Mrs. Bleatwobble* to each other. It put us in the battle together.

"I'm your dad and I've got you no matter what," I told them. In some ways it helped me more than them to name the family Fate doing the backstroke in their mother's bloodstream. I couldn't tell them that I believed Mrs. Bleatwobble was real.

The physical world can be fickle, the chemistry duplicitous, the particles and charges capricious. The physical world will betray us all. The expression about having nothing if you don't have your health is comic in its vacuous simplicity, coined by a healthy idiot while on a picnic in Bumpkin County, drinking iced tea, and eating fried chicken with Jed,

Fred, Buford, and Miss Molly. The physical world is ruthless beyond any deranged dictator, beyond *The Dear Leader* or *Der Fuhrer*, beyond *Uncle Joe* or *Pol the Cracked Pot*. We all must bow to our genetic fate and its power, more fearsome than St. John's seven-headed beast. Genetic fate is alive in every neuron that has ever been and will ever be. It inhibits or excites the physical world with a subatomic push that rattles the vast firmament of our personal universe. It's either an infinite boon or a malicious miracle delivered inside the brackets of three dimensions and time. That is the absolute inanimate deaf and dumb power that is the chance of our physical reality. No God is so vengeful.

As I told my sons, to name something is an attempt at control, domination, subjugation, even domestication … *attempt* being the key word. There are no guarantees, but you have to try when to give up means slow annihilation. So with childish cruelty we named our rapacious Fate "Mrs. Bleatwobble," the villain of our story and with that naming the idea of having a mother and a wife died. We christened her on a fine early spring morning, Saturday April 7th, 2012. Our timeless Fate was born into time and our priceless Deb began her exit, wheels locked onto rails, trains left stations, clocks gonged with precision, and stars maligned. The gears of Newton's predictable universe rotated to strike a Damocletian down-stroke.

* * *

I had just sat down on the toilet when my son walked into the bathroom, except he wasn't supposed to be home, he was supposed to be at work—or so I thought. He was very apologetic, dressed in work clothes exactly as I had seen him two hours earlier when I thought he was leaving for the farm. He and his brother had been working there for years, starting in high school as their summer jobs. Deb had always volunteered to help out my kind-of cousins, Annie and Maye, granddaughters of my grandfather's sister. Their farm was in Fort Langley. The family had 230 acres with a thousand feet of waterfront on the Fraser River. Farm Day was an open house they ran on the same weekend every fall along with lots of other local farms up and down the Fraser Valley. As soon as the boys were old enough, Deb brought them out to learn the ropes and connect with the functional members of my extended family. Adam and Micah learned the

WASP work ethic on a farm at the hands of their Germanic relations—ethnic irony if there is such a thing. Volunteering became summer jobs, which became college funding employment for both of them.

On this particular day, I had thought Adam was at work. Micah was at school, in grade twelve. I was using our shared bathroom downstairs, which was mostly mine during the day. My office was in the basement along with Adam's bedroom. He was nineteen, in university, had his own truck, and was working that spring after finals were over. The main door to the bathroom was off the hall but there was a cheater between the bathroom and Adam's bedroom. We had developed a protocol to maintain each other's privacy but did sometimes screw it up, so the occasional encounter was inevitable and eventually we lost any feelings of embarrassment. I sometimes joked with him and his brother that one day they'd have to wipe my ass like I had theirs when they were babies, so there was no point in being prudish about bodily functions.

So there Adam stood, apologetic, not getting to the point, not leaving. I could see something was on his mind; he was searching for the right words. Patience is one of my parental superpowers. My natural bent is a certain kind of learned watchfulness, a skill acquired under kitchen tables then perfected through a career spent observing the cosmos. Sometimes if I just waited a problem would solve itself, a task would get done, or the right decision made without any input. I was well passed the ten thousand hours required for expert status, according to Mr. Gladwell. Over the years I had perfected a tone and phrase that worked one hundred percent of the time with Adam and Micah in situations where the precise words wouldn't come.

"Yes, son?" I said and waited, steady gaze, kind eyes, slight tilt of the head.

"I'm sorry ... but I'm being crushed to death by the big tractor. I rolled it by accident. I took the embankment up to the dike too fast, at a funny angle, and before I could jump the tractor rolled. I was pulling the disker, which should have been a counterbalance, but the tow bar snapped so the disker stayed flat and the tractor flipped. I might be dead by now—I'm not sure, I don't feel anything so don't worry, I'm not in any pain. Everyone is doing what they can. Oscar is running to get the small tractor to try and pull the big one off me, but I don't think that'll work because the soil is too soft this time of year. Besides, I'm foaming out lots of blood, which means the crush wounds aren't sealed shut by the weight of the tractor, or maybe there's some gash wounds as well. I can't see from my angle, but it doesn't matter—at this rate of blood loss I don't have more than a few minutes. The ambulance is coming, but it's minimum twenty minutes, more if there's traffic. I'm sorry to leave you behind in this mess. I love you. You were the best father ever."

The bathroom wheeled around me in circles like Van Gogh's *Starry Night*. I lurched sideways and fell off the toilet onto my hands and knees, sucking in huge lung-fulls of air, trying to force oxygen into my spinning brain. I was making sounds that didn't seem human, goat sounds, while lights flashed in my peripheral vision. Cold waves of dizziness crashed over me as I fought to stay conscious. I closed my mouth tight and vacuumed in huge, damp swaths of breath through my nose, each one clubbing back the beast of unconsciousness as I battled my way back to lucidity. Finally I felt as if I could get back up on the toilet. After a few minutes of working to control my breathing I swayed to my feet, pulled up my pants, and stumbled forward, propping myself against the wall at the door into Adam's room. I opened it and leaned in like a man trying not to fall off a cliff.

Adam's room was all as it should be for a boy of eleven still in elementary school. My grip on reality strobed again. It had seemed so real. I had understood everything that was happening, accepted the situation as current and the context as history: university, working at the farm, having a truck and a driver's license. I was badly frightened. Was this a premonition, a hallucination, a waking nightmare courtesy Mrs. Bleatwobble, or a vision from some realm beyond our reality like a parallel dimension? Was I losing my mind? Did I have a brain tumour? Was this a symptom of a second life-threatening neurological disorder about to befall my family?

My head began to clear. Was there a rational explanation? I just had to figure it out. It was 2013, I reminded myself. Adam was eleven, in Grade 6, Micah was nine, in Grade 4. Neither were home, both in school, what day was it—Wednesday? I sat down on his bed. Slowly the here-and-now repopulated my awareness; though the movie reel hallucination wouldn't fade, the fear at least did. The fact of Adam's eleven years of life claimed more ground, gained mass, pulled me into its orbit, leaving the hallucination out on the edge of my still-spinning reality. That must have been what it was—a hallucination.

I once had a similar experience in a very different context, more of a waking nightmare. Long before kids Deb and I had watched a moving Bill Moyers documentary on dying, death, and the rituals different cultures use to make sense of having someone there one moment and gone the next. For two hours we were immersed in the grief of others, their thoughts, explanations, fears, and faiths. We cried with these people on TV, pondered and wondered, it was a deep and meaningful experience for both of us. We talked about what we wanted for our goodbyes, hopefully in the far distant future.

That night I had what I've always thought was a vision of the future. All my life, both dreams and nightmares have usually left me within moments of waking. At times I've dreamed beautiful music, songs, lyrics, moving poems that no one had yet written. But I could never get them down, not even two words or two notes, before they popped out of existence like an exotic particle the moment I awoke. This vision, on the other hand, has stayed with me all my life, never fading, never losing its power. I woke to a face looming over me, stretching the material of the bedroom wall as if it were a rubber sheet. I knew instantly it was Death. Just a face, ominous and indistinct, but with an expression that said, *You know who I am and why I'm here.* I was frozen. The brain expresses chemicals while we sleep that block the neuromuscular signals that control movement to avoid injury or even death during sleep. Some people suffer from somnambulism—sleepwalking—a short circuit in the system, the opposite of what I was experiencing. My mind was awake, I was conscious, but my body was immobilized.

I struggled as the face loomed closer, but I still couldn't move. Death was coming for me. It slowly descended, approaching, becoming clearer now, floating down beside me as if the body attached to the face was leaning forward to embrace me. Hands began to stretch the wall on either side of the face; I could see fingertips. I felt a decision being made within myself yet it wasn't me making it, as though I was lifted from beneath like an updraft by the decision to face Death. Suddenly full of courage, I left my body and began to sit up, though my physical body didn't move. As I rose, Death withdrew. I stood at the side of the bed and Death retreated to the top corner of the wall, its expression again becoming indistinct as the wall slackened. The impression in my mind became, *When you next see me, it will be your death day, but you will live a long life*, and then it was gone.

Instantly I was fully awake in body and mind, but I had not stood up, I was still in bed. I sat up and looked at the wall for traces of Death's presence, but there were none. The memory is still vivid. I've always understood the origin of the experience and I can easily explain it away as neurochemistry, but the subjective experience was so powerful that I've never been able to dismiss it. I can't believe it was just neurochemistry.

I remembered this vision from all those years ago as I slowly regained my presence in the here-and-now of Adam's bedroom. The vivid details of his imagined death deeply shook me and this wasn't the first time my mind seemed to have been derailed, there were other strange things happening that I couldn't readily explain. I was seeing things in my peripheral vision. Flashes of light, shadows, movement, the impression of someone just out of sight, these things had been happening for months. I would come to bed after reading to the boys, Deb sound asleep for hours by then, slip into bed beside her, and begin to close down into soft unconsciousness. Suddenly a muffled explosion would erupt from down the hall, where the boys' bedrooms were, and flames would shoot down the hall and lick around the corner of our open bedroom door, only to be gone in the fraction of a second it took to open my eyes. The most fleeting, momentary glimpse would remain, a whiff of smoke so subtle it seemed as if a thought. Always just beyond my rational perception.

Other times these almost-hallucinations came in the late evening when the house was quiet with everyone asleep, just me and Rhombus still up. I'd sense movement out on the deck, wind in the trees that turned into a figure at the kitchen window, there for a moment then gone, but the feeling of being watched wouldn't dissipate. The furnace would come on and the sound of a door opening would hide in the warm woosh. I would stop and hold my breath, straining to listen for the sound of footsteps in the house, a sound that refused to come clearly. Sometimes it wasn't explosion and fire but the front door being kicked open followed by automatic gunfire. A shooter I could see in video-game detail gone in an instant, just before the bullets flew my direction.

I told no one about these episodes. I had to hold it together. But I did go to our GP and ask for a complete physical, blood work, and an EKG. I would have asked for an fMRI if I wouldn't have had to admit what was going on. She surely would have booked it had I'd told her about a hallucination involving my future nineteen-year-old son's death, and probably a psychiatrist too. Regardless, I pushed back against my apparent insanity and kept buggering on the way I like to think Albert Brown must have, also with a brain that didn't quite work right.

I leaned on the famously fucked-up Nietzsche: what doesn't kill you makes you stronger. So smart, so happy, the Germans.

The most effective remedy, I learned, was to breathe, just breathe, controlled, slowly in through the nose, hold for a five count, then out through pursed lips. It always worked, but the amount of time it took for the rational world to return was a variable thing. I concentrated on Albert Brown and his legendary KBO spirit as I did these breathing techniques. I imagined his instantly lobotomized brain as against mine, slowly frying in excess cortisol. It was admittedly a bit of a long bow to draw but it helped—I felt a kinship. His ancestors were cruel. I resented their pasty English bodies projecting their epigenetic burden—a cargo of calamity—forward onto Deb and me. I felt as if the men of Deb's ancestry daily shat sorrow out upon the women of their lives, and I resented being made to be one of them when clearly I was not. I was an overcomer, a rise-above, I was not a drag-downer. I became convinced during those exceedingly difficult days that the denizens haunting my peripheral vision and half-sleep were the Fates of those weak, dead men come to pull me into battles their charges had lost generations ago. Explosion, fire, and machine guns were a recurring theme from their war history, sometimes inside the house, sometimes outside, but always threatening Adam and Micah. But it wasn't them, of course; it was my own Fate, Mrs. Bleatwobble the entire time.

She also used the old movie trope of a faceless menacing presence just outside a door or window. Someone standing outside under the streetlight, or a soldier fighting house to house as Berlin fell, a silhouette stealthing the dark ruins as I imagined Purple Helmut had done, slowly and quietly approaching our front door. These tormentors of my imagination always showed up when I felt least able to jump into action and save my sons—on the edge of sleep, lost in a thought, deeply dug into a calculation, or a bit drunk. She knew how to play upon my feelings of childhood vulnerability, bringing them forward from the past, ever dragging me back under the kitchen table.

One time, I had the strong impression someone was sitting in my car in the garage. I heard muffled sounds. I was sitting in the den on a Friday night, drinking Scotch and surfing porn while everyone was asleep. I kept having to mute the moans of women discreetly masturbating in public places, trying not get caught. It was a fantasy Deb and I used to play out before our sex life went to hell. Still, I couldn't shake the feeling of someone in the garage. Those old West Side houses weren't connected directly to the garage, it was usually a separate structure in the backyard accessed from the alley. I was getting agitated and annoyed but despite the alcohol and the hard cock I had to go check. I kept a martial arts staff in the closet near the back door, from when I used to train. I armed myself and very quietly opened the back door onto the deck.

I decided on the element of surprise. I quietly approached and put my ear to the garage door, poised a hand over the door handle, and listened. I thought I heard something. Maybe not. Maybe it was all my put-upon imagination. Fuck It! I burst the door open and hit the opener for the main doors, which also switched on the lights. I spun the staff into fighting position as the furry ass-end of a raccoon running for its life disappeared under the garage door and out into the alley. At least this time it was something real, not my punch-drunk brain, just a raccoon; not a wraith. Then I heard what I thought was the click of the back gate opening. Instantly in my mind's eye I saw that the raccoon had circled back, grown to five feet tall, opened the gate, and was coming to tear me apart. I could see it so clearly—a vicious were-rodent nearly as tall as me, toothed and clawed. I hit the button to close the door to the alley and stepped back out into the yard, my pulse pounding, breath pushing against the back of my teeth.

I tried to summon the will to cross the distance from the garage to the top of the sidewalk that ran down the side of the garage to the back gate. A twenty-foot, pitch-black corridor with a line of trees that hung low, smothering the sidewalk in darkness. Why hadn't I installed that light on the garage wall? A were-raccoon?! No doubt I was failing under all the stress but in that moment I couldn't ignore the possibility of threat to the boys no matter how insane I felt. Of course, there was nothing there when I plunged into the dark and stood my ground at the gates of hell—which was really just an ordinary gate into a typical Vancouver back alley.

I can't say for sure how long these troubles of the mind lasted for me—at least a year, probably longer. I became very familiar with the almost-apparitions that shared the quiet with me. I got used to a particular recurring dream featuring a fiendish grandmother with a mouthful of shark teeth and onyx eyes that absorbed the light. She appeared sitting in a rocking chair, wearing a peasant dress covered in tiny blood-red flowers. Her skin was the colour of polished cement, her hands all knuckles, her body thick and square. Like all good creatures of myth, Mrs. Bleatwobble came to me unbidden. She would read to me from a mysterious book on her lap. I could never see the title, I could never place the poem or the passage, but I always felt as if I should know it. These dreams were always ominous. She was always threatening. The readings were always cryptic. The most recent one had been inspired by a class I was teaching on stellar parallax, the method used to measure stellar distances. It didn't matter that the origin of the dream was obvious to me, the experience was still frightening. But unlike most of her torments this one arrived in the middle of the night when I was deeply asleep, as if to ensure I had no respite from her. Words percolated up like magma through fissures in the earth's crust, lighting my darkened consciousness with the red glow of an imagined hell, gradually making themselves known.

* * *

The gathering curtain of velvet black space
hangs like a question of casual grace.
The soon to be dead strike echoing steps
off tesselate stones in the crisp night blessed.
The cool silken air wraps a life that's receding
the wise night is silent, the daylight is fleeting.

Her voice crackled like fat in a frying pan.

"Who the fuck are you and what do you want?"

You know who I am, you named me. As for what I want, absolutely nothing, my dear. Nothing completely.

"Then why are you in my house? Why are you in my dreams?"

Can't you imagine the reason, David? You have a vivid imagination. I'm such an ugly old woman in your imagination. Your father beat you and abused you. Why am I not simply a grotesque version of him?

"I don't know."

But surely you must know, David. The women in your life have all been so beautiful and strong ... except for your own mother.

"I ... uh ..." My dream self tried to speak but couldn't, the words wouldn't come—like Albert Brown.

Perhaps your imagination is failing you, my dear. I don't know what that feels like. What does it feel like, David—to imagine, to dream?

"I'm imagining you, you're not real."

I see. So what does it mean for me to be imagined—for you to be imagining me? Do I live only in your imagination? Do I have no existence beyond your imagination? Does that mean I'm not real or does it make me only as real as you are?

"I don't ... I'm not ..." Again I fumbled. "I don't know who you are. I don't understand why you're singing songs to me and reciting poems."

That's a lie David, you know me ... you've known me all your life and they're your songs and poems—I simply find them in you. I can't imagine any thoughts of my own so they must be yours.

"Why are you doing this to me?"

It's my job, David. You're under my care.

"What job?" I began to sob. "Why am I ... under ... under your care? What does that even mean?"

Please don't cry, my dear. I have no power over you. After all, you're named for a great king, one who killed a giant with only a slingshot. You can do anything you want, anything you can imagine. I just record those choices and calculate the most probable consequences you bring into the world.

"I don't have any choice in this!" I yelled. "What the fuck do you want?!"

As I've already said, I don't want anything, David—I'm indifferent. I do know many things however, all of your ancestors, all of your past and all of your possible futures. You get up every morning and I calculate. It's very simple. Your future is entirely your choice.

"Get out of my house!" I screamed as loud as I could.

My voice echoed and suddenly I was standing alone in an old-world village square. Everything made of stone. All the buildings were dark, their windows shuttered against the night, not a light on anywhere, the sky alive with stars. I could hear a fountain burbling somewhere.

Sing that song again, my dear, she said in a tone as cool as graveyard mist. *The one about being your wife's willing plaything.*

My breath congealed. Had she really been there with Deb and me; sitting in the corner; watching us make love; watching us fall asleep?

"You were there on my honeymoon!"

I go with you everywhere, my dear. I'm part of you, I can't help but be with you. I've been under the kitchen table with you. I was with you at your grandfather's funeral. Your history is my history, David.

I felt caged by her gaze though she was nowhere to be seen. Fear locked me in place.

After a pause she continued. *Think of me like you do the gravity of dark matter. You know the science of dark matter very well, don't you, David? I believe that was your thesis subject, was it not?*

"I thought you said you're always with me." After hearing that my most intimate moments with Deb had been violated, I couldn't help but spit sarcasm; I needed to push back against the helplessness beginning to claim me.

Well, think of me that way then, if it helps you to understand. You create me like dark matter creates gravity. I'm the unseen result of something hidden. You're the dark matter, I'm the gravity.

"But I'm not *causing* you," I heard myself as a whining child.

All humans are always the cause of all their possible futures, as well as the result of all their possible pasts. You each attract choices for one another like water flowing down a mountain into a gorge. Your lives cascade together, creating a cataract of past, present, and future—yourself and your parents and their parents as well as your children's children—all these people are you David, all their thoughts and all their desires. I'm just one of that cloud of unseen witnesses your father preached about. I wouldn't be here if there wasn't a lifetime of consequences to calculate, David.

I felt as if I were looking at the night sky through the opening of a well from deep underground; only a tiny round escape high above me looking out at the billions of stars I knew were there but couldn't see.

You see only a very small circle of reality David; you have to imagine the rest. I can see everything but can't imagine anything. We're a perfect complement to each other that way.

I felt frustration and anger. "I don't have any choice in this. It's happening *to* me, not *because of* me."

That's a half-truth. You always have a choice, and the cause of all your possible choices is always you—your family, or your wife's family, or people whose lives intersect with yours, random strangers who may cross your path, and people not born yet or those long dead—all of these people are you. All these lives rain down the mountain side building the torrent to come, drowning your children's children in their fate long before they've gasped their first breath. The flood is coming, David, it's unstoppable. Humans are always the cause and death is always the consequence.

"*Fuck you!*" I screamed again, the echo bouncing off the stone houses into the night.

Then she released me. I awoke panting and panicked, in a full, cold sweat, as I had done so many times before.

* * *

Besides an overdose of stress hormones, two well-documented disorders could have explained what I was going through. I researched them both. Charles Bonnet syndrome is a rich source of hallucinations, but it's associated with macular degeneration and people see their hallucinations for discernible periods of time. Charles Bonnet hallucinations are exhibitionists—no ducking around corners or just-out-of-sight antics—and they usually aren't threatening. They're more absurd, like two-headed people suddenly appearing in your office, Klingons appearing in bed where your spouse should be, or an orangutan in chef's attire making you breakfast.

The other possibility was more frightening. A brain tumour could cause a vast number of symptoms, so recurring paranoid almost-hallucinations and dreams of Mrs. Bleatwobble were decidedly on the table. Even the appearance of Adam as his future nineteen-year-old self, a too-lucid hallucination, was possible but more akin to paranoid schizophrenia, which I was much too old for. Also, I didn't have the most common symptom, hearing voices—unless you included Mrs. Bleatwobble's, which I didn't. I knew she was real.

So, being the good man of science that I am ... or was... after much research combined with medical tests and a few actual events involving verifiable phenomena like raccoons or the wind, I settled into my self-diagnosis—namely, that the Fates are real and that my personal Fate, Mrs. Bleatwobble was torturing me, and I was stressed to the brink of collapse, drowning in cortisol. Medical science and Greek mythology explained all I needed to know. And although I did everything I could to control my anxiety and convince myself otherwise, my afflicter would not abate, so I lived in a world bounded by the aprehensive day and the ruthless night.

CHAPTER 13

THE BURIED YEAR

Mrs. Applegreen's living room was a shrine to the Dow Chemical Company. I counted eleven different forms of plastic, the most obvious being the clear plastic furniture covers. The fox-hunt motif wing-back chairs, the olive-green, crushed-velvet Georgian settee, the Victorian reproduction armchair, the brown Naugahyde tuck-and-roll hassock—all entombed in clear plastic wrap like Thanksgiving leftovers. Living room as time capsule, filigreed, polished, turned, and veneered; doilied, draped and valanced, never used. I had heard of living rooms like this but never seen one. Mrs. Applegreen was so proud of her *formal* living room, as she called it. I, however, didn't warrant the occasion to unwrap it. The irony was that most of the furniture protected under plastic was upholstered in various forms of plastic fabrics like nylon, rayon, and polyester.

The house faced west. Like most of the old Vancouver two-storey designs from the 1920s and '30s, the front steps led to a small covered porch with a single door that opened directly into the living room. There was no vestibule, just a small rectangle of dark hardwood border in the floor outlining where the mat should go. In front of the fireplace, where the hearth was in rich people's homes, was the same outline. In the Applegreen living room, the picture window was to the left of the door. On almost any street in Vancouver, if enough houses of that era had survived, you could see the pattern extend down the block, picture windows alternating from the left to the right-hand side of the front door. Obedient dreams.

The picture window in Mrs. Applegreen's living room was heavily draped in crushed velvet backed by white sheers, topped with an ornate valance covered in complementary wallpaper with crushed velvet flocking. It was a summer afternoon, nearly thirty degrees outside, but the inside was dim and cool. A thin sliver of sunlight persuaded its way in through an imperfection of age where the drapes no longer perfectly overlapped, allowing a threatening blade of light to fall across the vulnerable, crushed-velvet settee. From her perch on one of the plastic wingbacks, Mrs. Applegreen explained to me that the drapes had been custom made in the early '70s. That kind of craftsmanship didn't exist anymore, she said, so not only was there no one qualified to do the repairs but the fabric wasn't made anymore either. Proudly she pointed out her hand-crafted solution, which I had failed to notice, which caused her to puff out with still more pride because its camouflage had worked.

Mrs. Applegreen had sewn a tea-towel-sized piece of olive-green crushed velvet, very close to the original colour of the settee, which lay where the blade of molten anarchy fell. As the day progressed and the sunbeam tracked across the settee, she continually moved the sacrificial fabric swatch along until the day dipped into the forest canopy behind all those lush West Side trees and the republic of plastic became safe again. I pondered the fanaticism of this while she explained that it was only necessary seven or eight months of the year and even that was intermittent at each end of the calendar thanks to Vancouver's famously grey winters. Perhaps a mere two-hundred-ish days of vigil all tolled. Had Mrs. Applegreen known that April and I would slide around in juicy ecstasy, fucking all over that plastic-covered settee, using it like lubricated spandex, I have no doubt she would have toppled over dead, feet in the air, frilly knickers aloft like a cartoon bird.

April Applegreen had come along when I was almost completely broken. I had turned forty-three and decided to have my mid-life crisis a bit early. Given the decimation I was enduring, can you blame me? I was a late bloomer in everything else, so why not be early for once? Justification is not difficult, but while shaving in the mirror my advice is stay focused—looking into one's own eyes and deeply questioning oneself is begging to bleed. Once, April asked me whether fucking her helped me to fuck Deb. She had no idea of the level of suffering Deb was enduring, or the power of my crushing need for escape. I think she sensed my weakness, though, otherwise why would she have culled me from the herd of middle-aged men and brought me down like prey? Perhaps because I asked her to?

April was twenty-three. I was not her first older lover. Initially we recapitulated the power dynamic between Deb and me when we'd first met. Deb was in charge at the outset, as was April. Having a mistress was not something I had ever contemplated. I wanted for nothing with Deb until Mrs. Bleatwobble began her assault. I needed April to walk me through the etiquette of cheating on someone, which put her in charge. I was being trained again. The power dynamic swung in my favour, however; the first time I agreed to beat her up. April liked her sex very rough—she wanted me to leave a mark. I channeled my abusive father while cheating on my wife like my grandfather had cheated on his wife. I offer up the back of my neck freely to your judgment.

We met at a conference in Seattle in the spring of 2013. Judy was holding down the fort with the boys and keeping an eye on Deb so I could spend an entire weekend away for the first time since Deb's diagnosis three years previously. April was in communications for a not-for-profit agency promoting STEM education for girls in marginalized communities. I had decided on the drive down to the conference to find someone to bed. I wasn't proud of myself, but I could justify it. If you haven't ever experienced the deprivation of a lover's touch you don't know what your skin can do to your brain. Skin is our largest organ; it's connected to billions of neurons in trillions of ways. When your skin says you need to have sex with someone, hold someone, fall asleep with someone, it doesn't much care who that someone might be, and it doesn't take no for an answer. Whatever signals we humans put out into the environment when we're looking to hook up—pheromones, body language, tone of voice, dozens of other subtle clues (no doubt a primate biologist could fill me in)—whatever the suite of communications, skin is the conductor and all the other body parts are orchestra.

April was an experienced reader of these signals, an aficionado, a connoisseur, a virtuoso—choose your superlative. We happened to share a table at a post-conference dinner, one of those events where the organizers ask you to sit with people you don't know. She and I manoeuvred to sit across from each other. I was trying to be subtle, but I was decidedly attracted to her. Within a few minutes of being seated, she flashed her blue eyes at me as if to say, "I'll fuck you later if you want." No words were exchanged at that point. I was flabbergasted. I needed to see whether I was hallucinating—again—or whether this was real. I was convinced she was sending me signals. Later, over drinks we conspired.

"Hi, I'm Dave," I said.

"Hi, Dave, I'm April."

"Nice to meet you, April. What brings you here?"

She explained her position with the Wendell Foundation.

"Admirable cause," I said. "I haven't heard of them."

"It's new, only been around for a few years. What do you do, Dave?"

"I'm an astrophysicist at the University of British Columbia."

"Very prestigious."

"Thanks. I'm biding my time until NASA calls."

"Fancy yourself a bit of a space cowboy, do you?"

"Not sure how I'd look with a handlebar moustache."

"Very sexy, I think." She was baiting me, quite obviously.

"Coming from a girl as beautiful as you, I'll happily take that compliment, thanks."

"I've always been attracted to older men," she offered. "Especially the smart ones."

"Stop. You'll overfeed my innate egotistical asshole if you're not careful."

"I'm not big on careful. Discreet, but not careful."

"I hardly know what to say."

"As long as you know what to think."

"I think, therefore I can," I said, baiting her back.

"Well, I can too then." She tossed me a coquettish grin.

Then came the inevitable interruption—some guy wanted to hit on April and introduced himself as Don—or Bob or Ray. I can't remember his name but I do remember thinking, *Please fuck off.*

"Hi, Don-Bob-Ray. I'm April and this is Dave." She switched gears effortlessly, with charm and grace. I knew I was out of my depth but didn't care. After a brief but polite engagement with Don-Bob-Ray, we were alone in conversation again.

"How long are you in Seattle for, Dave?"

"I drive home tomorrow."

"Well, we'll have to make the most of tonight then, won't we?"

"I'd be happy to do that."

"But you don't know what I want from you yet."

"I'm excited to find out."

"What room are you in?"

"Four-forty-two."

"So you'll answer if I knock?"

"You already know I will. What kind of wine do you like?"

"I'm a Pinot girl. Gris or noir, depending on my mood."

"I'll be sure to have one of each. I want to be prepared for any mood you're in." I said.

She ended our conversation with, "Don't worry—I'll tell you what to do."

She went off to circulate, leaving me near bursting with excitement. Conversation bounced around the room, clusters formed and decohered, as we scientists like to say, pompous assholes that we can be. April and I philandered our way around the various conversations, always stopping in with each other, passing comments, connecting, leaving, reconnecting. She was better than me in the social mixer charm department. No one seemed to notice the signals we were trading. I was smitten. It felt so much like Deb when we'd first met. Simply writing these words twists the bayonet. Ignore all past and future invitations to judge me; I'm more than capable of that myself.

April was a surprise child, and I do mean surprise—though not quite to the hyperbolic degree of the biblical Sarah, who mythically gave birth at age ninety. Nonetheless, April was a big surprise to her forty-nine-year-old mother, sixty-six-year-old father, and twenty-eight-year-old half-brother. April's mother Fiona was the former mistress, now second wife, of her father Simon Applegreen. Fiona the shiksa had displaced the plastic-worshipping first Mrs. Applegreen, mother of April's half-brother Nathan. Simon Applegreen was aloof, self-important, always busy, always working on the family business. April was unabashed about her daddy issues; of course she wanted a combination of daddy and lover. Of course she wanted a man at least twenty years older than her. Being a mistress was normal, even noble; many cultures accepted this, even promoted the arrangement, and she was well convinced that almost every objection or justification was culturally relative. April believed very few taboos were actually taboo.

The mixer after dinner was posh, full of beautiful, charming, smart people and awkward, unattractive, brilliant people having great conversation, expensive drinks, and a great good time. The facilities were classic Pacific Northwest: warm wood, high ceilings, two stone fireplaces, two bars, comfy stylish furniture in clusters, a live jazz quintet, soft lighting, and floor-to-ceiling glass patio doors beyond which fell a fresh, light rain. Everything any self-respecting girl looking to get laid needed, not to mention a smorgasbord of middle-aged men to choose from for a girl with daddy issues.

April was tall and willowy with a small waist, ample, heart-shaped ass, long blond hair to complement azure eyes, smallish, perky tits with upturned nipples, beautifully handsome features, full lips, and a long straight nose. To me she was intoxication in the flesh. There were other, more beautiful women there, more turned out, but no one was as sexy as April in her understated, modestly fitted little black dress. She was discreet with the amount of attention she paid me, how much time we spent in private conversation versus small groups. She circulated regularly, leaving me for just the right amount of time. Watching her swish around the room was thrilling. Knowing she wanted me was heady, and the situation felt surprisingly easy and natural, assisted by alcohol and the lowering of inhibitions. The evening flowed like a warm bath.

Later, after midnight, April came to my room. What she asked me to do shocked me at first. April needed pain with her pleasure. More shocking was finding out I could hurt someone who asked me to. This personal revelation cut awfully close to the bone for an abuse survivor, but I submitted myself out of sheer desperation. She told me what she wanted in a soft, confident voice, getting more turned on as she gave me more intimate and detailed instruction. At first I couldn't tell if this was an act or the real thing, but as we progressed I realized I didn't care. She was making me crazy, and my desperation was fading into aggression. Surprising myself, I slapped her hard across the face. Then I pushed her down on the floor, unzipped my pants, shoved my hard cock into her mouth, and started fucking her face, gagging her repeatedly.

"Harder, Daddy," she choked out.

She was not surprised by my compliance. She told me afterward that she had broken up with men who couldn't find it in themselves to give her what she wanted. I pulled her hair, bit her nipples, pinned her against the wall, bounced her head against the door jamb, pinned her on her stomach, and fucked her ass. I inflicted pain, something I had never done before. April revelled in this mix of pleasure and pain with a lust that frightened me. But I kept that to myself—I knew I couldn't show any fear. Her needs were very clear and they obviously ran very deep. When I decided to let her come, I went down on her, asserting yet more dominance. She came hard. She rattled and writhed. Then I climbed on her and fucked her in good old-fashioned missionary style, as hard and as long as I could until I came. She said she came again, a claim no doubt aimed at my ego, but I didn't care—at that point I just needed release. I remember thinking, *Still got it for a middle-aged guy.*

What I imagined was going to be a one-night thing became a secret life. I had thought April was American, from Seattle. I found out at breakfast that she was an Anglo from Quebec living in Vancouver. I was filled with excitement and trepidation. I had crossed into some new place, into a new state that promised so much (but would deliver so little, like the old fantasy of lead becoming gold). I needed to see her again. Through April I was alive again in the midst of decay. The power of my need obliterated any landscape where April was a person with her own damaged history.

I chose delusion because that's what we humans do when we need to survive. We trade a year now for three years later, then a week for a month, then just one more day, and finally just one last moment before the axe falls. Had I been one of the whaling crew lost in the heart of the sea after surviving a sperm-whale attack like the one that inspired Melville's *Moby-Dick*, I too would have resorted to cannibalism. Unquestionably. Maybe there are whispers of Purple Helmut in me, epigenetic gifts wrapped in razor-blade ribbons and bloodthirsty bows. I was being shown things about myself that were previously hidden to me. I had opened the box, yes, but was it my fault kinky things sprang out, egotistical things, frightening primitive things? Mrs. Bleatwobble was having sport with me, but I put that out of my mind. I wasn't crawling back under that kitchen table no matter what. That was all the justification I needed.

On the drive home from Seattle, I screamed and cursed the universe for my newfound power, for new, rich, red blood. I blared my bile like a drunken sailor lashed to the mast in a hurricane. *Fuck you! Crank the music! Come get me, motherfuckers!* But all that bravado dribbled into my shoes the moment I walked back through the front door of my afflicted home. The windows misted over into darkness as if to imprison me and shut me off from the light of the outside world. The kitchen lashed an apron around me, the toilets gurgled a greeting, the washer and dryer boomed with bloodlust. The basement rattled its chains at me. I heard the crackling of unseen fires, glimpsed the *whoosh* of phantom explosions. The pots and pans, the dishes and cups—all clattered threats in a foreign tongue as if I were a slave stolen from far away and they my masters, the lords and ladies of the manor, threatening the whipping post.

The boys rushed at me with glee. Deb smiled, then glowered, then looked away. I thanked Judy and she went home. I didn't know how to be or who to be so I stuffed it all down—the shame, the excitement, the anticipation, the fear. Faithless in Seattle. I was already planning. It's frighteningly powerful for a middle-aged married man to be targeted by a beautiful woman twenty years younger, someone who has a deep need that you can answer. How did April know that I would be willing to abuse her? Make no mistake, it was abuse, consensual, but abuse nonetheless. A kink I now know many people enjoy but one that wasn't in my sexual vocabulary before April. She told me she could tell I would comply. What could she see in me? Someone who knew what it was like to get beat up? Someone who knew how to rationalize? Someone who understood desperation? Someone malleable? Someone with an epigenetic sadist living in his metaphorical attic? I have no idea.

My affair with April—sounds like a Rodgers and Hammerstein musical, doesn't it?—lasted through the worst year of my life, and it kept me alive. Adam and Micah also kept me alive. Both statements are true but only one is public. I guess my sons kept the virtuous hero-me alive, and April kept the villainous carnal-me alive. How fortunate that I got to maintain a fulsome version of myself while Mrs. Bleatwobble fucked me over in new and unforeseen ways. Self-pity and rationalization marinated in red wine and despair—maybe that's why the French can eat and drink to excess without getting fat.

April certainly acted French, though her family was Jewish-Anglo-Quebecois from Montreal. Her father and the new-and-improved Mrs. Applegreen still lived there while original-recipe Mrs. Applegreen had moved to Vancouver, where she took April in for a time at the behest of Simon Applegreen and a renegotiated divorce settlement allowing April to follow the tug of the West Coast after graduating from college, which embarrassingly for me was only a year before we met. *I love a cliché*, sung to the tune of *I Love a Parade*. What does it mean for me to be a cliché? Maybe I'm not. Maybe, like so many other men, I'm just deflecting blame for my own sexual desires, fantasies, deviancies even, onto the woman, or women, in my life. Or maybe that does make me a cliché, just not the one where an older man needs a younger woman to prop up his fading virility, but the one in which men blame women for what women *make* them do.

At this point, I'd like to invoke Satan, or victimhood, or genetics, or failing brain chemistry. I think I could build an impressive list of possible causation, the best one being the hard reductionist idea that everything I did was predetermined, set in motion at the very first moment of the big bang. An absolution even the Catholic Church couldn't match. Philosophy can be useful when you have your twenty-three-year-old mistress bent over a chair, plaid school-girl skirt flipped up, fucking her from behind, pulling her long ponytail with one hand like Bronco Billy at the rodeo, slapping her ass hard with the other while she moans, with pleasure, "Please, Daddy, fuck me harder, harder, Daddy, harder." How could any man be expected to resist? Maybe better men could, but I certainly couldn't. Maybe my history of abuse and loss made justification easier, or maybe I would have done it anyway. Maybe I am my father's son but with a different peccadillo. I don't know. I can't know because it didn't happen any other way than the way it did. My life was broken beyond repair—twice broken—and so was April's, long before she and I met. We all have to rise above, or not; be resilient, or not. Like duplicitous dough, there are times we rise and times we fall. Such poetic justification of weakness and failure, don't you think?

I was getting a feel for what addiction must be like, which made me think of my father, and I hated that. Certainly my life was not consumed with April, she was a respite, a distraction. She claimed to love me and was perfectly fine with my love for Deb and the boys, but I couldn't bring myself to tell her I loved her back because it would have added another lie to the one I was living. She teased me about it but never complained. She was completely invested in our shared double life, confident in her position as the mistress, delighted with her savage needs being met and my willingness to perform without qualm or apology. A beautiful young woman with everything she thought she wanted. Part of me wants to go back there, to that eve of destruction that was so damaging, back to the majestic sex and the deep emotional solace that came with the living, breathing, naked opioid that was April Applegreen, but I can't. I made my choice and created the consequences. She was nuclear, she was radiation, she cracked my walls and split my veins. I had never felt so much raw emotion, so much energy, hormones turning my bloodstream into a 1920s speakeasy; all booze and smoke and sex. Not short on hypocrisy, me. And now that I had introduced it into my personal life, why not import it into my professional life as well?

Some of my close friends either knew or suspected. Bob Chow had a fiftieth birthday party in Chinatown at the Pink Pearl Restaurant. He bought out the second floor and invited a hundred people. He and I were close; of all my friends and colleagues, he knew the most about what was going on at home. I took April to his party. He understood immediately, or maybe I just thought so. Her demeanour toward me was far too familiar for her to be simply a young colleague, and my behaviour toward her was almost like public paranoia, but she didn't care and Bob said nothing. He was gracious to April, as were his wife and the others who knew me. The cover story was, of course, one of pity. My beautiful young colleague April had volunteered to take my arm and cheer me up, even making light of the fact that I seemed uncomfortable at times. Though she played the role perfectly in my eyes, I doubt anyone was fooled, at least not those who knew my situation.

"Relax," she said. "It's not as if we're having an affair. You're way too old for me." That caused both laughter and sideways glances.

She was hiding us in plain sight with just enough innuendo to titillate. Bob certainly wasn't fooled but he wasn't lurid either, and I got the impression he wasn't a stranger to this situation. April continued to be charming as usual, making the rounds, engaging all and sundry. I eventually relaxed and slipped into the ruse. Of course, all this cheating fried my already frying brain more, and I had to lock things away inside secure compartments but holes were blown in my emotional barn and my cows wandered too; just like Grandpa Felix. It seems almost anything can be justified this way if you're okay with too many locks and not enough keys. April suffered her own dissonance, but hers was not the result of our relationship. Hers came down the line directly from her father. No need to search farther back on that family tree. Women with daddy issues always have a shit father, so April and I had this in common despite the decades between us. Shit fathers are much more common than shit mothers. Some of us are lucky and get both.

Simon Green was a bad Jew, at least according to his orthodox family. Adding "Apple" to the front of his last name gave him, he believed, both an alphabetical and cultural advantage in multicultural Montreal. Although, according to April, he associated freely with his orthodox relatives he was not religious at all, only going to synagogue for the high holidays, weddings, and the occasional funeral. Simon Applegreen was an executive with IBM. He spoke four languages: English, French, Russian, and Gaelic—yes, Gaelic. The Gaelic Jew is truly another unicorn of this story. He travelled the world for business and pleasure, had many affairs with blond, blue-eyed women, and he self-identified as a reincarnated Celtic chieftain named Cynbel—meaning war chief. Hence he taught himself the language and was an avid participant in the English Historical Battle Re-enactment Society of Upper Canada, participating in the Battle of the Plains of Abraham re-enactment between Montcalm and Wolfe eleven times.

His orthodox family mocked this aspect of his odd and complex psyche, calling him Majestic Warrior for the exaggerated confidence and leaping stride with which he crossed the battlefield. A Jewish/Celtic John Wayne. Simon a.k.a. Cynbel was a complex dude indeed. Fiona Applegreen was his Celtic trophy wife, a gorgeous woman with auburn hair, blue-green eyes, and alabaster skin. April was a study in the image of Fiona, and I guess I was just as smitten as Simon. For April, I was the conflation of father and lover. She was working out her complex (some would say fucked-up) relationship with her complex (some would say fucked-up) father— Inaccessible, unfathomable, and often unavailable. I was giving her things Simon Applegreen either couldn't or wouldn't or shouldn't.

By April's account, Simon Applegreen was a viciously intelligent Greek statue of a man with skin the colour of roasted peanuts and the exceedingly rare and arresting golden iris you find in parts of Southern Spain and North Africa. He was also funny, charming, and had a beautiful singing voice born of a naturally warm, oaky baritone speaking voice, which he used to narrate his lovemaking to Fiona with flourish and creativity in multiple languages both spoken and sung. April said she heard their passion for each other often and was proud of them. She told her girlfriends in school all the things her father said to her mother in flagrante delicto. No doubt April's view of her father was as idealized as my view of my father was demonized. Regardless, I was happy to be a carnal father for her, rather than be my father for anyone. This was another strategy I used to fend off the guilt, focusing on the void April needed filling in her life rather than the void that was opening in mine. I could understand April's void, even though her father was a half-truth I couldn't live up to. What I could do for her should be exceedingly clear. To quote a bloated, veiny, and mediocre movie hero, "We fill gaps." Mine were expanding like the canyon always opening between Wile E. Coyote's feet. April's were fixed and immutable.

We were together for a little more than a year. You might think April could have been a new lease on my next life, that I could have kept my relationship with her going, bring it out into the light and enjoy it. You might think I would have embraced the possibility of legitimate love, wallowed in the sticky sex like a fat hog, recharged my empty soul—but that wouldn't have been real. Instead, I grew to hate myself. I could see the inevitable end of my relationship with April, that I would eventually disappoint her. I would age out. She would eventually be revealed as not having the strength to be a stepmother. Our relationship was all fantasy, nothing more. So I went from having difficult emotions that I'd worked hard to understand to a kind of numb, free-floating emotional limbo. That was when Mrs. Bleatwobble moved in and lit the fuse that would burn toward my ultimate devastation. She graced me with yet another poem in yet another dream. This one was meant to show me that pain always wins, that I was a fool, and April was to be my lesson learned. It was feeling like a fool that burned the poem into memory, no matter how hard I tried to forget it.

* * *

Was raining grey the day we met, wish I knew that flash of blue you showed me.

The next time we spent some time the day was alabaster, words got inked and stories told of sexual disaster.

Wish I was the wind that blows through your hair, across your skin that you showed me.

Wish I knew the reason, wish I felt the pain, wish I lived the moment, wish I knew the way to stay unchanged.

Was raining red, we met again, secrets bloomed, the dance resumed, said to you I wish I was your lover.

Was raining silver, pink, and purple, the conversation on that day was naked, kneeling, beating, reeling, breathing slowed, anticipating what we knew that we would do if we were lovers.

Wish I couldn't leave you, wish I felt something else, wish I knew the buried years, can't seem to find the time or tears, perhaps the flame's the only answer, rich red blood the only cancer.

Wish I knew what she would do if she knew we are lovers.

* * *

A short time later, with speed and mercy, Mrs. Bleatwobble administered the *coup de grâce*. You may still think she was just a figment of my imagination, a convenient way to excuse my own behaviour. You may not yet be convinced of her reality, her malicious intent, of the lightning bolts she was capable of wielding. Think of those old 1950s movie reels of atomic bomb testing. That was how it felt the second time in my life that words decimated me—the first time from Deb; this time they were April's words. Nothing was left standing after the shock wave blasted through. Surgery is never perfect. Surgery is performed by humans on humans, and no matter how minor the procedure—a vasectomy, for example—mistakes happen, and the body does what the body will do. Of course I got April pregnant.

CHAPTER 14

BIRDS OF PREY

My memory wasn't working. I stood in the vestibule searching for numbers, glass dividing the world of the vital from the world of decay. This made me think of God and death. Did God have a plan with a prepackaged meaning provided just for me? A plan with no need for me to look for it—it would be there even if I didn't see it or understand it, spiritual batteries included? Could I take comfort in knowing that what was happening to Deb, to me, and to the children we'd made was part of something larger, that there was somehow a reason for all of this suffering, a spiritual home at the end of the day, lights on, fire crackling, dinner on the stove, a kid practising piano, conversation, security, love? We all want that. I wanted that. Why couldn't I have that? Or maybe I could if I could just let go. Maybe all I needed to do was a cosmic trust-fall like you're supposed to do in a cheesy group encounter weekend and let God catch me. Given all the inexplicable things that had happened thus far in my life, what was wrong with an alternative all-encompassing, beautiful, simple, uncaused, unexplainable thing ... God? I wanted simple, comforting relief and rest. I could admit that. I was close to the edge of endurance. If Jesus Christ had shown up in my living room and told me it was all true, that

God did have a plan for me and I didn't have to worry anymore, I would have broken down and cried like a child.

I remember being lost in these thoughts as I see my arm rise and my index finger extend to push the buttons. I remember forgetting the code. I try and remember the sequence of numbers but can't. I think of numbers, of all the people who have stood exactly where I am, remembering numbers, not remembering numbers. My heart drops down into the unknowable infinity of numbers. Maybe that's what God has over numbers; he claims to be knowable.

There are so many mysterious, mathematical structures, ancient pillars made of numbers. Famous ones like the Fibonacci sequence, prime numbers, the golden mean, infinite numbers like pi, and Euler's equation, (which is a mathematical acid trip) but I like Zipf's Law and its cousins because it turns numbers into aliens living in our midst unseen, showing up in almost everything we do without our knowledge. When we write a book, build a building, play baseball, or run a stock market, Zipf and his gang of aliens show up. All Zipf ever said was to take the most common thing in any group—for example, the word *the* in a book—and count the number of times it appears, then take the next most common item in that group—let's say it's the word *and*—and count the number of times it appears, then continue that process for each less common item in the group and watch as a formula magically appears from nowhere without anyone having designed it into the system—a *power law*. And that premise holds for any collection of things in any complex system, whether human engineered or natural; a map of roads or veins in a leaf. What is a big-brained primate who needs love to make of all this random chance?

If Zipf and Jesus went for a beer and I got to hang out and listen, would I have been comforted or depressed? I think Zipf would say that in this reality there's a tiny sliver we understand and within that sliver we see order, life has order, and things make sense, so it also makes sense that there's a deep underlying order we *can't* see. We each have to find our personal purpose and meaning within this order. That's the essence of being human.

Jesus would ask how order gives rise to meaning. Zipf would reply that as part of an ordered universe we are part of something larger than ourselves, and in that belonging there is personal meaning. Jesus would ask whether belonging gives you the ability to lay down your life for someone you love. Zipf would answer that in belonging there is love, which is simply a more intense and subjective kind of belonging created by relationships. Jesus would ask whether Zipf could calculate the scaling frequency of love as a product of belonging and if a power law that emerges? Zipf would have to admit he couldn't answer because love is not a force or matter, it's a personal, subjective experience, so even though he could calculate belonging from the distribution of social groups, like families, there would be no way to calculate the existence, or non-existence, of love. Jesus would then offer that perhaps love is contingent on consciousness and is thus a mysterious epiphenomenon of a complex, dynamic system—the self-aware human mind—and that as part of an interdependent whole—the set of all humans— love is beyond calculation. Zipf would agree, and Jesus would say, "Fucking right on, Zipf! Love is incalculable!" He would slap old Zipf on the back and chug the rest of his beer.

Then memory offered up the number I was searching for—4505, the exit code and address of the Arbutus Lodge long-term care facility, which I couldn't leave without punching in because people with dementia wander through unlocked doors out into the wider world, get lost, and die.

* * *

Is there a word like the German *schadenfreude* for a strange mix of relief and guilt? I don't know, but the combination is real. I felt it. Deb's apartment was half bachelor suite, half hospital room. The bed was more hospital, with rails and adjustment hardware, motors and belts. The room itself was more apartment, with a bedroom area, sitting area, TV and stand, tiny counter and sink, one cabinet above, one below. But the two things that filled me with trepidation were the oversized bathroom muscled with chrome handles and pulls, and the thick metal rails with heavy bolts and fasteners hanging from the ceiling above the bed like something from an abattoir. I was long used to the simple, almost friendly handicapped sign with its wheelchair logo that appeared everywhere in the building. We'd had one hanging in the car for a few years, four aces in the poker game of parking. But the overhead lift track was new to me. I had no idea such things existed, though it made sense. What do you do when a person can't lift themselves up to a sitting position anymore? How do you get them out of bed and into a wheelchair? We had installed a shower grab and toilet rail at home about the same time as we got the handicapped hanger for the car. Lester had come in to do it—he wanted to be sure everything was anchored properly. Anthony helped him. I could have done it but was glad for one less thing to worry about.

Lester could barely look Deb in the eye. The boys and I were used to her diminished body and blank expression, but it shocked people who hadn't seen her recently, and Lester had seen her only three or four times in the last few years. Every time he came by for a visit she cried uncontrollably, then cursed him out for having lived instead of Katherine, then told him what a bad father he was. Who could blame him for not visiting more often? Her vision was so clouded that she looked in your general direction not at you. Her optic nerves were almost completely demyelinated. The struggle to comprehend was a mask she wore constantly. Lester wasn't used to this new version of his once extraordinary daughter.

I asked the administrator about furniture. The previous family was happy to let us keep what we wanted; they would donate the rest. We politely declined the ancient television and fussy old-lady dresser. We had an extra smart TV at home and Deb liked her dresser from our bedroom, so those we moved in. The boys were big enough to help, and it gave them the satisfaction of service to their mother. Anthony helped too. He'd been an almost weekly fixture since sobering up. The house hadn't been that well serviced since Lester was a young man.

Helping Mom had become a healing theme for Adam and Micah—pushing Mom around in her wheelchair, getting things for her, helping her up the stairs to bed. She was less threatening to them that way, less alien, and they regained some control of their home life as Deb's control of her body ebbed. Now we were entering this next unknown phase. Deb was going to live in a care home, in an apartment that was empty because the previous occupant had died, as had the one before that, and the one before that. Crumbs of death were piled up in the corners, the heavy sighs of the survivors still damp in the walls.

The boys went through Deb's things as she sat in her chair in our bedroom for the last time, showing her this and that, asking if she wanted to take this or that. I had made up a few boxes, which they were dutifully packing. Deb seemed happy. The anger had drained into resignation since the hospital had let her come home for the day before going to her new home. How do you accept the broken body you inhabit? What does it feel like as it breaks a little more each day? Those were questions I wanted to ask this woman who used to be Deb, but the thoughtful and wise person capable of answering them was long gone.

The morning moved into afternoon; check-in time approached. The hospital had given strict rules for the day. I was allowed to pick Deb up and bring her home to pack. We were expected at Arbutus Lodge by 3:00 p.m., where Dr. Scarlatti would take charge as captain of the foundering ship the *Deborah Becker*. I never liked Dr. Scarlatti's name; it sounded like scleroti, like sclerosis. She made a baker's dozen of doctors that had been on this voyage to the edge of the map with us. Once Deb was sure the boys had packed what she wanted and I was sure she had everything she would need, Adam and Micah loaded up the boxes. The new TV and Deb's dresser were already there waiting for her.

With one son under each arm Deb struggled down our stairs for the last time. The boys aimed her at the chair by the front door. She plopped down while I set up the wheelchair. I had been taught how to do a seated transfer. You place the wheelchair perpendicular to the patient, close their feet together, and place your feet on the outside of theirs in a wide stance and lean forward. They then clasp their hands together behind your back or neck, you reach in around their chest, clasp your hands behind their back, and pull them up into you while arching your back and lifting with your legs. Once you feel their full weight you spin on your heels, maintaining your squatting position, and place them on the wheelchair seat as gently as you can. Don't forget to lock the wheels. This was not a skill I had anticipated the need for, but I became a pro. I used the same technique to transfer her from the wheelchair into the front seat of the SUV, but it was tougher because the SUV was higher than the wheelchair. No matter—I had this down pat as well. The boys scrambled into the back seat as I folded up the wheelchair and slid it in the back with the boxes.

The Arbutus Lodge was only about ten minutes from our house. The front entrance had a circular driveway, and as we pulled up, Dr. Scarlatti and Deb's section manager, Anton, were there to greet us. They provided a flat-deck dolly for the boxes, which the boys took charge of, while I went through the Deb-as-patient wheelchair process. Dr. Scarlatti and Anton welcomed Deb, but her mood had turn dark again and she refused to speak to them. Her face pulled into a deep scowl as the reality of her new home full of geriatrics settled in. The doors slid open and the boys followed Deb and me with the dolly. Dr. Scarlatti excused herself. Anton took us to the elevator and we all rode up to the second floor, west wing, where Deb's apartment was; number 208. Anton walked us down the hall into the room and assured us he and his team would take good care of Deb. He tried to address her directly again but she wouldn't have it. She needed someone to punish.

The boys started unpacking as I transferred Deb into the armchair. They asked her where she wanted things to go, which lightened her mood. The space took shape, taking on some of her personality as the boys set out her things. These reminders of our past life stung me, but she became happier as the boxes emptied so I accepted the pain and let it pass. Staff dropped in to introduce themselves. Friendly residents poked their heads in with welcomes, all well past seventy but for one woman that I pegged for maybe sixty-five. We had the apartment set up in about an hour. Outside the window, it was a beautiful spring evening in May of 2014. Deb had spent four months in VGH waiting for this opening offered by someone else's closing. The apartment looked out on a courtyard, gardens, arbutus trees, and the setting sun filtering through their leaves; the room wouldn't be too hot at the height of summer. There were two dinner times, 5:00 and 6:30, and I suggested Deb choose 5:00 knowing her usual bedtime was 7:00. She chose 6:30 just to contradict me. Her notion was that now that she was rid of us, she would be less tired.

Just as the time came for us to say goodbye, Annie and Maye showed up, perfect timing! They were jovial and glad to help, and the strange emotions of the situation drained from the room. My guilt misted away, and the boys and I left to the sound of Deb laughing. The last thing I heard was something about her finding a boyfriend. These women had made the decision to be family when they could have remained merely related. What causes a person to choose messy involvement based only on a tenuous genetic connection? It's more understandable when people choose family based on a relationship beyond genetics, when there's an obvious relationship behind those decisions—maybe an emotional connection, maybe friendship, maybe a shared hardship. In the case of Annie and Maye, they just showed up at the house one day. Maybe because of what their grandmother told them about growing up with my grandfather, maybe because their definition of family required it of them, maybe out of religious convictions. In the end it didn't matter.

At home the rest of the evening was a new quiet. Rhombus was confused. Dogs are such creatures of habit and labs especially like to have a job. For years, Rhombus had had the happy job of cleaning up after Deb. He had become a dog navigator, responding to Deb's increasingly mercurial moods with either the comfort of his presence or scarcity when she raged. He always sensed what the situation required while benefiting from an endless string of treats bestowed by an incurable tremor. Now he looked at me as if to ask what had happened to his job, where had she gone. As people with progressive debilitation leave the wider world they shrink from the outdoors but take up more space indoors. The term *shut-in* is old-fashioned but accurate. Deb's presence in the world outside our front door had shrunk as she came to dominate the world inside it. When someone dies, the spheres of people that rotated around them in life pause to say goodbye. When someone is forced to retreat from the world in stages, without finality and definition, the spheres go out-of-round like a bent bicycle wheel and nothing stops. All of this in the expression on a dog's face.

After Deb moved out the load was so much lighter, but the guilt was bitter. I cried in my Scotch after Adam and Micah were asleep. The next day began a new, old normal: school, work, dinner, groceries, all of it happily mundane but with a giant hole in the middle. We went to visit Deb that day after school, to check in and see how things were going. We brought Rhombus; family dogs were allowed in on a leash. The front doors slid open, the inner doors slid open, and a new country beckoned, like a border crossing. We learned the emotions of our very own Checkpoint Charlie, crossing from the world of the free to the world of the constrained. The lobby was scattered with chairs in clusters, small sofas, recliners, coffee tables, and side tables; the carpet was commercial, neutral, and tough as a week's stubble. The front desk was off to the left, the sign-in clipboard and pen on a little peninsula, almost an outstretched arm reminding you to stop. We would become very familiar with the coming and going process as well as the administrator Gail, who sat behind the desk. She was always sunny and helpful; she could find the staff member you needed or give you a she-went-that-a-way to help you find your inmate. Such a nice prison guard.

The lobby was dotted with elderly people. There was one severe dementia patient accompanied by his personal aide. Families with money could employ a full-time care aide assigned to their loved one, lightening the load considerably on the institutional staff. Others were government-subsidized residents like Deb. We got our handout because of our family status with young children still in school; it didn't cover all our expenses but was a huge help nonetheless. I had spent our entire savings over the last five years, trying to keep up with not only the things we needed that weren't fully covered by medical benefits but with Deb's mental-health spending, unexpected things like a half-dozen car accidents in one year, house upgrades, and a new wardrobe for Deb every six months as she shrank out of the old one—all while trying to maintain the full set of activities that Adam and Micah were used to. I was given dispensation by the many kind store staff in the places we frequented with Deb. They would let her "buy" whatever she wanted and would allow me to return the many things, tags attached, that usually remained in the store's bag, untouched.

The denizens of the lobby lit up at the sight of Rhombus, so we had a kind of informal receiving line that took some time to get through, the wheelchair residents being slowest to arrive and the longest to remain. This was another custom of our new country that would take some getting used to. Things moved at the pace of a dirge, doors were reticent, elevators were slow. Because of Deb, elevators had become a habit for us. But Rhombus hated them and had to be coaxed in, where he would then lie flat on his belly like a cosmonaut pulling Gs, until the doors opened to freedom and all was instantly forgotten.

We went up to the second floor, down the beige hallway, and past the nursing station and supply room. Many of the apartment doors were open, making it feel more institutional, less residential. Rhombus said hello to all the passersby. Deb's apartment was on the left about three-quarters of the way down the second hallway. The door was closed so I rapped lightly, opened it, and poked my head in to be sure the coast was clear. She was sitting up in bed and staring out the window. It was hard to know if she was still angry, depressed, or lost in progressing dementia. She gave us a weak smile and the boys took Rhombus over to her and kissed her on the cheek. I closed the door and unhooked Rhombus's leash so he could explore the apartment. Micah told her about his day at school. Adam asked her if she liked her new apartment. She listened half-heartedly and answered sparsely, like a person weighted and dragged down.

Rhombus curled up on a spot he would come to adopt. Our little family stumbled along over this new and awkward terrain, quietly negotiating the fog until ever so slowly it lifted. It was approaching five o'clock, time to head home for dinner and a deep draught of survivor's guilt. We said our goodbyes, hooked Rhombus up for his dramatic descent, and left. I deliberately left the apartment door open in the hope that some of the life of the second floor, such as it was, would sneak in around the corner and lighten the heavy history wafting up from the carpet.

The ten-minute drive between countries became our twenty-first-century cold-war reality. I explained to the boys why I called the entranceway Checkpoint Charlie. Later, I tried to get them to watch *The Spy Who Came In from the Cold* with me but that lasted less than fifteen minutes. When I imagined Deb in her new life-not-life my thoughts became a cocktail of guilt, nostalgia, and if-only speculations. She wasn't dead but everything about this disease and the process it imposed was like an incremental death. The losses piled up over days, weeks, and years.

We stopped on the way home and got burgers, fries, and milkshakes to bring home for dinner. I reminded myself that this kind of eating would have to end quickly, or it would risk becoming a bad habit. I checked my pockets for more emotional energy but got only lint. The evening folded down around us as an inaugural small victory—we'd made it through our first full day without spontaneously combusting.

I cleaned up after dinner as the boys finished their homework and started gaming. Deb used to laugh at the language she heard emanating from each of their bedrooms. The first time you hear your tween-aged child say "Eat my ass, motherfucker" in a prepubescent voice, you either roar with laughter or your heart sinks. We roared. Our theory of child-rearing was to never force their behaviour underground. We preferred shock to ignorance. Now I had to carry that alone. There was guilt around every corner for me those first few weeks, not over the decision to move Deb—which had been Alfred Ba's, not mine—but over which one of us was supposed to carry on. Of course I should have been the one in the apartment and Deb the one to maintain the family and see the boys into adulthood. That would have been easier for Adam and Micah. I tell myself it would have been easier for me too, but that would be a lie.

As weeks turned into months, the new routine grew like weeds in the sidewalk, unwanted and unbidden but green and insistent regardless. I struggled with the frequency of visits. Quantity or quality? The boys' lives were busy with school, music, sports, and friends. I turned down every opportunity for research and advancement, putting my career on the lowest flame possible without ending all possibility of tenure. The powers-that-be understood but I knew this was not a grace unending.

There was usually at least one weekday when we could all make it at Deb's dinnertime. Rhombus got his job back, and Deb loved it. We learned how to time our arrival so he could clean up under the dinner table Deb shared with three other ladies. They all began to save things to accidently drop onto the floor for him. Thus began the highlight of the day for Rhombus and Deb, whichever day it happened to be. The boys took turns pushing Deb back up to her apartment, which gave the staff one less person to collect. She had lost the strength needed to wheel herself around. Her left arm was so weak that when she did try to wheel herself she travelled in arcs. We would take her up and I would transfer her into bed, sit her up, and we would talk or watch TV. As summer approached the days stretched, staying light until past eight, so plenty of evening was left for us to walk Rhombus when we got home. But this routine was also changing, it felt less like therapy because Mrs. Bleatwobble had moved out too. She was now always in Deb's apartment, sitting in one of the chairs. She'd melt away when we showed up and sit back down as I snicked the door closed. No one else saw her, but I still believed.

The most singular thing about travelling in the new country, the Country of Affliction, was its smells. Our sense of smell is the only sense directly connected to the emotional and memory systems of the brain. Smell can save you from death; remembering a smell that killed a fellow hominid can save you from variations of that same demise, though we don't need this skill much anymore. It's an evolutionary inheritance from a time before the development of our uniquely human prefrontal cortex, the part of the brain that abandoned Albert Brown when a bullet razored across it and that was now slowly forsaking Deb, one scleroti at a time. The smell of age is unmistakable; even the first time you encounter it you know what it is. There's an undertone of decay, a hint of death—not putrefaction, just bodily systems no longer flushing and cleaning effectively. The smell of commercial disinfectants, the smell of institutional building materials, concrete and carpet, the smell of bland food, coffee urns, medications—all unmistakable—these were the mnemonic agents of a foreign power, like informants in our midst, always there no matter what side of Checkpoint Charlie we were on.

Summer seemed to arrive quickly that year. I didn't notice the changes in the boys' schedules or the winding down of classes. It was a bit like driving on autopilot, lost in thought only to find yourself safely home. I had arranged for no work all summer. With one day left in the school year we took the ferry to Salt Spring. Thursday was always the best day to travel; the Canada Day long weekend made Friday on the ferry a zoo, a modern-day Noah's Ark.

We had five days to run the island guilt free, no Deb left glowering in the cabin, angry because she couldn't manage the terrain and we dared take a hike or go to the beach. Still it felt odd, no guilt but no real joy either. All our traditions were encrusted with memories of four, the smell of coffee and cinnamon buns, the creaks and echoes of the old schoolhouse turned art gallery, the blues band at the vintage car show, the peculiar mix of seaweed, salt water, and gunpowder from the Canada Day fireworks. Yet despite the strangeness, we had fun. In those moments when we missed her, one of us would voice our emotions. Mom used to love this or that, do this or that, say this or that. We had all learned to stand in our pain—to ignore it was the real suffering.

We took the 10:15 a.m. ferry home on Tuesday and went straight to visit Deb. Adam had bought her a scarf, Micah a First Nations healing rune, a stamped silver disc in a tiny carved wooden box. It was near 3:00 by the time we arrived. Deb was napping. We woke her gently, opened the curtains, and let the bright afternoon sun push Mrs. Bleatwobble out into the hall. Deb's face lit up when the boys presented her with their gifts. I remember thinking I hadn't seen joy on her face in at least two years, maybe longer. We spent more than an hour telling her about the trip and catching her up on the changes around Ganges, reporting the boys' final marks on their report cards from the previous week—it was all a joy for Deb. Even just a month before, she had reacted to news of the outside world with resentment. I was happy for Adam and Micah. The chronicle of their daily lives was welcomed for the first time in a long time. It was another turning point for them—doors that had been closed reopened.

We left in high spirits. We were eager to get home and retrieve Rhombus from the One-Legged Norms. Throughout that summer of 2014 Adam and Micah continued to recover from their mother's absence at home; the speed of their bounce-back was astonishing. I had been told to expect it but didn't believe it would be so quick. I underestimated the resilience of children. I knew there were prices yet to be paid, but we would face them when they arrived; there was no point in worrying about tomorrow's problems today. What I hadn't expected was how alone I would feel without even a severely diminished Deb in the house. We were a one-legged family living beside one-legged people. Some single parents are better than two, but most aren't. I can only know how I felt: spectacularly inadequate. Replacing a mother like Deb was impossible, replacing the feminine enchantment she graced our lives with was more than impossible, and replacing the icon that is a mother was the most impossible of all.

I focused on security and love and as many visits to see Deb as we could manage. The three of us became well used to the residents, routines and broom closets of the Arbutus Lodge. Even the smells dropped into background eventually, waiting for memory to call them back to espionage. Deb loved to be pushed around the grounds by her sons, through the court-yards, gardens, and meandering pathways. We would find a place to sit and visit, usually bringing her coffee in a to-go cup with a lid, which she could drink from despite the tremor. Rhombus usually came along, sniffing out the residents he knew, getting treats, doing clean-up duty, and exploring. Happiness is an infection; the happiness of a dog can make people happy. You could look at us sitting there in the sun as a broken family or a happy family—both were equally true.

Deb's brother Anthony visited her regularly. Their routine was more adventurous than ours. He could roll the neighbourhood with Deb, go to Quilchena Park or up to Kerrisdale for shopping or a coffee. Her brother John had all but disappeared; he moved around a lot and no one knew where he was at any given time, Lester heard from him only once or twice a year.

School started up again, with new teachers, new hockey teams, more carnage in the rear-view mirror; smoother roads ahead. Our days weren't done until seven o'clock at the earliest, ten at worst, so weekday visits became impossible. We made up as best we could with longer weekend visits. Hockey got in the way, not to mention the need for free time for Adam and Micah and downtime for me. Anthony had dinner with us once a week. He would take one of the boys to his game if I had the other's game and no teammate rides were available. The house became testosterone heavy. Judy dropped in regularly, checking up on us, measuring the slow shallowing of the crater where Deb used to be.

Deb settled into her diminished life. Maybe having all her daily needs met by someone else was a relief to her given all the disabilities she was battling. It's hard to know because the view from outside is so bleak for the one left to carry on. Carry on—what does that mean? It felt more like leave behind, leaving the mother of your children for dead and skipping off into the sunset. Now that she wasn't in the house, in need of constant care and a threat to the boys' emotional safety, affection between Deb and me started to return, or maybe it was unearthed. Maybe it had always been there but had been buried under the daily avalanche of pain. Maybe I wasn't that different from Adam and Micah. Once we'd established a daily distance, I started to feel safe again.

Trauma lives in your flesh and bones. I'm an expert—it's what I know. That doesn't mean you can't overcome it—you can. It does mean you are forever changed. That's what I feared for Adam and Micah. How would they be changed? They wouldn't know for years. Maybe I wouldn't be around to help them. Would they remain close enough to commiserate and help each other? I didn't know.

We had our first Christmas without Deb at home that winter. That Christmas Eve saw a rare snow. Adam and Micah were happier than they had been in years; though they loved their mother deeply, the progressive pall she had cast on the household was gone. My stress level had sunk back down to its normal state—background. I was watching the snow fall outside. The boys were asleep. The stockings were full and Rhombus was asleep on the couch beside me. I was sipping Scotch, softly humming "Silent Night" to myself. The lights were low, the fire was crackling; candles burning on the mantel. I cautiously ventured out into thoughts of the future and how we might remain a family without Deb there to anchor us.

* * *

Every generation is fettered to its ancestors like a Mississippi chain gang while simultaneously experiencing the mystery of brooding self-awareness. Sipping Scotch on a Christmas eve, watching flames dance in the fireplace, snow gently muffling down around the world outside makes one ponderous. As my thoughts began to curl into the seduction of sleep the phrase *terminal velocity* crossed my mind. Is there a terminal velocity associated with a falling snowflake? I doubt it. At first I thought nothing of this mind-wandering sidebar. I had learned the calculations in a fluid dynamics class years ago. My brain was digging up intellectual fossils. Then words began to form as I drifted down into sleep; singing began.

In your eyes are my wings and the ocean in which I drown,
I can't control your choosing.
In your sky I can see heaven excluding me,
I can't control these feelings crowding me.
I'm a river you take me up and hold me high,
your sky enfolds me until I'm dry,
You need pain with your pleasure,
I need pleasure to ease my pain,
you open your arms wide as the world, and I fall like rain.
David?

"Yes … ?" I was in a lecture hall. It seemed crowded with students yet utterly silent at the same time. The stage lights were bright but the seating light was dim and I couldn't make out any faces, only forms and shadows. The voice I recognized continued from somewhere in the back.

Why are you a river?

"I don't understand your question," I said in my professorial dream state.

In your imagination you see yourself as a flowing river.

"I suppose I believe I'm impermanent but part of something larger—maybe the flow of humanity, maybe the flow of time."

She resumed her singing, unseen, somewhere behind a pastiche of dark grey set against the glare of the stage lights.

In your clouds are my dreams and the blindness of my despair,
I can't control your passions.
In a vision came to me a bird of prey and spoke of you,
but I can't make out what he's saying to me.
I'm a river you take me up and hold me high,
your sky enfolds me until I'm dry.
You need pain with your pleasure,
I need pleasure to ease my pain,
you open your arms wide as the world, and I fall like rain.

Deb entered my dream. She was curled up under a streetlight, she looked dirty and homeless, asleep on the sidewalk; snow dusted the street, dusting her; falling on her as she slept, gradually deepening. No one was around, no one to give her shelter.

And eventually you'll be used up, dried out. Does that represent your death? the voice asked.

"Maybe." Soundlessly the setting changed. I found myself standing outside, under the streetlight beside Deb's sleeping form, snow falling all around us. "But you can predict when I'm going to die—you might even know already. You've done the calculations, haven't you?"

Yes, I have, but that's not important now.

"You're a product of my imagination," I said to the snowy street.

I'm not imaginary, David, I'm real, Mrs. Bleatwobble said. *I don't have to be physical to be real do I? Thoughts can become physical things, but someone has to think them first. I'm your words, your thoughts, your ideas.*

Don't you feel the snow falling on you? I do. Can't you feel it falling on your sleeping wife?

"I don't believe you," I said stubbornly, finding myself back in the silent lecture hall.

You imagine, and you believe. That's your reality, therefore I must be real—logically speaking. Your parents imagined you before you were born. You imagine things, believe them to be true, then those things become real, like the measurements you've taken of cepheid variables or your papers on dark matter. You create your very own reality that you inflict on others— perhaps afflict *is a better word—based on your boyhood experiences—logically speaking.*

"I didn't imagine space and time into existence."

But you did *imagine those things into existence, David—or, more accurately, you* do—*every moment.*

The stage of the lecture hall was now the street outside. I held out my hand and watched the snowflakes fall and melt on my palm. I imagined a snowflake falling in increments that divide in half at each point in space so the steps become infinite and the snowflake never hits the ground.

Reality is just your imagination David. Mrs. Bleatwobble continued. *The building blocks of your personal reality are the same building blocks every human uses to create a personal reality, you're all living in a story you tell yourselves..*

Did you know Deb was going to get MS?"

Yes I did, my dear.

"So that night when I looked over at her, across the pillow, after you read to me from that book and I knew she wasn't going to survive—that was you?"

You like to describe yourself as a sentient bag of meat, don't you, David? You enjoy that turn of phrase. Where do you, the sentient bag of meat, suppose that insight came from? I think you know it wasn't me. I'm neither a cause nor an effect, I just tabulate your ledger. Think of me as your life's boring old accountant.

"But why? What's the point? Who do you keep my records for? God?" I wanted to provoke her.

Hahaha!

I'd never heard Mrs. Bleatwobble laugh before.

For the future, of course, and for you, for your future. I was there with Albert Brown. Without him there wouldn't have been a Deborah. Without your family Deborah wouldn't have found a man she deemed worth marrying and your children wouldn't exist. All these records I've faithfully kept, all the causes, all the effects, and all the consequences.

"I hate my family. I'm not a violent drunk, and I'm not a deluded fool looking for answers from an imaginary deity."

And yet here you are, David.

"What the fuck does that mean?" I jabbed out the words.

It means you're a consequence no different from the consequences you abhor.

"How can I be just a consequence if I have the power to imagine my own reality into existence?"

Consequences are finite David, imagination is infinite.

"So how many ancestors do we trace back? Where do we start to count consequences from? Who can I blame?" I roared at Mrs. Bleatwobble, "I want someone to fucking blame!"

That's an unanswerable question, my dear. Even I can't tell you where your equation began and where it ends. When you step off the curb and have just a split second to ponder the chain of events that has brought you and that onrushing bus together, in that instant you will know this truth in every cell of your body.

"Is that how I'm going to die?"

You have many Christmases yet to come, she answered without answering. *Your rescue, reclamation, and redemption aren't complete yet. You're a modern-day Scrooge David, you still have causes to contribute to other lives—you and I are not done yet my dear.*

"I don't want to be just a cause in someone else's life and death," I said, almost to myself.

But you are David, you all are—that's a choice you most certainly don't have.

I pondered the abyss of this logic in silence.

Remember that vision? I made a promise to you then. Not that I have jurisdiction over life and death, but I do know when either are about to arrive … or both.

"Yes, I remember."

Until then, my dear. With that, she vanished from my dream.

I was back outside, standing in the falling snow as it became heavier. I looked under the streetlight where I had seen Deb. Her outline was there, drawn by drifts on the sidewalk—but she was gone.

CHAPTER 15

COLD GLORY

As soon as I heard Dr. Scarlatti's voice on the phone I knew something was wrong. She said Deb had entered what was called the active dying phase of the disease. The term *active dying* was new to me, an ominous oxymoron, it hadn't come up in the living-will meeting Deb and I had had with the doctor—at least I didn't remember it. That meeting was surreal for me. Deb was matter of fact. Sometimes her understanding of the disease and its consequences appeared beyond even the doctors' knowledge, as if there was this little Princess Agnes the Navigator somehow still alive in Deb's brain looking down on the landscape and seeing the entire picture long before the other people in the room did. The experience rattled me, as if a core Deb still existed that the disease couldn't touch and I couldn't access either. This Deb was going to show up at some point and hold me accountable for everything I did. This Deb would kill me if I didn't do everything possible to give our sons the rest of their lives back.

Dr. Scarlatti did most of the talking. I listened and asked a few questions—mundane questions, technical questions, process questions—at this stage of the disease I had no other kind of questions left. I hung up and looked at the boys, searching for the right way to explain what was happening. I had learned through the counselling process to tell them everything and then help them deal with whatever it was. Holding back wasn't saving them from anything; it was only delaying the inevitable and depriving them of learning how to be resilient and feel their feelings. That was a difficult lesson for me. Growing up abused made me default to protection, which I interpreted as standing in for them and taking the blows. Counselling had taught me what a big mistake that was early enough for it to make all the difference. I knew our sons couldn't escape the damage that came from their mother's suffering, but they would avoid extra baggage down the road because I pulled my head out of my ass in time.

I told Adam and Micah their mother's body was beginning to fail and she wouldn't live much longer. I remember this conversation making my breath slow and thick; trepidation squeezed my lungs. My mind was filled with dread over how they would react, but as they had done before, our sons surprised me with their outsized wisdom. They were calm and resolute. Dr. Scarlatti suggested we allow the medical staff to get set up and we come by first thing in the morning but they wanted to go right then, and so we did. It was October 2017, evening had fallen, and the short ride over to the other country was dark and silent, with no quips about Checkpoint Charlie. The lobby was quiet when we arrived. The day wound down early at Arbutus Lodge; so easily hum slumped into hush. I had always avoided bringing the boys later in the evening, not because of them but because it depressed me. Sunny and supportive while not avoiding reality—that was my go-to dad stance. Getting depressed was for late at night, alone, just Rhombus and me. Dogs always know when you're sad. He would curl up beside me, head on my lap, the dog version of *enough said*.

Day One

We made our way up to Deb's room. Adam and I were apprehensive, Micah was wide open. How he always managed that attitude still amazes me. He must have gotten some of the Princess Agnes gift. The counsellor said he was an extraordinary child, and I bowed to her convictions. I saw it many times when he took his pain full frontal, with no attempt to defend himself. He suffered and I watched, which was one of the hardest things I've ever had to do as a parent. Adam and I built defenses to retreat behind when the pain became too sharp. I went into full-on retreat and desertion

188

with April for a time. But Micah? He never ducked for cover, not once.

When we arrived at the room, the curtains were drawn and the lights dimmed. Equipment sat in the corner, not yet set up. Micah approached Deb, sat down on her bed, hugged her, and started to cry. She lifted her arms weakly and wrapped them around him. Adam stood beside the bed, where he too began to cry softly. At the sight of this I burst into sobs; the knowledge of our impending and final loss knifed into me, my breathing hitched, and sounds came out of me I hadn't heard since I was a child under the kitchen table. It was my turn to feel the entirety of the deep pain I had swallowed in only small doses until then, my turn for catharsis.

Adam sat down at the foot of her bed. She still clung onto Micah, eyes closed, but she sent out a probing hand to find Adam. She gripped him fiercely and pulled him close, as though all of her love had only one withered arm left to flow through. I cried and cried until I was dry. My sobs and staccato breathing eventually softened. A sinkhole of emotion had opened up and the ground dropped away, I had no power to stop it even had I wanted to, and I didn't. I was crying for everything. This was the beginning of my redemption gifted by the only human on the planet who could gift it.

I sat on the chair beside the bed. Deb opened her eyes and looked at me, croaking a word that was impossible to understand. It didn't matter because everything she wanted to say to me was in her eyes.

"It's your time, Deb," I said. "We love you, we're here with you, my darling. You won't be alone, not for a minute. Whether you know it or not, we'll be here."

Those were the words that came out. I don't know if they were the right words. The last time I did this I was a bit player, at the double death of Katherine the Great and Princess Agnes the Navigator. Platitudes had been fine then; no one expected more.

Dr. Scarlatti came in, greeted us, and talked to Deb in her Dr. Bedside voice, comforting and confident. I needed that too. She settled us in for the test of endurance to come. Mercifully there was no beeping, whirring, or hissing equipment to be used. Those machines were for *all measures*, and that was not what Deb had wanted. No life-prolonging interventions, no breathing apparatus, no hydration, just comfort. Dr. Scarlatti asked us to wait in the hall while staff prepared her.

I called Anthony, Lester, Judy, and the One-Legged Norms, then Annie and Maye. I explained the situation to them all, that we needed to take shifts. Anthony and Lester would take midnight that night until the next morning. Judy and the OLNs would take the rest of the following morning and afternoon. The boys and I would be back from late afternoon to midnight. Anthony and Lester would do overnight again. Annie and Maye would take the following day all day until dinner, Judy and the OLNs would take that evening until midnight, and that was as far ahead as we planned. They all made it clear that the boys and I should come and go frequently no matter who was on duty.

A nurse emerged and told us we could go back in. They had connected an IV to Deb's left arm and hooked up a heart monitor, but the sound was off. Micah went back and sat on the bed, and Adam pulled up a chair beside them. The three of them talked for a long time—that is, the boys talked. Deb couldn't reply but I could read the conversation on her face and fill in the missing words; I was her Ginny, she Albert Brown. We had had many conversations like this with Adam and Micah before the bad days started. It was easy for me to imagine what she might say. Unlike the boys, I had a head full of memories of the real Deb, the woman I had fallen in love with.

When you create new life with another human, the bond is unbreakable no matter the losses, no matter the failures, no matter the betrayal and the pain. Deb's face was alive in a way I hadn't seen in years. Of course, I knew this wouldn't last so I sat and drank her in, deeply. I tried with intent to pull these moments into every cell of my body. If I could live half a lifetime with images of my father raging through me, then I would live the second half of my life with images of Deb, Adam, and Micah huddled together in love, talking, laughing, smiling, animated, defying the deathbed if only for a time. I could feel the seed of my redemption cracking open.

Adam found *Braveheart* on TV, a family favourite. Deb always cried at the love story, felt the deep satisfaction of the revenge scenes, became angry at the betrayals and the injustice of noble William Wallace's sacrifice. She had the warrior's fortitude of her mother and the vaulting humanity of her grandmother. In another life she would have married William Wallace and died for him just as Marion Braidfute had done. I couldn't live up to a fantasy like that. For a time I buckled under the load but I consoled myself with the fact that I got up, albeit as a different man—nothing so noble as William Wallace, twice broken, but still I got up.

My blistered soul gained a great deal of solace that evening, watching Deb with our beloved sons. There was a joy in her eyes that I thought had long ago died. *Braveheart* is a long movie. Deb fell asleep about three-quarters through. The boys didn't notice until the movie was over. About then Anthony and Lester showed up. Anthony hugged his nephews, Lester stood off to one side, just like his emotions, beyond arm's length. The five of us shared the room for a time, we talked. I gave them the update such as it was, then the boys and I went home, leaving the night's watch to occupy the dark.

Day Two

The next morning I called the school and told them what was going on. Micah had refused to go even before I asked them how they wanted to handle this. Adam agreed with Micah that school should be on hold until *this was over*—that was the euphemism we used. After a late breakfast we went straight back to Arbutus. OLN Sr., OLN Jr., and Judy were there. Anthony and Lester had gone home to get some sleep. Deb was asleep but her sons' voices soon woke her. When they approached her bed again, she slowly rose to consciousness and smiled a soft, fragile smile. They each hugged her and sat down on the bed, the conversation started again, bouncing around the room.

Judy and the Norms asked questions of the boys, made comments. OLN Jr. told stories of his growing up with Deb, Anthony, and John. The boys learned of the mythic Mrs. Rain and her old-lady ninja skills, the back-and-forth battles over hockey balls, and the way Lester or OLN Sr. would have to go, cap in hand, to get the balls back. Sr. interjected that sometimes he had lied to Judy and just gone out and bought new hockey balls because he was afraid Judy, or worse, Katherine, would get into a fight with Mrs. Rain. Judy spent a long time telling Adam and Micah stories about their grandmother, Katherine the Great, with Judy interjecting "Remember that Deb?" every now and again. By this time Deb was fully awake, her eyes beaming. They discussed what Katherine liked to cook, her career in politics, her favourite movies and music. Judy told the story of Lester buying the station wagon and how Katherine turned it into the flagship of her personal political navy.

By noon, everyone was getting hungry so OLN Jr. and I went out to get burgers. OLN Jr. was light on his one foot, and it surprised me how easily he hopped into the car. The first thing he said after we got in was how sorry he was for all of us, including himself. He confessed his lifelong crush on Deb and joked about how if he'd had two legs I wouldn't have stood a chance. "Pun intended," he added.

"I agree," I said, but I knew it wasn't true. He wasn't the blank canvas Deb had needed back then. I was the unicorn she could paint, the My Little Pony of university boys ready to be named and trained.

I was taken aback to learn that he knew more of Katherine and Agnes than I did. He said he wasn't surprised that Deb had many of those same gifts. He saw all three generations of women in Adam and Micah—particularly in Micah. This was gut-wrenching to me. My sons had never had Agnes and Katherine in their lives and wouldn't have Deb soon, yet they had their legacy alive in their genes, but I was the one being charged with shepherding them into their future. It wasn't fair. I was inadequate. I should have been the one to die, at just the right moment, when they were old enough to handle it but young enough to cry in their mother's arms. That's what should have happened. But it didn't.

When we got back with the food Deb was asleep. Judy and OLN Sr. were playing the role of surrogate grandparents with love and wisdom: to my utter astonishment, they were planning the funeral. I hadn't even thought about it let alone broached the subject with Adam and Micah. I stopped myself from interjecting and just listened to them openly discuss how they wanted to commemorate their mom. That afternoon we ate burgers and planned Deb's celebration of life while she slept. It wasn't surreal; it was the most real thing we could do. It opened up a vast territory of remembrances that Adam and Micah could participate in creating—what kind of flowers she liked, what music and which books she liked, particular family keepsakes, stories that made her laugh, stories she liked to tell, milestones and significant events in her life, in our lives, in their lives. There's beauty in trying to capture the essence of a person's existence in the thoughts, experiences, and representations of the loved ones left behind. I had never looked at it that way before, but watching Adam and Micah eagerly participate in planning their mother's funeral struck me as profoundly meaningful for all of us. It was literally the outward expression of the version of Deb that would live on within each of them.

I started to cry. The five of them looked at me, bewildered. They were having moments of sheer joy and I was crying. I explained how beautiful and profound an experience it was for me to hear from Adam and Micah what Deb was leaving behind, and how those things marked who she was in their eyes and how she would live on. It also sparked the bitter remembrance that somewhere out there, maybe still alive, maybe not, I had a mother who had left me less than nothing. In truth this explanation for my tears was a half-truth. Yes, I felt all those things, but I also felt, again, as though the wrong parent was dying.

The dinner rodeo had begun out in the halls. The first time we had seen this show, the boys and I were dumbstruck. The staff, outnumbered at least ten to one, had to round up all the mobility impaired and dementia sufferers and get them into the dining room to the correct table at the right time. It was tragicomic. That first time we had simply watched, amazed and silent. But after we learned the routine, the boys would always wheel Deb to the dining hall should we happen to be there at dinner time.

It was shift-change for Judy and the Norms. I suggested they wait for twenty minutes until the elevators cleared, but both Norms said they would take the stairs. Again their abilities surprised me, and I'm not sure why. I suppose I somehow always pictured them more impaired than they actually were. I should've known better by then. We all learn to cope with our longstanding wounds, whether physical or psychological, and they become so much a part of us that we can't imagine ourselves any other way.

The commotion in the halls died away, but we wouldn't be joining the flow—Deb was dying and didn't need food anymore. What a thought. Daily we living organisms have to convert fuel to energy to sustain ourselves, and now one of us had opted out and decided to die. Although Deb couldn't have eaten even if she'd wanted to, other ways of prolonging her life were available, but she had refused them, and with death approaching she remained steadfast. She was a mountain, dominant and immovable—her true force was, as always, still in there somewhere.

I went out to get us pizza. Who knew fast food was death-watch suste-nance? The days of casseroles on the dining-room table while the soon-to-be dearly departed lay ensconced in a bedroom upstairs were mostly gone. When I got back Deb was asleep again and Adam and Micah were watch-ing TV—*Alaskan Bush People*, which they found hilarious and fascinating. They added *Hillbilly Handfishin'* and *Trailer Park Boys* to their repertoire not long after. We ate and talked, eventually turning off the TV in favour of playing music over Deb's Bluetooth speaker. Both boys had inherited an eclectic taste in music and enjoyed finding new artists; they roamed the downloads on their phones, choosing songs Deb liked or new songs they thought she might. We were convinced she knew we were there and could hear the music and conversation.

Deb and I hadn't told the boys many stories from our time at univer-sity together, mostly because many of them weren't age appropriate and some would never be parent appropriate—no kid wants to hear about their parents' sexual escapades. That night I chose to tell them the story of the Naked Pagans vs. the Salvation Army. I omitted the fact we were high on acid, but other than that it was pretty much a blow-by-blow description. They were astounded their parents had ever been so young and rebellious. Some of the humour of that story was lost with the acid-trip omission, but they still found it hilarious and surprising. It was then I realized they should know more about who Deb and I had been before them. I went into great detail about the station wagon and how many people we used to load into it; they loved that the car was a part of Katherine's history too. It also helped overwrite some of the fears they'd had while riding with Deb as her driving skills evaporated.

All of these stories helped the three of us recapture life before multiple sclerosis. Deb was restored and I wasn't in need of redemption. I told the boys how we met, how pathetic I was, how smart and beautiful she was. I described meeting Katherine and Agnes for the first time, how I could feel the brilliance and strength in them, how I understood then why their mom was so extraordinary. I even hinted at how different this was from my own mother and my childhood, which was a mistake because they immediately wanted to know more. It wasn't a happy story, I said, and this wasn't the right time for it, but I promised to tell them all about it sometime in the future when it wouldn't detract from the good stories about their mom.

The song "Sweet Surrender" by Sarah McLachlan was one of Deb's favourites from a Vancouver girl who had made good. When it came up on the playlist, she stirred and floated up into the conscious world. We gathered around her and watched her wake. I studied every nuance, every twitch of her eyelids, the changes in her soft breathing. When her eyes finally opened, we were so close we must have looked like disembodied heads. She smiled, with her eyes especially, and we each leaned in and kissed her on the cheek. Her skin was old-lady soft, papery, much more so than her actual years. *Active dying* popped into my head, thoughts about the things I had seen, images of her suffering, uncontrollable bodily functions, furniture surfing, countless falls, how light she'd been the last time I transferred her into her wheelchair. As quickly as the mental pictures came I pushed them away. I looked into her eyes and said, "I love you, my darling wife."

Micah was holding one of her hands, Adam was holding the other. Their bond was wordless. The music had moved on to another Sarah McLachlan favourite of Deb's, "Witness." Beautiful words, Sarah, questions hanging like smoke in the air.

Anthony and Lester showed up early. Deb was still awake so they had a chance to talk to her and join the conversation. Lester was an old man now. He was still unable to acknowledge being one of the sources of dysfunction in the family, and he mainly talked in platitudes and weather reports. Anthony had missed the early years with Deb and me and most of the boys' early lives as well, but he was fully present now. He straightened Deb's hair, searched her eyes, smiled, comforted—his was an empathy born of total loss. He had no life outside of us, at least not yet; I hoped he could make one for himself someday.

Deb's favourite music continued beneath the sparse conversation. Adam and Micah were growing tired, and I was in that fidgety stage before the crash. As the clock threatened midnight Deb fell asleep, so the boys and I left and Lester and Anthony took the graveyard shift for the second night.

Day Three

Annie and Maye arrived just after 7:00 a.m. loaded up with food, photo books they had made, keepsakes from the farm, and mementos from their side of my family. They brought a picnic of bread, muffins, butter, jam, cheese, sliced ham, pickles, cookies, fried chicken, potato salad, and a cooler of beer. We got there around eight. The boys had already eaten breakfast but they dove into the picnic basket. Family made food was destined to be Adam and Micah's favourite thing about a day's work at the farm, and there was no passing up this feast. We had been there for less than an hour when Deb woke. Adam and Micah said good morning, kissed her cheek, and told her Annie and Maye were there too. They closed in around Deb's bed and she began to cry. Maye hugged her, Annie hugged her, they cried, the boys teared up, and I slumped into a chair, crying yet again.

The reality of the situation swam over us all, unspoken but understood, that this could be the last time we would all be together with Deb. At times there is a wistful joy alongside the pain; at other times there's only pain. This time it felt as if gravity had ceased to be, and untethered we floated, heartsick in the knowledge that soon Deb would not awaken.

Annie and Maye prayed with Deb. We weren't a religious family; we were an irreligious family. I hated this God being prayed to, this God who was represented by my abusive, alcoholic father. But, in that moment it didn't seem to matter that it makes no sense to hate a fictional being. Their words to their God opened deep wounds in me. Years of sorrow poured out.

Annie prayed, "Lord Jesus, please be with your servant Deb in her final hours as she prepares to meet you. Bless her with your peace that passes all understanding, and fill her with the love of her children and her husband and all of us who love her down here. Fill her with your divine love and open your arms to her as she crosses over to you."

After a pause Maye continued, "Comfort those of us left behind with your holy spirit and keep us secure in the knowledge that we will see Deb again one day in your heaven, where she will have no pain and no suffering. Hold her in your loving arms until we get there. In your name we pray."

"Amen," everyone said in unison—except me.

In that moment my hate for my father was disembowelled. I don't understand why. My sons clung to their weeping mother. Annie and Maye touched them, rubbed their shoulders, stroked their arms, and whispered private prayers to them in words I couldn't understand. I never believed in God, and I don't to this day. But I do believe in something, I'm just not sure what. Rationally I understand that this display of love from these two women had pierced the tumour I'd hosted all my life. I acknowledge my profound emotional deprivation growing up without this kind of love and the damage I took. I understand that we all crave love. We need love like we need oxygen, and the lack of either will kill us, immediately or eventually. I understand how these things are. I don't understand *why* these things are.

As we all eventually ran out of tears the sorrow lifted, replaced by a deep joy equally as inexplicable as the death of a lifetime of hatred for Carl Samuel Becker, the Tin Man. Another profound mystery from the same infinity that we each come from and will each return to. Not heaven, nothing so simplistic. Something like our source, like the ancient concept of the well of souls, or like the Buddhist idea of reincarnation but for particles and forces, we are star stuff said someone once between tugs on a hookah. In the end it doesn't matter—pick your story, imagine your own version of Shambhala. What matters is finding beauty and joy in how temporary we all are and in the time we have together, be it short or long. Pain taught me to always choose vulnerability and love. End of sermon.

The rest of that Saturday was the Woodstock of death vigils—no drugs, but lots of music and open hearts. Maybe this was what church was supposed to be like; I wouldn't know because it was never that for me. Deb was in and out of consciousness, her sleep becoming deeper. When awake she was increasingly a spectator, as if she were moving away from us, floating up toward the cheap seats, leaving us to watch her recede.

So much good food meant we had no need to leave. We talked and talked and talked. We covered all my family history from Graf-Otto and Purple Helmut to Grandpa Felix and my father, thankfully not in gruesome detail but enough that the boys were shocked. They looked at me with new eyes. Other than the prayer, there was no talk of God or Jesus. Annie and Maye were not proselytizers; they simply lived their lives by the paradigm they chose. The way all people of faith should do, in my irreligious opinion.

Besides family, we talked about farming, school, and sports, we checked in on how each person was doing—their thoughts and emotions—and we discussed the future. The most profound conversation of that day was a tear-filled exchange Annie and Maye had with Deb. We were back to chronicling family again, this time their side of my relatives. Unlike my side of the Beckers, where only Adam and Micah comprised the next generation, kids galore filled Maye and Annie's side of my family. Sensing Deb's thoughts, no doubt because they were also mothers, Maye sat down on one side of the bed and Annie on the other, and as they took Deb's hands they promised to love and care for her sons, to fold them into their families, to always look out for them, and to teach them how to work, how to be good men, how to be good husbands, and how to be good fathers one day too. They repeated these promises over and over until they were overwhelmed by their own tears.

Adam, Micah, and I watched silently, full of wonder. This was a country we couldn't travel to. It seemed almost an ancient ritual of motherhood around a sacred fire. Love, power and wisdom poured into the room on a feminine tide. We were speechless. It's sometimes wise for men to be speechless when it's so obviously feminine power ruling the moment.

I had always imagined Deb, Katherine, Agnes, and even Ginny, who I knew only from family lore, as dreadnought mothers. Great battleships displacing history by the ton as they ploughed through their times, bringing their families safely along from one generation to the next. I could see from this sacred ritual of motherhood unfolding before me that there is dreadnought in all mothers, and again I wondered what had happened to my own mother's sacred power. I felt an overwhelming sense of gratitude at the great good fortune I had found in Deb and her family, though we were losing our very last dreadnought mother.

Afternoon turned to evening, and Maye sent us home around eight; the women would stay until Anthony and Lester showed up. We were exhausted from the emotions of the day. Deb was asleep again. When we got home the boys went to their rooms to game and I walked Rhombus. I needed some fresh air to help me puzzle out why sacred words directed at a mythical being had affected me so deeply. The many kindnesses of Annie and Maye had loosed my tears, both that day and in the past, but that I could understand. Why prayer had so pierced me was and still is a mystery to me.

Day Four

When we got to Arbutus Lodge on Thursday morning, Anthony and One-Legged Norm Jr. were there, but no Lester. Anthony had gone to get him, but he was falling-down drunk. Lester had plumbed his emotional depths and found them to be twenty-six ounces. When Anthony showed up alone, Maye insisted he call someone else, and OLN Jr. was the obvious choice since they had history. They had slept in chairs most of the night. The graveyard shift was tough: Deb slept the entire time, so there was no opportunity to talk to her. The hours were thankless.

I sent the two of them shuffling off down the hall toward the elevators. Adam, Micah, and I settled in for the day. That morning sank into me like teeth, an old familiar sadness—the gloom that was my constant shadow before my life with Deb began. The birth of first Adam then Micah had, I thought, banished this part of me permanently. The joy of parenthood is powerful magic, and I thought this beast was gone for good. But this particular Thursday morning was the full-on malevolent black dog, as though the healing of yesterday was just a dream. The weather was grey, the light was swollen, even the texture of the fabric on the chair was intrusive—everything was an assault. Institutional smells soaked the air. Deep cleaning took place on Thursday mornings. Floor polishers droned. My psyche was burnt skin.

The boys found sports to watch on TV, ski-cross from Quebec. The hum of voices helped. Deb slept. Her breathing seemed shallower than it had been the day before; that was only my impression, which I couldn't trust. I did notice she no longer shifted position in bed. Another ability lost. The morning rose slowly toward noon, interminable until Judy and OLN Sr. showed up with lunch. I hadn't thought about feeding Adam and Micah, but thankfully Judy had. She'd made a casserole. Who decided that finger sandwiches and casseroles were the homemade synonyms of death?

The arrival of Sr. and Judy helped to lift the shroud off the day. Sporadic conversation misted the room but Deb didn't wake. I was afraid that yesterday was the last time she would consciously join us, and if so, that would have to be okay. Yesterday was the best dying day anyone could want. She deserved that to be her last conscious memory of us.

Would that memory stay with her in some way? Was she aware of it in her current unconscious state? Would it dominate her memory only for what little time she had left? One thing I was sure of: I wanted our sons to have at least one more day like that, a memory of their mother that would remain as bright on their own dying day, hopefully many decades in the future. But I had wanted lots of things that hadn't happened over the last few years. I had wanted things to not happen that did. I had learned the illusion of control.

Staff came in, which cued us to leave. The physical body required daily maintenance tasks that were better left out of memory. The boys and I decided to go home for a few hours. Judy and Sr. would stand watch for the rest of the afternoon. We took Rhombus for a walk in the park which never failed to lighten our collective mood. He was good therapy. We foraged but found no food in the fridge for dinner, so I ordered pizza … again. It was past six when we got back to Arbutus and sent Judy and Sr. home for dinner. Deb was still asleep. As a family we'd always watched nature or science documentaries together. It was a ritual we all enjoyed. After the boys were in bed, Deb and I would watch English murder mysteries. This particular day the boys and I needed a distraction, so over the sound of Deb's shallow breathing we watched *Nature* and *Nova* after which I introduced them to *Luther*. The pin stripes and tweed of English murder mysteries became a thing for the three of us from that day on.

OLN Jr. and Anthony showed up about eleven but neither boy was ready to leave. I left them there with their uncle and Jr. for as long as they wanted to stay. I had no trepidation on their behalf; they could handle whatever happened during the night. I went home alone, unsure of how *I* might handle it. When I opened the door and stepped inside an obstinate silence greeted me. The house refused to speak, the pots and pans slept, the furnace snored, the toilets and the laundry sat stoic—all ignored me. No fleeting catastrophe flashed in the periphery of my vision, no malign presence sat knitting in the corner, no Mrs. Bleatwobble. I was annoyed with my former tormentors for being absent. I didn't deserve to be ignored. If I wasn't the one dying, I should at least suffer along.

I took Rhombus for another walk. Anthony brought the boys home about 2:00 a.m. I had left the front door unlocked and was asleep on the couch when they came in. I thanked Anthony and locked up. The three of us went to bed. I was helpless over what to expect tomorrow, Friday the 13th but Saturdays were always my nemesis.

Day Five

I had no idea what time it was. Rhombus woke me, wanting to be fed. What day was it? Friday. I needed coffee. I always needed coffee but this morning was junkie level. Adam and Micah were sound asleep. It was almost eleven. A shot of panic jolted me, then I remembered Judy and Sr. had planned to spell Anthony and Jr. that morning. The Friday morning world had no doubt lit out with the starter's pistol while we slept. School would be pulsing with adolescent energy absent Adam and Micah. The global Rube Goldberg of people and cities everywhere spun on, heedless of the time-less Greek tragedy we were living. Maybe I was dead and this whole thing was a nightmare. Maybe Deb was at home with the boys and the dog and I was the one dying, trapped in a hall of mirrors, a kind of unconscious awareness. Maybe that's what being dead is—infinite reflections of yourself devoid of time and context, with no future and no history, just a hollow now populated by a déjà vu of fleeting, inaccessible memories. Holy fuck, my mind could be the master of morbid. My mind has a mind of its own; what a shame I couldn't control it. Where was that coffee?

Two hours later we walked into Deb's room at Arbutus Lodge. Judy and Sr. were eating sandwiches. Judy said Dr. Scarlatti had come by and wanted to speak to me so I called down. She was in her office. I left the boys with Judy and Sr. The weather had turned from grey to rainy. The windows in Dr. Scarlatti's office were at an odd angle; in fact the entire east wall of the building was lined with these narrow windows high up that started at the ceiling and projected down and out over the gardens at a shallow angle before they notched back in, a kind of transom letting light in from outside but keeping the offices private. The whole thing looked as if it had been designed behind the Soviet Iron Curtain.

The last time I was in this office, Deb was telling Dr. Scarlatti her *wishes*, the ones now dictating her dying process. We had also talked about phy-sician-assisted dying, but the laws at that time were asinine. You couldn't request it in advance, even if you knew you were going to suffer a lingering, painful death. Without the ability to communicate your desire during the active dying process, when all that's left of you is suffering and your ability to speak is buried under pain meds that render you barely conscious, you are expected to ask for assisted dying? And your loved ones can't do it for you; they are to be spectators only, taking in every grisly nuance of your suffering as your parting gift of memory. Stupid fucking politicians and their moralist asshole constituents ... but I digress yet again.

Dr. Scarlatti said she thought we were within twenty-four to forty-eight hours and Deb would likely not wake up again—no euphemism was offered. Pain or discomfort were not evident, she said, so she felt no need to increase the dosage of meds in Deb's IV. I was to make sure everyone knew the time was close and to be on standby. The more loved ones who are present to share the final moments, the better for all, especially the person dying. Dr. Scarlatti was sure, based on her long experience, that the dying person had an awareness of other people in the room and that bulwark of family and friends had a soothing effect on all present. I thanked her for her kind words and the care she and the staff had given Deb. I thought about the receiving line at our modest wedding in that West Side backyard all those years ago and the thanks we had given out. The juxtaposition was cruel.

When I got back to the room all was as I had left it, with Micah, Adam, Sr., and Judy in soft conversation and Deb asleep. I was about to sit down when Deb groaned loudly. We were jolted. She began to twitch and moan, unintelligible words burst forth like muffled explosions, her sunken face was writhing. Before I could think of what to do, Micah was at her side and Adam was out the door to the nursing station. Deb's breathing was panicked, spit bubbled on her lips. I felt my face blanch with fear. *Please don't let this be how her final moments will pass.*

The nurse bolted in and went straight for the IV, releasing a bolus of meds with the breakthrough plunger. We watched for a timeless minute until the calming began. Dr. Scarlatti entered a few minutes later and took control in her usual calm way. She increased the level of drip meds slightly and told the room a version of what she had just told me, then explained that what had just happened was a form of nightmare. They would turn on the sound of the heart monitor to its lowest level, she said, so we would default to looking at it rather than focusing on Deb's breathing—this was less stressful for the family in her opinion. She again encouraged us to put everyone on standby. She had given this talk many times in the past, yet her empathy was genuine and fresh. I was grateful for such compassion in what must have been a rote response, and I thanked her again. She and the nurse left.

I made the calls: Annie and Maye, Anthony, and of course Lester. He didn't answer, so I left a voice message. Judy called OLN Jr. before we settled into the rest of the afternoon a bit rattled. I watched Deb's breathing closely; the background beeping of the heart monitor didn't help. I noticed everything whether I wanted to or not—the expression on her face, the geography of each inhalation, each spotty exhale, the sounds in her throat, listening for fluid, the interval, the regularity, the depth of each breath. I sat and listened for changes, and watched, transfixed.

I watched.

I watched.

I watched as her breaths rose and fell. We think we breathe with near mechanical regularity but we don't. It's the same for the beating heart—irregularity is built into the system, an indicator of health. In this process, I watched the irregularities becoming infrequencies.

I watched.

I watched.

After what must have been an hour of this silent, fraught observation, I couldn't stop myself from descending into a kind of sympathetic OCD, so I offered to go out and get burgers for everyone. That way Judy and Sr. could stay and I might be able to reassert control over myself.

The post-burgers evening puttered along without the drama of the afternoon. The closer the end comes, the more this watching process leaves the modern world behind, reverting back to a time before knowledge and control, when mystical incantation prevailed and the death watch was shrouded in sacred ritual. Birth and death, the great and ruthless equalizers.

The boys had turned on the TV to watch the evening lineup on Cartoon Network: *Adventure Time, Futurama, Rick and Morty*. Deb and I loved these cartoons, the *Bugs Bunny* of our sons' day, with levels of humour for kids and adults and even the odd PhD. We all settled in to have our brain chemistry adjusted by cartoon humour. I doubt Judy and Sr. had ever seen these cartoons before but they laughed along and asked Adam and Micah questions about the plot and the characters. It was surrogate grandparenting at its finest.

Anthony and Jr. showed up early, just before ten. Anthony had gone by Lester's apartment, but there was no answer. It took some convincing but I got Adam and Micah to agree that we'd go home, get some sleep, and be back early in the morning. I would set an alarm for six o'clock and we would be back by seven. We left Judy, the Norms, and Anthony on the watchtower.

Day Six

She was so drunk. I was in bed. She was in the living room on the sofa, singing along to the Holly Cole version of "I Can See Clearly Now." She was loud, off-key, and fumbling the words, and I couldn't help it—I started to laugh. She couldn't hear me. The music was cranked, she was cranked. A SWAT team could have come through the windows and she wouldn't have heard a thing. I got up, got the video camera and snuck into position. What a video that made. I caught the back half of the song. God, she sounded bad. God, she sounded drunk. I stood out of her line of sight, sniggering, recording, planning. She rarely got drunk, but when she did her naturally bright disposition became silly. Yet even in this soon-to-be very embarrassing moment she could do no wrong in my eyes.

The song ended and I skittered back to bed. It was past one in the morning, after a house party on the Labour Day weekend of 2001. She shut down the living room very quickly for a drunken woman, came into the bedroom, fumbled her clothes off, and tumbled in beside me. I pretended to be asleep. She pressed her luscious nakedness against me.

"Let's make a baby, I want a baby," she slurred.

"Let's make it, baby, I want you, baby" was what I heard.

When had she turned into a 1970s soft-core porn star? I covered my mouth and snorted into my hand. She ignored my response, or maybe didn't even hear me. She found my cock, which responded on cue as it always did, climbed on top of me, and guided me inside her.

We were making Adam when the phone rang and woke me up. It was just after five thirty; my alarm was set for six. It was Anthony. Deb was stirring, not exactly waking, but something was happening. I woke the boys, made myself coffee to go, and we were out the door in under ten minutes. I called Maye from the car. OLN Jr. had already called Sr. and Judy. The boys and I got there just before six; Sr. and Judy were only five minutes behind us. It would take Annie and Maye a lot longer. Arbutus Lodge was over an hour away from the Fort Langley farm. If they could get on the road before the morning traffic it would shorten their travel time.

The night nurse had been in before we arrived. Anthony and Jr. had asked her to wait for me before changing any settings. They weren't sure if she was waking up or in distress, and neither of them wanted to make that call. The boys and I surrounded the bed, each of them taking a hand. I studied her face, looking for something that might tell me what to do. Sounds were coming from deep in her chest, something between wheezing and words. Her head was moving a little but the rest of her body was still. Her breathing was barely perceptible as the heart monitor beeped a quiet hopscotch pattern of pauses and pulses. Still she seemed calm with no sign of discomfort on her face. When the night nurse came back, I told her we wanted to wait and see, so she said she would stay close. We settled in and watched.

Not much changed for the next hour, but as daylight seeped into the room her breathing seemed to become a little stronger, as if a circadian response mechanism was still working as it should. Judy opened the blinds to a grey fall daybreak. Deb's body twitched.

The boys burst out with "She squeezed my hand, she squeezed my hand, she's squeezing our hands! Mom, Mom! Wake up, wake up!"

Her eyes opened, then swam—even the dull daylight seemed to be an assault. It wasn't clear whether she could see us, and an eternity of seconds slid by as she struggled for purchase of the outside world. She worked to crest the fathoms of deep unconsciousness holding her down; you could see it happening, a physical effort. She struggled to find our tiny island of loved ones in the vast, trackless blue.

To this day, to this very moment, at any moment I choose I can see the dilation of her pupils as her eyes went from blank to aware. In the split second it took for her gaze to focus into perception, she hitched my breath and stopped my heart. She looked at me with a knowing love I hadn't seen in years. She was more than there—this was the Deb I would have died for. Why wasn't it me? It should have been me.

She still couldn't speak but neither could I, and words weren't necessary;

this Deb could read my mind. I felt forgiven for being the survivor, forgiven for all the things I had done and said during our darkest days together. I was to be a better man in future; she had given me all the legacy I needed. All of this went unspoken in only a moment that left me hanging in an infinite present like a cartoon astronaut, suspenders hooked on the crescent moon. The bond we had created through Adam and Micah was indestructible—maybe all unconditional love is. That was certainly what I felt for our sons, and for Deb—again. Her gaze had made me whole. I thought my unconditional love for Deb had died of conditions but it was there all along, buried under miles of pain and loss.

She looked at Adam and Micah with yet more love. Her face barely moved, but her eyes smiled, and they both dug into her frail body and cried. They told her how much they loved her, they promised to be good and kind, they promised to remember her. Micah said he would talk to her every day, play her music, and write her songs. Adam promised to help people with their pain and suffering, to find her strength and kindness inside himself, to always be the best of her. The final gift I had hoped their mother would be able to give them—one more day of being with them, being fully present and able to love them—had begun.

We all crowded around her and consumed the moments like mannah from heaven. More than an hour had passed, but no one noticed the time until Annie and Maye arrived. They went to Deb and hugged her. They renewed their promises of how they would love and care for Adam and Micah, and this time they mentioned me too. I crumpled into a chair and cried loudly and long, bitter tears that felt like failure. Each person present got their chance to speak to Deb one last time, though she couldn't answer. Those of us who needed it—Anthony and I—got our redemption, but Lester left his gift unopened, and the opportunity to be forgiven for his alcoholic failures was lost to him.

Adam and Micah clung to her, alternating between uncontrollable grinning and sobbing as their awareness whipsawed from immersion in the sublime now to the inevitable cruelty of the immediate future. We all felt it. We all drank in every sweet drop of time against the bitter absence to come. The spirit in the room was powerful, thrumming with life, a harmony focused into one perfect note of shared experience. I was not prepared for the transcendence of these two perfect hours, and even less prepared as Deb began to fade back into unconsciousness. We had been gifted a bright burning before the flame went out. The Fates are faithful in the execution of their duties.

Deb smiled softly with her eyes one last time before she closed them and slipped back down into darkness. The room was resolute: we would see her through to her final moments, bear her up on the storm of wild love we were blasting out into the universe, as if a solar wind for her shinning transport.

I watched.

I watched.

I watched.

Her breathing was shallow and raspy. The heart monitor had begun to stumble. We were silent in anticipation. The nurse had come in and opened the drip up to maximum. There would be no more waking up and no sensation of organs shutting down. The seconds ticked over between breaths. There was no colour left in her face. It was grey and sunken. Her mouth was tightening around her teeth. The creeping progression of the death mask had begun. The rasp of her breathing gradually grew to the rattle of fluid replacing air. The force needed to fill her lungs was increasing, her inhalations were becoming convulsive, oxygen was becoming scarce. Judy pulled the covers up to her neck, sympathetic to the cold that was taking over her body. The shutdown cascade would start soon. At some point there wouldn't be enough oxygen to go around. The autonomic life-support systems would take priority. Her extremities would be left to die. Secondary systems like the endocrine system and nervous system would be starved of oxygen in favour of the cardiovascular and respiratory systems. Organs would begin to fail.

Her breathing steadily gave up momentum. The intervals between breaths stretched. The beeping heart monitor dawdled, its path becoming crinkum-crankum like a lost child. As death approached we instinctively closed our circle ever more tightly around her bed. Hands reached out to touch her. Hands reached up into the air, beseeching palms upturned, prayers were whispered, mixed with sobbing. The stuttered beeping of the heart monitor and fading death rattle slowed in unison as all became stillness. Mrs. Bleatwobble was quiet and watchful in the corner. Clocks ticked. The sun rose and fell and rose again. We were carbon petrified beneath the stacked plates of generations, watching one of us turn to diamond. Time and place ceased to be as Deborah Jane Becker, the last dreadnought mother, ceased to be. It was Saturday, October 14th, 2017, one hundred years and one day from Albert Brown's incomprehensible, death-defying fate.

CHAPTER 16

THE OPEN SEA

And then she was there, alive in patterns and colours, snippets of song, words exchanged and moments shared, all erupting like fireworks—feelings, smells, emotions, a starburst from some deep chamber of my catacombed memory. My head swirled with concussion, and as my vision cleared I could see her, I could hear her, she was right there in front of me.

"Hi, Dave," she said simply.

I stammered.

"Pensive and nonverbal," she said. "How charming."

Our first exchange of words all those years ago.

"Kabalarian," I said.

She smiled. "I'm glad you remember."

"Deb, there's nothing about you I will ever forget."

"You forgot me for a while," she said. "But I was gone too so it's okay. I don't blame you."

"I'm so sorry, Deb, so sorry. I love you, I always will. Can you find a way to forgive me… for everything I did? All of this—" I groped for words as I flailed an arm at the room. "It should have been the other way around. Adam and Micah need *you*—this should have been me." I thumped my chest with a closed fist. "It should have been *me!*"

She put a finger to my trembling lips to quiet me. "But it wasn't you. It is what it is."

"I hate that stupid expression."

She grinned with mischief. "That's why I said it."

"Remember our honeymoon?"

"Of course," she said, "every precious moment."

"I can't go anywhere on that island without seeing you. I see you in our house, on the street out front, in the garden, on campus—you're half of me. I can't believe I'm losing you!"

"Dave …"

"Yes?"

"I know you have a daughter."

"Oh God, oh God, oh God," I wailed. "I'm so sorry, Deb! I'm as bad as my father and my grandfather."

"No, you're not. And even if you were, it wouldn't matter now. You know what matters. You know what you need to do."

"Forgive me please, Deb."

"I forgive you, Dave, and I love you. I always have, even when I was saying all those horrible things to you on my worst days. Underneath it all I always loved you." She paused. "Now it's your turn to forgive me."

"I forgive you, Deb. I love you more than my own life. It's so hard for me to be the one left behind."

"Promise me you'll look after our sons."

"I promise."

"And take Annie and Maye up on their offer to help, and let Judy and Norm Sr. be grandparents, especially since they don't have grandkids of their own. See, I'm leaving you with a ready-made replacement family."

"From the moment we met you were everything to me. You gave me a family, you gave me people to belong to. You made me a whole person, you gave me a new life, just like you did Adam and Micah."

"And you gave me the Battle of the Naked Pagans." She smiled again, a wide, radiant smile. "Dave, remember that video?"

"The 'I Can See Clearly Now' video?"

"Yes."

"Remember the cat? And don't say the name you gave him—you can be vulgar sometimes."

"I know," I said. "Rafael."

"Remember the night I came home from the double-vision basket-ball game?"

"Of course."

"Remember, Dave. Help the boys to remember. Give them good things to remember. The bad years need to be burned along with me."

"I promise."

"Tell them lots of stories, and when they're grown up and they can handle it, tell them *all* the stories."

"I will."

"Dave?"

"Yes?"

"I could hear everything. I knew you were all here. These were the best six days of my life."

"*Don't go!*" I yelled.

* * *

I don't remember much, at least not in the "do you remember the time when" sense. The vision was all encompassing, with no time or place to fix it down. The experience felt not so much beyond time and space as somehow devoid of it. I lost sense of the room, of Adam and Micah and the rest of them. I was alone in a moment that had stopped, and only the past existed, only memory, but somehow much more—spirit, energy, infinity. I don't know. I didn't understand the experience then and I don't now. It was mystical, transcendent, an eternity spent at the edge, looking across an abyss. I knew I would never be the same. She was gone, then she was there, then she was gone. A kind of void followed the thunderclap of revelation, first a roar so loud it was nearly silent, then only the electric buzz of blood flowing in my ears as she filled my embattled senses with her presence. She appeared there in front of me in less than an instant as though the quantum universe had chosen to reveal itself to the naked eye. She kissed my lips and I sank down into the timeless deep with her, unable to float my disbelief. She spoke to me. I felt her words on my skin.

"Goodbye, Dave."

I remember gasping. I remember the feel of Adam's shoulder under my hand and the seam of his t-shirt, the image of the flatline on the heart monitor, the scent of Micah's hair under his baseball cap, Anthony's profile against the window, the presence of the others in the room. The smell of worn leather came to me with the sound of a baby crying. She smiled beautifully; her eyes locked on mine and words began to form in my mind.

* * *

Memories crack, cobblestoned moments beneath a heavy footfall,
boots climb the hills to find a view of the ocean scape,
bearing away words and smiles on tides of remembrance.
Paced and timbred hearts sound 'round the rocks and piers;
we hold each other in paper arms while the swelling pools rise,
soaking in the water's cool destruction,
a slumped sinking that folds us down as we gently accept the sea,
leaving treasure trunks behind to float the beaches of green tomorrow.

Now that we are gone and the sight of land is lost, we can turn to fishing,
the boat gently rocks and slaps the rhythm down while we fix the line.
Soft sounds on subtle breezes, scents that mingle with our breathing,
coffee and sandwiches wait for sunrise, the sky the colour of purple lips.
We fix the tiny fish to the hooks, one treble through the upper jaw,
one treble beneath the dorsal fin; our game is bigger.
It's easy to forget the land, the beach, the streets, and houses
once the bait has plopped over the side and the line has whizzed out
of sight;
prop the rod and plant a foot, now it's time for coffee and morning buns,
the best time of a fishing time, the best morning of a fishing morning.
Open the lid and lift the thermos, open the spout and fill the cup,
the first smell that isn't sea is bitter rich and liquorice creamy.
We can think of no better time or place in the whole history of the
whole world,
so perfect there's no need to forget what came before because it never was,
that's the power of morning, and coffee, and a fishing sunrise

... waves lapping wood
... orange canvas life jacket
... polished oars with crackled varnish
... pewter-coloured oar locks
... navy blue peacoat and tan cabled sweater
... sturdy black boots and a fine red cushion to sit on
... not a sight to be seen but the smiling ocean, teeth glinting in the rising sun.

* * *

Day One
David?
"Yes, you old hag, I'm here."
So am I. Mrs. Bleatwobble ignored my insult.
"Is it time?"
Soon.

We were in my father's church on Fraser Street in the old neighbourhood, in the sanctuary. The walls were lined with stained-glass windows high up near the ceiling. Their Gothic arches offered little colour; it was night and dark outside. The wooden pews were finished in a soft satin sheen and red carpet filled the room, running up to a small stage dominated by a pulpit in the centre made of the same blond wood. Choir pews stood behind the pulpit, flanked by two small sets of stairs. On each of the flanking walls above the stairs hung a wooden bulletin board, crafted of the same blond wood and shaped like small Gothic windows. They were posted with removeable numbers and letters, gold on black, displaying church attendance, the date, hymn numbers, and Bible verses for the week's theme. A retractable projector screen suspended from the ceiling above the pulpit was rolled down, obscuring Jesus on the cross hanging on the back wall above the choir pews. On the screen, a porn movie was playing with the sound off; the scene showed people having sex in the pews of a church. The stained-glass windows of the movie church were dark too. And in the movie church a movie was playing with people having sex beneath darkened stained glass windows and in that movie church yet another movie played of people having sex in a movie church with darkened stained glass windows; ultimate night was outside the infinite regression of movie churches. Night was eternal.

"Why did Deb have to be the one to die?" I asked. "It should have been me."

Her answer echoed in the silent sanctuary. *No reason. It could just as well have been you...or somebody else, a slightly different you, perhaps a slightly different her. It still would have been meaningless..*

"Was there a connection to Albert Brown?"

In a manner of speaking. The probabilities were inevitable, and your wife just happened to arrive at the right time.

"And what about my family?"

Your ancestry created so many probabilities even I can't say what consequences may yet manifest from their history. Don't worry, your children will find out. Whispered violence, rumours of war, said Mrs. Bleatwobble, quoting my thoughts.

"Fuck You!" I said. I felt no fear, only hatred. "Deb had to die to rescue me."

She was the one all of the consequences ended up connecting to. In the crosshairs so to speak...like Alber Brown. Sorry David, I'm being ever so callous. And did she? Rescue you? You've had all these years to reflect.

"I was a fool, all the things I didn't understand, things I didn't see, I hate the person I was but she didn't. That was the person she rescued. She killed that person a little bit every day, in the same way the disease killed her. Her version of me survived and I saved our children from you so because of her we were all rescued."

And what have you told your sons about the things you did? I overheard you make a deathbed promise.

"Everything. I told them *all* the stories," I said, sinking beneath the innuendo of infidelity and clandestine fatherhood..

Even the ones you hate yourself for?

"I told them I love them more than every day of this life," I said in a penetant whine, "and anything that might come next—if there is a next." I felt my sureity drifting. "And I would have traded everything for it to be me. But it wasn't."

And your daughter? Mrs. Bleatwobble asked.

A calico cat appeared from under a pew, came over and sat at my feet.

"I told the boys about her, and I told her about them, and about myself"…a second calico cat appeared, "and all my failures, even the ones she already knew about." A third then a fourth calico cat came to sit by me and more were coming from under the pews, some ignored me, some watched me unflinchingly, fear pooled in my loins. "She's kind and wonderful, so are my sons," I struggled to stay composed, "all three of them turned out the best any father could hope for."

I caught movement in my peripheral vision, a lick of flame and a wisp of smoke, then Mrs. Bleatwobble walked out onto the stage through the hidden backstage door my father had appeared from every Sunday for decades. The cats took the stage with her as more came from under the pews, by now there were dozens. She looked demonic, as if all the sins of all my ancestors, and my grandfather, my father and I animated her. She crossed and stood behind the pulpit. She smiled at me and the movie froze in place with a woman dressed as a nun forcing herself on a man's mouth while she pulled his hair. All the movie churches froze. Infinity stood still.

Is this what you imagined it would be like, David?

"Dying?" I asked.

Looking back on your life and asking your children to see and understand all the different yous who bumbled about in the course of your days.

I chased a fleeting feeling of uncertainty to the edge of a chasm, searching for the right words. "I didn't imagine how small it would make me feel."

What about your beloved science, all your personal accomplishments, the insights you're leaving behind for others to build on? Don't those make you feel important? You spent your life on them. Did you waste your life, David?

A memory of roman candles came into my mind; the smell of gunpowder, the shapes of fireworks against the night sky on Halloween when I was a boy. I always thought those shapes were so beautiful, so delicate, but when the fireworks stopped they disappeared. "My work is insignificant compared to the vast unknown," I said, "but I still love the mystery of it all."

All humans are insignificant, David. You come and you go. Even when you're alive you're not conscious most of the time—you sleep, you daydream, and even when you are conscious you live in an imaginary world. You are ephemeral, my dear, in your very essence. Didn't your father ever quote James

4:14 to you? You do not know what will happen tomorrow. For what is your life but a vapour that appears for a brief while then vanishes away.

I looked around the sanctuary. All was so familiar, inexplicably comforting. "My father was wrong."

So to spite him you chose to explain yourself as a map of neurons firing or a grand correlation of information processing that builds in loops then erupts forth a person? Isn't that just another way of saying the same thing? Another hope of things unseen? Superstition?

"I don't know. Can't you tell me?"

I can't begin to imagine how you see yourself, David, unless of course you can, then I can see right through you and beyond, into your future. All the answers you've so desperately sought all your life but failed to find aren't accessible to me, otherwise I would surely tell you, my dear.

I could feel anger returning. "No you wouldn't. Everything you say is a manipulation. I've lived without answers and I can die without them too."

But you are weak David, you've said so yourself.

I walked toward the stage and picked up a cat, held it in my arms and stroked it's fur until it purred.

What do you think Deborah felt as she greeted her death without answers? Mrs. Bleatwobble asked.

"She felt loved. That I know. She told me herself."

She was sacrificed for you, David. Do you think your children understand what was lost so that you could live on?

"Fuck you and your inquisition!" The cat leapt from my arms and I looked away, pondering the red carpet, feigning bravery.

It's your life, David, not mine. I just record your choices..

"You're the same old harpy you always were," I said, gathering a few pebbles of courage. "I know what you can't do—imagine, dream, question, wonder why. You can't even *change*! All you are is history and probability, you're a nightmare made of yesterday's choices and my yesterdays are over so fuck you!"

You're powerless against history and probability, David. The only thing you have even the least power over is the moment, and once you make a choice even that ort of power is gone. All of your choices were made in chains.

"But I still made those choices," I yelled back as my anger rose. The movie started again but this time with the sounds of moans and sighs echoing in doppler effect from the infinite dark. "They're the most meaningful things I did in my life," I screamed, "the choices that created Adam, Micah, and Andi. They are my choices!" My scream echoed down into slience. The movie froze again. Mrs. Bleatwobble replied in calming tones as if giving comfort.

All of you are just tiny ripples in an infinite ocean, including your beloved children, David. Your problem is one of scale. You're a finite self-aware creature with an infinite imagination imprisoned in a doomed body alive in only a tiny raindrop of spacetime. I can't imagine the suffering you were born into…pun intended, my dear. Each of you pops into existence then passes into nonexistence soundlessly, with only the slightest twitch of energy in universe upon universe of endless energy—just a twitch.

"And you're assigned to me, so that means when I *twitch* out of existence you're gone too. I christened you, and soon you'll die with me. Mrs. Bleatwobble is dead; long live Mrs. Bleatwobble." I raised an imaginary toast to my imaginary tormentor.

You're right, my dear. When you're gone, I disappear.. I'm merely your witness and there won't be anything more to witness..

"Witness!" I found myself screaming again. "You've picked through my life like a junkie rifling through a trash can."

That is my job, David, distasteful as it may be. And what did I find in that trash can called David Becker? I found Graf-Otto, your grandfather Felix, your father Carl, and even the infamous Purple Helmut. The only one I couldn't find in you was your mother. The only women I found were the ones you lost too soon; Deborah, Katherine, and Agnes. Imagine what things would be like right now if Deborah were here with you. I can't but you can. What if your sons had their grandmother Katherine to grow up with, or if Deborah had had Agnes just a little while longer? Use your imagination, David.

"Andi wouldn't have been born."

You're right, your daughter wouldn't exist. Perhaps her Fate will be different than the rest of your family.

"I know she won't be toremented by you. And I can imagine all those things; I do imagine all those things. I can dream about Deb anytime, and

Katherine and Agnes too. I can call them up and have them with me whenever I want. They're in Adam and Micah too—even Katherine and Agnes who they never met. We're all in each other and we never leave. Adam, Micah, and Andi will have me all their lives, and pass me down the generations. My body will live on in the bodies of people hundreds of years in the future; my thoughts, my ideas, my genes will be alive—tiny bits of me, a manner of speaking, a gesture, an attitude, a tint of hair colour. You'll be gone but I'll still exist in my future family. You hate that."

You like the thought of my hatred, David. I've heard you think it before.

You may calculate the consequences of my decisions and foresee the future, but wherever it is that I'm going, whatever becomes of *me* next you can't follow. You end when my imagination ends."

Fly, fly, slip away, Mrs. Bleatwobble whispered softly into my ear, beginning to weave my ending, *through the steel and concrete, through the frowning doors.*

Fly through the night over sleepers on still wings, through indigo shadow and dreaming streets.

Fly from the binding to the wide-open lands, deep and secure in long, cold glory.

Fly from the pain, from the endless inquisition, from the marionette strings of a staggering dance.

Fly from home, from walls wet with memory, from the dirge and desire of bright, bloody day.

Fly from your body, numbered and nothing, fast through the flesh like the arc of an arrow.

Fly from us. Waste no more breath here. We love you, a prisoner in our busy bones.

"I wrote that for Deb."

It's time, Mrs. Bleatwobble replied.

* * *

"Dad—Dad—*Dad!* Wake up! You were dreaming."

I feel a hand rubbing my arm and wake to the beautiful face of my daughter, Andi, her eyes full of love and care, hovering over me. She gives me a few moments to fully find myself in three dimensions plus time.

"It sounded like a nightmare," she says.

"An old one that came back," I agree. "It's gone now."

"I confirmed with the hospice society's loaner program person." She continues, hovering and fussing over me, fixing my hair, touching my face. I love the attention but don't want to admit it. "They'll be here this afternoon. I thought you'd want to be awake for that."

"Fine with me," I say. "But it'll be a bitch to get in the house, and I'm not crazy about dying in the dining room."

"We've talked about this, Dad." She is clearly a bit exasperated with me—again. "There's no way to get a motorized bed upstairs and around the corner into your bedroom. The smaller equipment's no big deal, but there's nothing we can do about the bed." I can see the annoyance on her face.

"I just want you to be sure you're up for this." I don't know why I feel so conflicted about my daughter's ongoing help. I suppose I feel I don't deserve it.

"Enough already! I'm not changing my mind, and all you're doing is offending me by asking every other day."

"Sorry. Accepting help isn't my strong suit."

"You mean accepting help from *me*."

And there it is—my buried insecurities unearthed, even after all these years.

"Your guilt is *your* guilt," she continues. "It's not mine and I don't want to have any of my own, so I'm doing this. Please let's not debate it yet again."

"Okay, point taken. I'm sorry." She goes silent, which always makes me uncomfortable. "Everything goes back when I'm gone—literally?" I try to rescue the conversation with the cheery fact of my impending demise.

"Yes. Gone just like you, but we won't cremate the bed."

Smartass, I think. Was her mother that sharp? I can't remember, or most likely I never noticed. "Nice comeback," I say.

"Micah or Adam will help. Both of them offered, and Jake too, so don't worry—we have your corpse covered, Dad."

"Smartass." This time I say it.

Andi is here often, now that my time is short, most of the time with her husband Jake. They're not married; no kids, but I refer to him as *husband* because *partner* reminds me of Peter Sellers in *The Party*.

Turns out April found her sugar daddy and he was a good stepfather to Andi. They didn't hide the fact that he wasn't her biological father so she came looking for me when she felt the need. I guess I didn't give April the credit she was due. My excuse is the me that was involved with April was a colossal mess second only to the mess I was before I met Deb. The grind of losing Deb so slowly and painfully dragged big chunks of me back under the kitchen table. Understandable don't you think? Maybe even pitiable.

"You do realize I understand what happened between you and my mom—and why?"

"It's the only thing left in my life that still makes me feel foolish," I confess, "like I used to feel when I was a teenager."

"So the relationship that created me was foolish?"

"Not the relationship. Me, I was foolish—and sometimes I still feel that way. You're not the first person who needed to understand. I'm sorry to have put that on you and your brothers. They had to find that same charity of spirit."

"Charity! What the hell, Dad! My love isn't charity. I understand because I love you, not the other way around."

"You're not hearing me." My voice rises despite my effort at control. "Maybe you'll understand when you're old and take stock of your own life. Listen, sweetheart, I don't know why feeling like a fool is such a trigger for me, and I don't understand why embarrassment burns so hot for me. I do know it has nothing to do with you or your mother, or Adam and Micah or their mother. This goes all the way back to my childhood and it's never left me. I can't help it and I don't understand it. I love you to bits, no less than I love Adam and Micah."

"Okay." She pauses to consider my words, then says, "I guess I had issues of my own. I spent a lot of my teenage years fantasizing about what you were like. I had some pretty bad relationships in my twenties while I was trying to decide if I loved you—the real you—or if I loved a fantasy. That's what happens to girls with daddy issues. Or have you forgotten?"

That hurts. "No, I haven't forgotten." I feel like a fool all over again but I don't share my feelings this time.

"I'm sorry," she says, "that was mean and Evan was a good stepdad."

"Did I mention I love you to bits?"

"About a million times."

"Good for me," I crow.

She smiles. It's the same arresting smile as her mother once seduced me with. The same crystal-blue eyes.

"I've lived a good life, Dad, despite not having you until I was eighteen. Mom was a good mother—she *is* a good mother. I had friends who grew up stepkids, they did fine. I did fine. Better once you were in my life. Even better after Jake came along."

"He's a good guy, Andi. I'm happy you found him."

"You ended my daddy issues, Dad. He's a lot like you, so I guess you did more than end my issues, you showed me what I needed, not what I thought I wanted. Does that make sense?" She looks thoughtful and a bit shy.

Andi isn't the brash woman her mother once was. I'm in there somewhere, introspective and unsure. "You grew into a smart, confident woman, my darling daughter. I saw those qualities in you on the day we met. I was so nervous. I was afraid you'd hate me."

"And I was afraid you wouldn't love me, that something from your and Mom's relationship would poison us."

"No chance. You were the second last person on my list to ask forgiveness from, your mother was last. That was tough. Regardless, I'd decided to love you no matter what, whether you'd forgive me or not; whether she'd forgive me or not." I pause for a long moment, reflecting.

"Dad?"

"Yes?" I tilt my head, waiting.

"Did you really have a conversation with her ... with Deborah"—she pronounces the syllables carefully—"after she died?"

"Yes, I did, Andi. I know it sounds insane, especially coming from me, a sometimes atheist, sometimes agnostic astrophysicist with a history of throwing FUs at a God I don't believe in. There's not supposed to be anything after we die. There shouldn't have been anyone there to have a conversation with. As I said to your brothers, I'm fine if you decide I was hallucinating in my grief. That's a perfectly plausible explanation, and you'd think of all people I'd believe that—but I don't. This life is complex, unpredictable, and uncertain, and we're all incomplete. That science I know with one hundred percent certainty. That's why I believe I had a conversation with her after she died."

"And what about your dream-demon, old lady Fate? Is she real?"

"As real as rocks," I say. "At least the ones in my head."

"I don't know what to say, Dad."

"You don't have to say anything, Andi."

* * *

At eighty-nine, I've outlived almost everyone I know. The whole clan is pulling for me to make it to the next milestone. Colon cancer has other ideas, I think. Stupid fucking disease. Happily, though my ass is broken, my brain still works. I'm fine with imminent death. I know how to die.

Five grandchildren, six great-grandchildren—don't ask me their names, but when I see them I know each one of them—almost. I'm sure you understand. And of course there's Andi, and her Jake. I'm happy to be the patriarch of a good number of good humans, and very happy with the legacy I'm leaving behind in them all. Forget the career and the money, it's the pieces of me in them I'm most proud of—not myself per se. All three of them were smart enough to take the best of me and leave the worst, which is a bit surprising in Andi since I didn't meet her until she was eighteen. I wish I'd had more time with her but I didn't know she existed, though I suspected, until then, and she had a father, or so she thought. I wasn't there to give her as much as Adam and Micah, obviously because of what the boys and I went through together, but also because I didn't have the courage to face April and ask the obvious question. No matter the choices we make we're always three people. That's the real trinity. If I had the cheek to invent a religion, my hell would be a single chair in a locked room.

* * *

So here I am, a broken down superstitious old man and former scientist at peace with his contradictions or blind to them, a well reationalized life. It's my turn to die. The drips and beeps are now mine. The years sneaked by on padded feet, trailing footprints of molecular memory, imprinting my cells with all the people I've known as if they were fossilized in the once-wet sand of my forming. That's where Deb is now, in what's left of my body.

Behind my rheumy eyes, in my wrinkled dreaming, she's a tide that rises in me and floats away the hours, pooling up into me whenever I need the salt and swish of our slattern summers. Blue and bluer, on she goes, an endless warm ocean all bump-and-grind enticing. Floating on my back with my eyes closed I see clumps of watercolour clouds roll lusty-fat and lazy across the voyeur sky. In my memory speckled thoughts of silver mercury bend around a grassy point, a welder's plume of flashes and sparks sprayed wide by the sun across a crystal skin of water that undulates in my wet ears, softly rhyming ancient incantations to me as it ripples. The shoreline looks different from down here, the headland is unfamiliar but I know the history in those reeds and rushes, my days hang from the crabapple and the Garry oak like old moss; my time and my place, grown into the people I love like roots running in reverse, up from the generous ground into their bloodstreams, pumping them full of my story, my genes, my history; beautiful, ugly, poignant, and proud. The outgoing tide rolls and pulls me along. I open one eye and see their smiling faces. I wave as I sweep past, no second thoughts or reservations. I round a grassy point surrounded by coins of copper in the redshifting dusk, past the very last spit of land, on my way out to meet the persuasive depth of the smiling sea.

POSTSCRIPT

The Inspiration Behind the Story—
Songs, Poems, and Real-Life Events

I very much hope you enjoyed my first novel; there will be more to come. If you did, please leave a review on social media and start a conversation with me. You can find me on Goodreads, Facebook, Instagram, and TikTok, or at kenevren.com. Thanks!

This novel was inspired by one cataclysmic, real-life event: the death of my then wife, mother of my two sons when they were young boys. The *if only* questions buried under the rubble of our once-easy life were unearthed for this novel, though the story itself is thoroughly fiction the emotions are real. The plot and characters were crafted from decades of reading my favourite writers—Salman Rushdie, Margaret Atwood, John Irving, Ray Bradbury, Isaac Asimov, and Stephen King, as well as classic writers such as Edgar Allen Poe, Charles Dickens, J.R.R. Tolkien, and C.S. Lewis, to name only a very few of both sets. After all, what is story but the adornment and decoration of real life, our own or an imagined one. And some of the jewels I used to adorn this story I hope you'll find interesting in origin. Albert Brown? That really happened to my maternal grandfather in WWI. He did survive, and he was overtly kind and almost completely nonverbal as a result of his battlefield lobotomy. The story of Gomp and Zophie rafting down the Fraser River in the early twentieth century in search of land to squat on is a snippet of reality from the family history of my late wife applied to fictional characters. Mrs. Rain and her front lawn? She lived across the street from my childhood home; she was not a ninja but did look like the Queen. She died with many of the neighbourhood hockey balls still in her possession. The One-Legged Norms? My wife Barb's maternal grandfather was named Norm and he had one leg, she also has a one-legged cousin named Norm. I thought having the fictional characters be father and son, and missing the opposite leg would make for one of those shiny pebbles of fictional reality. Most importantly the extraordinary women of the story are one hundred percent true in essence if not name. Real women inspired the fictional characters of Ginny Waggstaff, Princess Agnes the Navigator, Katherine the Great, and Deborah Becker. My extraordinary wife Barb, my sons' fierce stepmother, sat at the deathbed of their extraordinary mother and promised to love and nurture them as her own, that transcendent event really happened. We have been rolled and folded into a new family dough, three of this and two of that now five of us ... plus dogs.

Also an inspiration for this story is my own mother. She could not be more different from Dave's non-mother. I grew up loved, protected, and nurtured. My mother is an extraordinary woman who is most definitely a dreadnought, and my late father was not an abusive alcoholic, he was loving and kind. Deb, Dave, and the boys are fictionalized, idealized, then humanized characters built around the real-life events of our personal tragedy.

Using bits and pieces of story, truth, fiction and fact, I fashioned what I hoped to be a beautiful, intriguing, tragic and inspiring metaphysical mosaic of one family's surreal multigenerational history. If you're reading this, I'm going to guess I accomplished that for you. The writers I love have done this for me many times over. From countless hours of living with fictional characters and their stories, I've come to believe that there is a new trinity born with every story: the writer, the reader, and the story. Each new trio creates a new being, one that is elements of all three yet ever so slightly different than each before the story was shared and so always unique. Story as a form of cultural DNA—that's what I believe you and I have done together. I find this idea immensely rewarding and the process some of the most legal fun a person can have.

The other aspect of this novel I'm very proud of is the collaboration of my musician friends, my sons, and their musician friends we've christened *Wove the Poet*, and we're creating an original music soundtrack for this novel. As of this writing, there are eleven songs planned, eight of which are quoted in the novel; the other three explore major themes of the story. Eight of the eleven songs will showcase the gorgeous voices of my wife Barb, my son, his friends and friends of friends, two are spoken word over music, and one is a combination. This is something done for movies all the time but rarely for novels, though the concept is gaining in popularity since the advent of audiobooks. You will find a link to purchase and download *A Body of Fates: The Soundtrack* at kenevren.com/soundtrack once it's ready for release. I hope you enjoy the music as much as Wove the Poet enjoyed making it.

With thanks,

Kenneth Evren
kenevren@kenevren.com

A BODY OF FATES – POEMS AND LYRICS

BENEDICTION

Fly, fly, slip away
through the steel and concrete,
through the frowning doors.

Fly through the night
over sleepers on still swings,
through indigo shadow and dreaming streets.

Fly from the binding
to the wide-open lands,
deep and secure in long cold glory.

Fly from the pain
from the endless inquisition,
from the marionette strings of a staggering dance.

Fly from home
from walls wet with memory,
from the dirge and desire of bright bloody day.

Fly from your body
numbered and nothing,
fast through the flesh like the arc of an arrow.

Fly from us.
Waste no more breath here.
We love you a prisoner in our busy bones.

CHAINS AND CHOCOLATE

You're my magic you spark me
fearsome fiercely into flame
your deep cadence calls to me
I'm helpless, I'm hopeless
you are spinal final
so beautiful I can hardly breathe.

The salty lick is mossy sweet
a precious gem profound
so hypnotized I cannot fend off
this gentle madness
so I ride reckless
I can hardly breathe.

You were made for me Terpsichore
shelter shade for me Terpsichore
a welcomed blade through me Terpsichore
You're my dream.

Before there ever was you knew me
chains and chocolate afternoons
desperado virtuosity
the alchemy of wonder
sacred in your nakedness
and oyster philosophy
I can hardly breathe.

You're my willow to weep my pillow to sleep
you're the chills that run up and down my spine
you're my willow to weep my pillow to sleep
my cross my empty veins my funeral wine
you're my willow to weep my pillow to sleep
you're a thief of grief my refuge my divine
parallel lines intertwined.

Why are you so sharp your hooks in me

fastened tight with polished fingernails
close your eyes while I close mine
penetrate the ground and stand fixedly
while I descend to find you in your goddess bottle
I can hardly breathe.

FISHING WITH FREDO

Memories crack, cobblestoned moments beneath a heavy footfall,
boots climb the hills to find a view of the ocean scape,
bearing away words and smiles on tides of remembrance.
Paced and timbred hearts sound 'round the rocks and piers;
we hold each other in paper arms while the swelling pools rise,
soaking in the water's cool destruction,
a slumped sinking that folds us down as we gently accept the sea,
leaving treasure trunks behind to float the beaches of green tomorrow.

Now that we are gone and the sight of land is lost, we can turn to fishing,
the boat gently rocks and slaps the rhythm down while we fix the line.
Soft sounds on subtle breezes, scents that mingle with our breathing,
coffee and sandwiches wait for sunrise, the sky the colour of purple lips.
We fix the tiny fish to the hooks, one treble through the upper jaw,
one treble beneath the dorsal fin; our game is bigger.
It's easy to forget the land, the beach, the streets, and houses
once the bait has plopped over the side and the line has whizzed out
of sight;
prop the rod and plant a foot, now it's time for coffee and morning buns,
the best time of a fishing time, the best morning of a fishing morning.
Open the lid and lift the thermos, open the spout and fill the cup,
the first smell that isn't sea is bitter rich and liquorice creamy.
We can think of no better time or place in the whole history of the
whole world,
so perfect there's no need to forget what came before because it never was,
that's the power of morning, and coffee, and a fishing sunrise
… waves lapping wood
… orange canvas life jacket

... polished oars with crackled varnish
... pewter-coloured oar locks
... navy-blue peacoat and tan cabled sweater
... sturdy black boots and a fine red cushion to sit on
... not a sight to be seen but the smiling ocean, teeth glinting in the rising sun.

GIRL ON THE GLEN

Softly sang the girl in the willow tree,
gently floated her voice on the glen.
Came the wind asking her why she sang sadly.
Answered the girl, I was hung here by men.
They wanted my sweetness each one at a time,
and when I refused them they beat me,
and raped me and left me here hanging.
The girl in the willow tree,
sadly singing,
a corpse on the glen.

GRANDMOTHER'S KITCHEN WHILE IT RAINS

Tiles of smooth, faded linoleum, the woodpecker's log full of toothpicks,
massive white and black, porcelain and iron, fired by gas and tears,
the stove squats dominant, brooding, a hulking spectre on lion's feet,
the burners popper to life by uncounted matches struck uncounted times,
the plain cupboards laden with the charms of learning to cook during the Great Depression.
Chrome, vinyl, and Arborite stand utilitarian under the window that looks out over the alley,
the perfect place for little boys to watch the busy lumberyard from.
The fridge is bright white, art deco, an Oldsmobile stood on end.
Strong switches on the walls, heavy, round and brown, guard the lights from small hands.
Cross-shaped silver handles flank the graceful spout over the white sink.
A door at the back opens onto the long porch where we all ate perogies.

The light is the weak light of February.
The window is slick with the exhalations of the labouring pots.
The alley's activities are blurred.
Paint is layered, year upon year, over the window frame,
many painters having lost their hand, smearing the panes
while trying to paint the wooden frame, like emotions run amok.
The cactus, that foreigner dressed oddly, stands erect and silly in
his little pebbled pot protected from the rain outside that he can't need.
I can smell the loaves of kuchen cooling on wax paper,
laid over a plain linen towel on the plain wooden table that lives in
the porch.
Did that plain table once live in the prairie dustbowl kitchen too,
where all these other mute children of history once lived?
The woodpecker knows but he won't say.
The black porcelain cat, the mason jars, the broom only knuckles now,
the thin aprons, they all know.
She is beautiful as a child's peaceful dreams.
Nickel-grey hair pulled back into a practical bun,
her peasant dress a monochrome of tiny flowers
flowing loosely about her square shape.
Her face is cracked with lines and channels
that speak of love and security to me.
She is humming a hymn, German humming—
she talks to me in both languages.
Her back is turned, she is at the stove.
I see her now with my adult eyes, the incarnation of loving sacrifice
spent on the hopeful golden plain of a breadbasket life I can never know.
The rain jangles musically and thuds softy on the six imperfect
window panes,
six square eyes watching old Mr. Ginter limping under lumber loads
that would buckle a younger man.
The singular scent of butter frying mixes with her cooing and clucking
while she creates a meal from little and memory from nothing,
inked black and deep and powerful, then pressed into diamond
by her children's children's children and the stacked plates of time.

She is epic in the bone-spur labour that mercilessly bent her,
the gaunt hobos who owe her a meal still after sixty years, they all think so.
The land, vast and flat that first cradled her boot and felt the bite of her
plough as she and her husband shook the empty, mournful prairie
into a cold and stiff-jointed isolated first winter's home;
that land knows her titanic grip.
But we were quicksilver, young and bent on play,
her grip could not hold us long as we raced out,
leaving her to watch from her living-room window,
old and small, even then more memory than flesh,
closer to heaven but fighting for the purchase of gravity
so as to watch her beloved second seed at play
just a little while longer.

ROSE THE MOON

The gathering curtain of velvet black space
hangs like a question of casual grace.
The soon to be dead strike echoing steps
off tesselate stones in the crisp night blessed.
The cool silken air wraps a life that's receding
the wise night is silent, the daylight is fleeting.

SLEEP IN BLISS

Sleep in bliss and dream of me
nothing to fear or feign
only us deep inside our skin
a sacred creed calamity
a kind and crumbling destiny.

Kiss me like the Joshua sun
snapping sheets of humming heat
softly bind me blind and stay
sweetly cut my blues away
pierce the past and drink the sorrow
forever quenched against tomorrow.

Hold me known and be my love
holy bones we burn
crimson in our chemistry
sapphire in our savagery
nothing more than hollow now
bound in pearls of littered light
we are glitter cast against the onyx night.

TERMINAL VELOCITY

In your eyes are my wings and the ocean in which I drown,
I can't control your choosing.
In your sky I can see heaven excluding me,
I can't control these feelings crowding me.
I'm a river you take me up and hold me high,
your sky enfolds me until I'm dry.
You need pain with your pleasure,
I need pleasure to ease my pain,
you open your arms wide as the world
and I fall like rain.

In your clouds are my dreams and the blindness of my despair,
I can't control your passions.
In a vision came to me a bird of prey and spoke of you,
but I can't make out what he's saying to me.
I'm a river you take me up and hold me high,
your sky enfolds me until I'm dry.
You need pain with your pleasure,
I need pleasure to ease my pain,
you open your arms wide as the world
and I fall like rain.

THE PINWHEEL GALAXY

The Pinwheel Galaxy spins and spits its spangled load,
rhythmic, regular, fantastic it goes 'round pounding.

Alone in the silver night we dart from snippet to flash,
quantum-timed to saxophones and Epiphones and unknowns.

We are augmented minors,
perpetually passing chords,
born to blend in come-round resolution,
to harmonize church-organ fat in tasty four part,
thick-bottomed bass, creamy middle, high thirds keening up sharp,
a chill-the-spine purple magic only the vow-takers can't feel.

DaVinci vanished in strokes of holy oil,
Mandelbrot made drunken cats,
Sky Church sustains then fades,
Jimi stratocasts from the stratosphere,
all ancient beasts that stalk our soul-barrens,
an alchemy of star stuff and winter nights,
rock-a-bye below the incandescent arcs of meteor tails,
wet-electric, alive and alone.

There is a certain voice in the strings' vibrating whine,
calling way-far,
drawing dust from the Belt of Orion,
blowing hot plasma from black hole jets,
heavenly harps slaving to the draw and blow of God's sloppy old black lips.

It will always arrive, that thing, whatever it may be,
dizzying down from all the possible futures,
like games of chance tumble-dumped from a bright celestial box,
ringing with notes of joy pink with pathos,
singing with sighs of sweet, bluesy sex.

Hammer-on and snap-off Jimi.
Let's hear it licked like every woman wants to be,
slicker than any spin doctor's harlot tongue.
It's 3:00 a.m. on a winter's night,
and the pinwheel galaxy needs no spin doctor.

WISH I

Was raining grey the day we met
wish I knew that flash of blue you showed me.
The next time we spent some time the day was alabaster
words got inked and stories told of sexual disaster
wish I was the wind that blows through your hair
across your skin, that you showed me.

Wish I knew the reason.
Wish I felt the pain.
Wish I lived the moment.
Wish I knew the way to stay unchanged.

Was raining red we met again
secrets bloomed the dance resumed
said to you I wish I was your lover.

Was raining silver, pink and purple
the conversation on that day
was naked, kneeling, beating, reeling,
breathing slowed anticipating
what we knew that we would do
if we were lovers.

Wish I couldn't leave you.
Wish I felt something else.
Wish I knew the buried years,
can't seem to find the time or tears.
Perhaps the flame's the only answer,
rich, red blood the only cancer.
Wish I knew what she would do
If she knew that we are lovers.

Printed in the USA
CPSIA information can be obtained
at www.ICGtesting.com
JSHW021933210324
59696JS00004B/10

9 781738 938001